DOCTOR WHO

MATRIX

ROBERT PERRY AND MIKE TUCKER

B B C

Published by BBC Worldwide Ltd,
Woodlands, 80 Wood Lane
London W12 0TT

First published 1998
Reprinted 1999
Copyright © Robert Perry and Mike Tucker 1998
The moral right of the authors has been asserted

Original series broadcast on the BBC
Format © BBC 1963
Doctor Who and TARDIS are trademarks of the BBC

ISBN 0 563 40596 1
Imaging by Black Sheep, copyright © BBC 1998

Printed and bound in Great Britain by Mackays of Chatham
Cover printed by Belmont Press Ltd, Northampton

For Marc and Daniel

Thanks to:
Andy (as always)
Mark Morris (for the perfect set up in 'The Bodysnatchers')
Phoebe (for the walk)
Alan Barnes (for suggesting the walk)
Sophie and Sylvester (for their characters)
Steve Cole (for everything else)

'I'll rest, sayd he, but thou shalt walke;'
So doth this wandring Jew
From place to place, but cannot rest
For seeing contries newe.

Thomas Percy

Part One

'Longinius.'

The Roman turned. 'Yes, Procurator?'

Pilate crossed the marble floor from the judgement hall. 'Have you seen Cartaphilius?'

'The doorkeeper? Yes, but two hours ago.'

'Then bring him to my chamber. I would speak with him.'

Pilate swept away, grinding his hands into the front of his robes, a habit that had not left him for several days now, not since...

'Your pardon, Procurator...'

Pilate stopped. 'What is wrong, Centurion?'

'Cartaphilius is no longer in the palace.'

'No longer in the palace? Then where?'

'I know not, but when I last saw him he was making for the desert.'

'The desert?'

'Yes, Procurator. As if he was embarking on a journey.'

Chapter One

All that is outside, all that walls are supposed to keep outside, was here focused, concentrated, entombed in stone and iron.

Through endless stone passageways the silence was audible, the stillness somehow tangible. The occasional stagnant pool of dull yellow light, seeping from sources unseen, was lanced with murdering shadows, shadows that flickered with eerie half-life, voices ringing like whale-song.

In one tiny room a figure was huddled over an old roll-top desk trying to shut out the cries in the dark. The room was a clutter of archaic scientific instruments – theodolite, sextant, an old brass microscope, a huge floor-mounted compass – all dusty from disuse. The walls were practically invisible beneath mounds of books; hundreds, probably thousands, of ancient volumes which hadn't moved for years. The figure was working.

The only signs of movement were his hands moving quickly and precisely; the rest of his body remained still. His eyes stared from beneath a dull black cowl, unblinking, never straying from the work in front of him. He was juggling, twisting, scratching at a lump of clay, vaguely man-like in shape, his long nails gouging out lines and hollows, the clay peeling off in lumps and falling unregarded on to the desk and floor. He made no mistakes, there was no hesitation in his movements. It was as if he had been programmed for this task. And, slowly, a figure was emerging from the clay. Not human; barely even humanoid. A bizarre anatomical jigsaw. Huge, rough head, bulbous fish eyes, enlarged arms ending in bony, clawed stumps, short, squat legs, web-like feet – it was more than just ugly, it was a distillation of pure, destructive malice in miniature. The hideous toy appeared to afford no pleasure, no pain, nothing to its creator. His face, deep in shadow, was impassive, almost unaware, as if his concentration was focused not on his task but somehow beyond it.

It was finished. The little beast was complete. The man rose from his chair and swept into the corridor, disappearing into its prehistoric, vertebral shadows.

Somewhere deeper in the labyrinth he came to a set of huge double doors wrought from hammered metal. At his silent approach they swung open, with no creak or clang or apparent propelling force, as noiseless as his spectral footfall. Beyond the doors was an immense spider's web of Gothic architecture: pillars, screens and high vaulted ceilings, grinning carved faces distorted by flickering braziers, all woven in intricate, continually unfolding patterns of light, shade and stone, leading with many a twist and turn to a huge central nave. Here, the mad cathedral architecture of the complex was more concentrated, more oppressive, more threatening than anywhere else. The other rooms and corridors were just tributaries; stray strands far from the arachnid nerve centre. Here the weave was strongest, here some ghastly, predatory spider power was concentrated. The very walls were intense, magnetic, like some fairground maze of mirrors, forcing energy continually back to the crucial central point.

Like a shadow, the hooded figure was suddenly snatched into the lattice of darkness; at once invisible, momentarily arcing across a shaft of light from somewhere high above this elegant, primal generator. He walked with unchanged mute, blind assurance through the stone circuitry to the nave. There he stopped, lowering his head for a moment, then placed the clay mannequin on the floor. It sat at the centre of an array of lines and figures, circles within circles and a huge pentagram, which radiated out into shadows.

For the first time the man appeared to tense, throwing his head back and his arms wide. He looked slowly around him, his eyes burning into the dark cloisters, his lips drawn back over tightly clenched teeth.

He sang. Low at first, deep, quiet, rumbling, blending with the lost anguished cries of the shadows. Then gaining in confidence, volume, snaking up the register, wordless, sweet, almost ashamed. His voice died. Silence. The emptiness swallowed his words. He stood, his arms still outstretched, waiting.

With the gentlest dilation of the liquid stillness the shadows appeared to bulge and break, giving birth to new forms – solid, almost; if they had any colour at all it was grey fading to black. This was no illusion, no trick of some devilish master builder. The soulless hunger of this place had found physical, mobile, living expression in these children of shadow, looming around the cloaked mentor. Called by the sweet, desperate promise of the song, they seemed to ripple with the darkness, sparking with sudden, quick infusions of bright, necromantic energy, as they passed across the strident gold symbols which gashed the floor.

They formed a ring around him, the one who had called them. Twelve in all, waiting. He brought his hands together as if in prayer. His eyes snapped shut, his lips began to tremble, to twitch, finally to shape the words of a new song, a circular incantation, at first inaudibly, internally, then with each sweep of the cycle a little louder, again, again, again. His ghost-coven began to hiss, to inhale and spit back his words, tunelessly, voicelessly, like wind among dead trees. Louder and louder, feeding the sound-swallowing cloisters. Louder, until finally those cloisters became full and began to regurgitate the dread litany, the very building lending its voice, spilling sound back at them from its dark recesses; a hysterical wall of echoes, out of time, finding strange rhythms of their own. The cloaked mentor stopped. He began to recite now, slowly, his words lost beneath the maelstrom he had made. He dropped to his knees before the clay statuette; imploring, charging with desire.

He pointed a pale, bony finger at one of the coven, who let out a voiceless, hissing wail. The shadows closed around the one he had chosen, pushing him forward, pushing him towards the clay figurine. Spectral hands clutched and clawed at the stonework,

3

fighting to be spared this. The very essence of the one he had chosen, ghost-essence that it was, seemed to be sucked, distorted, drawn into the figure like water into a gully.

Gradually, slipping away beneath the raging sea of sound, the clay figure faded and was gone.

Chapter Two

Dull grey waters gathered, hurling themselves into exploding crystalline fragments against the rocks; recombining to repeat the assault; again, again, again.

The Doctor stared into the ocean. Squatting on a rock where the spume would occasionally graze him at the very limit of its flight, his eyes were fixed on the distant horizon, blinking occasionally to ward off the sea's outriders. His straw hat blew off and away. He let it. He was lost in the swirl of the sea.

Ace was worried. For the best part of an hour she had waited outside the TARDIS. She pulled her badge-strewn jacket tight around her and stared at the puppet-like figure propped awkwardly between rock and sky many feet below. He had been there the whole time, hardly moving. She had never seen him like this before. Their time together had been one of machine-gun bursts of activity; a manic game of tag across time. The lifestyle suited her; the constant hot breath of danger, the violence, the never-standing-still. A life of reaction, not reflection. Periods of hyperactivity would be interspersed with periods of total shut-down, when the Doctor would sleep, deep, for days while the TARDIS drifted through the space/time continuum and Ace ate, slept, moped around.

She caught his hat as it tumbled across the grass towards her. Hell, what was wrong with him? Since leaving blitz-torn London he had hardly spoken to her. No bright idea about a new world to visit or something she must see, no let's-just-see-where-we-end-up enthusiasm and the anticipation of the unexpected. Nothing. He had set a course and stood, glowering at the console, willing the TARDIS to arrive. It was strange; the atmosphere in the TARDIS – the very fabric of the ship – seemed to lock into his mood; a thick, unbudging curtain of despondency. The mood penetrated every room and corridor, following Ace wherever she went. She couldn't shut it out. In the end she had just retreated to her room and switched on her ghetto blaster. The TARDIS corridors had reverberated to Bowie, Happy Mondays, James; anything to lighten the atmosphere.

When she guessed they were no longer moving she had returned to the control room. The doors were open and the Doctor was not there. She had emerged from the ship – just a battered old police box to look at it – to a biting wind and the imminence of rain. Earth again. She was on a cliff-top. She could hear the movement of the sea and the cry of storm-winged gulls feeding. There was bracken under her feet, no sign of the Doctor. She had looked over the edge and seen him, bounding down some invisible path, not even looking where he was going, his eyes already fixed on the sea. His trotting speed hadn't slowed when he had reached the foot of the cliff and begun picking his way across the rocks towards the disintegrating surf. Finally he had stopped on a large boulder, paused for about a minute, then sunk on to his haunches. He hadn't moved since.

Now Ace was fed up. This had gone on long enough. She set off towards him, her feet finding a path she could hardly see; sandy, earthy, covered with close shrubs and nettles, often vanishing into smooth, difficultly angled rock. Fine. Now, across the rocks themselves. They were much bigger than they had looked from above, with crevices as deep as she was tall, and slippery. A wonder he didn't break his neck. She half-crept up behind him, timid for once.

'Professor, are you all right? You've been here ages.'

At first he didn't reply. Then, almost drunkenly, 'I'm with the dead. I'm among friends…' Slowly, he drew out the words. They made Ace feel uneasy. He paused, his gaze following the course of a gull. 'When I was a boy on Gallifrey I used to visit the sea a lot. Just sit there, watching and listening. I used to think that was where the dead went, that they were all out there, in the sea. I used to think you could hear them whispering to you from the waves.' His voice was distant, itself dead. It seemed to Ace that it might have been the voice of the sea, and the Doctor just a shell held up to her ear. 'The dead are very important to Time Lords. They are always with you, making their presence felt, all around you. More so than the living. We preserve the minds of our dead.'

'Professor, what's brought all this on?'

'You…'

Her?

'Susan…'

'Susan… Who's Susan? Professor, what are you talking about?'

'There was a Susan once, you know. She used to travel with me, just like you. She used to call me Grandfather… She's out there now.'

'Dead?'

'Dead… Gone… What's the difference? She left me a long time ago. You have to know when to let go, you see. You will leave me too, before very long.'

Ace didn't reply. It was true, of course. She had always considered her time with him essentially an interlude: a journey, albeit a wayward one, at the end of which she would simply walk away and pick up the abandoned threads of her life. Of course she was fond of the Doctor. Maybe she even loved him in a way. But… to be in the TARDIS was to be a part of his life, to live his lifestyle. Other things just seemed to go into suspension. Which was great for a while. She would leave the TARDIS stronger, wiser, better… but what about him? Would he be at all changed by their relationship?

'It's funny, you know, Ace… My people – the Time Lords – all but eliminated pain, suffering and hardship from their society… but somewhere along the way they lost their compassion, their ability to relate to each other on an individual… on an emotional level. Their humanity… for want of a better word. I really thought I was different. I was bored with their stupid rituals, their ancestor worship, and sickened by their high and mighty attitudes. So I left. I thought I could escape it. I was wrong.'

'What do you mean? You're free of all that. Free to do what you want.'

For the first time his eyes left the slate water. He swung to face her, an intensity and anguish in his gaze that Ace had never seen before in him.

'I'm still a Time Lord, Ace. I'm as socially and emotionally impotent as the rest of them. Incapable of forming lasting relationships. Oh, I'm always up to my neck in other people's problems, but what then? I help them if I can and then move on. Never any long-term commitment.' He appeared to deflate again. He turned back to the compelling sea. 'There have been lots like you, Ace. People who have travelled with me in the TARDIS. They're all out there now.'

This wasn't fair. Ace didn't want to hear it. For God's sake, she was only seventeen. She suddenly felt burdened, tied. This was something she couldn't understand, let alone cope with. She was shaking, and silent. The Doctor seemed to sense her fear.

'Anyway, you're home. This is Earth. England. You can go now if you like.'

'But I don't want to go.'

There was nowhere she *could* go. Nowhere she wanted to, anyway. The Doctor once more turned to face her. He took both her hands in his.

'A little longer then, eh?' He smiled his gentle, warm, crooked smile. She felt her vision beginning to blur - tears - oh damn, damn...

They had both lost interest in their surroundings: the sea, the ragged and bony fists and fingers of rock that formed the shore, the lighthouse that stood at one end of the inlet, abruptly cutting off the sea's expanse to their left.

Out in the water something was happening. Something not right. If they had been listening now they might have heard, above the roar of the ocean, a distant, hysterical chanting. A hand emerged from the waves, then went under again. A shape was moving just beneath the surface, towards the shore. They never noticed. Just off the rock where Ace stood and the Doctor crouched, his back now fully to the sea, the water surged, bubbled, heaved upward. With a scream, a snarl of deep-seated, guttural malevolence, the thing broke the water's grip and lurched shoreward, huge, hunting, clawing its way on to rock.

The Doctor was on his feet and facing the thing in one movement. Ace let out a hoarse yell of surprise that felt like sandpaper in her throat, then the Doctor was pulling her roughly from rock to rock towards the cliff path. The rocks jarred her legs, cracks and caverns reeled towards her, her head was spinning, her heart was pounding. They were alive again.

The beast lumbered after them, huge, rough head, bulbous fish eyes, enlarged arms ending in bony, clawed stumps, short, squat legs, web-like feet. Its skin was scaly like a fish, its mouth a mess of irregular, pointed teeth, its voice deep but curiously shrieking; almost birdlike. It had the colour and consistency of clay. Its movements were almost apelike on land, its arms steadying it on its inadequate legs. It was half-scrambling, half-leaping over the rocks, occasionally flailing wildly at its new-found prey with a savage arm. The Doctor and Ace reached the start of the cliff path, breathless.

'Get back to the TARDIS. I'll try and head it off.' Moving away from Ace, the Doctor picked up a large stone and threw it hard at the thing's head. It turned slowly, turned back, turned again, confused. Its prey was now two. The Doctor shouted and threw his arms above his head, jumping, dancing and waving. That was enough. The monster leaped towards him with a screech. The Doctor dived to one side. The creature missed its mark and sprawled on its belly, riding on a scree of pebbles, head first into a deep gully. The Doctor leaned forward, his hands on his knees, taking deep, urgent lungfuls of air. Ace was vanishing up the cliff, no longer worrying whether there was a path or not.

Claws scrabbled with stone by the Doctor's feet. It was time to move again. He turned and ran in the direction of the lighthouse. There had to be a way on to the cliff-top from there. He didn't yet have any idea what to do about the thing chasing him, or what sort of grievance it was pursuing with such venom. He hadn't even begun to consider what on Earth it was, or why it was on Earth at all. He reached the base of the lighthouse. No road – ridiculous! No way up the cliff he could see, just steep, blank foliage and rock, and, on his right, the sea. He was trapped on a promontory. Only one way to go.

He could hear the drag of flesh on rock as he mounted the dozen or so steps that led to the lighthouse door. He hoped the thing would be too big to enter the lighthouse. The doorway was small and at least then he would have time to think and get his breath back. The door was wooden, ancient and sea-stained with long-rusted handle and hinges, and it was locked. No, it was open, just stiff from disuse. The place must be deserted. Good. A quick glance over his shoulder: the thing was mounting the stairway, slowly, low on all fours, its underbelly slapping on each step. The door began to give a little. The Doctor threw his full weight against it, forced it creaking and groaning open a few vital inches, just enough to squeeze through. Scrambling inside, he slammed the door shut and bolted it.

He looked around him. Inside the lighthouse was cool, damp and dark. A doorway led to an empty stone room; the winding stone staircase, spiralling up into dark, began at his feet. There was a scratching sound at the door, then a muffled thump. The Doctor began to climb the stairs; perhaps in one of the rooms he would find a weapon. There was an echoing crash at the door. Another. It shook. A third and the door splintered, bulged inward. The rusty bolts gave way and the door swung open, limping on its hinges. An immense arm and a head came through the doorway. A shoulder butted against the heavy doorframe. Too tight. The Doctor smiled. He was safe behind walls that had withstood the battering of the sea for two hundred years. They wouldn't give way now. The creature snarled. Its arm thrashed uselessly against the walls and floor, its head butted the doorframe. Then, unexpectedly, it began to push against the inside wall of the lighthouse; to squeeze itself through a gap obviously too small for it. The Doctor watched in horror as the doorframe started to bite into the creature's shoulder, tearing off the clay flesh. Shoulder and arm were gone, abandoned to the rocks and rain. The creature was inside.

It showed no pain. It didn't even slow down. The Doctor was bounding up the stairs two at a time. A door. An empty room. Higher. Another, also empty. They must have cleaned this place out when they left. Nothing to use against the creature. He ran on. An idea struggled to take shape in his mind. Only one feasible course of action. The thing was getting closer. He had to get to the lamp room. Not far now. He flung open the final door, at the top end of the staircase. Light drenched him, dazzling from all sides. He was in a bubble, trapped by glass and breathtaking daylight, he and the enormous, paralysed lamp mechanism. Where was the door to the balcony? His only hope. He lunged towards it, but at the same desperate moment, the one massive arm of his pursuer descended, catching him across the back. He fell to the metal grid floor, his fingers gripping instinctively through the holes. He swung himself on to his back, and for the first time actually stared his attacker full in the face. Full in the eye. The creature bellowed and the sound echoed around the Doctor's imagination. That voice... those eyes...

Time paused for the Doctor. The creature's eyes locked with his. There was something terrifyingly familiar in its gaze. He could hear distant chanting above the wind that battered on the glass. He felt consciousness beginning to slide from him.

Suddenly, in the distance, there was a voice he seemed to recognise... Ace?... was it?... 'Doctor!'... calling... 'Doctor, get out of the way!' He was lying on metal. He saw Ace framed by the creature's legs, holding two large flasks. He knew what to do. He threw himself to one side, rolling around the huge lamp, and lay face down, covering his head with his hands. There was a loud explosion, a shattering of glass – he felt it shower down on him in fragments – and the cry of a felled monster, the cry of lost children.

Chapter Three

When he got up, the wind hit him full force. There was little left of one side of the glass dome of the roof and walls, or of the lamp, and the balcony on the same side was broken and buckled. Ace was standing in the doorway, grinning, throwing her one remaining flask into the air and catching it. The Doctor leaned out over the broken balcony. The creature was gone, just an ugly statue smashed on the rocks below.

He stepped back, gripping a piece of twisted lamp machinery. He felt dizzy, sick, drunk with memory. Deliberately he focused his attention on Ace.

'I thought I told you not to make any more of that stuff.'

Nitro-9: a powerful, frighteningly unstable explosive. Ace shoved the flask carelessly into an expansive pocket of her bomber jacket. 'Come on, Professor, you'd be dead without it. What was that thing anyway?' Mentally she was carving another notch on her gun barrel.

The Doctor shook his head slowly. He was confused. He felt threatened by some indistinct horror; something he had as yet only glimpsed. Something frighteningly familiar. 'Some kind of golem... inert matter animated by an external force.' He almost laughed. 'The stuff of folk-tales.' For a moment his tone was bitter. He paced around the lamp room, tapping his teeth with his fingers, his brow furrowed. 'That creature had a mind, a soul.'

He wasn't talking to Ace. His words vanished like water through the holes in the grid floor. The rain started to fall hard now, carried almost horizontally across the top of the crippled light-tower. The Doctor didn't seem to notice.

'... A borrowed soul. Not its own.'

'Professor.' Ace prodded him. 'Let's get back to the TARDIS.'

'What?... Oh...'

They carefully descended the dark stairway, for the first time aware of how slippery each step was. The Doctor moved slowly and uncomfortably. The blow to his back, unnoticed in the rush of events, had been heavy. He pushed Ace unceremoniously past the shattered beast on the rocks, not even glancing at it, harshly dismissing her plea for a 'souvenir'.

'It's only a lump of clay.' He knew this wasn't the reason. He knew he should examine the creature's remains. He was scared. He didn't want to find out what lay behind the attack. The physical danger hadn't bothered him, but an instinct told him that something terrible and unbearable lay barely veiled and he dared not look too hard.

They reached the cliff path, now streaming with water. Clutching at each other for support, the two of them stumbled through the rain towards the waiting TARDIS. The door was open, the warm glow of the interior like a beacon. The Doctor vanished inside. Ace took a long final look at the bleak seascape, then closed the outer door. She had had enough of this place.

The Doctor was once more leaning over the TARDIS console, glowering at it as he made rapid instrument adjustments. The time rotor – gaudy cylindrical centre-piece of the hexagonal structure – began its familiar rising and falling motion.

'Where are we going?'

'I don't know. I need to think.'

The Doctor seemed as keen as she was to get away from here.

'Something's wrong, Ace. We're not moving.'

The time rotor was sluggish, getting slower as they watched. Suddenly the lights in the control room dimmed to a foggy yellow. The time rotor shuddered to a halt. The familiar dull whirr from the console died.

The Doctor's head was erect, his neck arched back, eyes darting, almost sniffing the air for sound. And there was something, minute, a distant echo, far behind the silence.

'What is it, Professor? What's that noise?'

He fixed her with a steady glare. 'Something getting in.'

Like a bloodhound the Doctor sailed from the control room, into the guts of the ship.

'Professor…' Fed up, indignant, confused, she followed him through the door and into the corridor – dim now, like the control room – which led past the living quarters he had allotted her. She remembered how she had been offended at the time; the cupboards were full of clothes, knick-knacks everywhere. How many people before her had used the room? How quickly had they left? Didn't he ever clear up after them?

He was vanishing around a corner ahead of her. She didn't know this part of the ship. She could get lost if she didn't keep up.

'Professor…?' He was getting away from her. She arrived at a crossroads. Three possible ways. All dark, all unfamiliar.

There – to the left – something vanishing around a distant corner. Trainers pumping, she pounded down the dusky corridor. She was starting to panic. Why didn't he stop? Was she in fact following the Doctor at all? She had sensed she was following him – something had told her – but now she was beginning to doubt her instincts.

More to the point, she was lost. All the corridors looked the same, especially in this half-light. She walked, slowly now, hands slightly extended, her eyes darting about her. Things were changing gradually. The walls and floor looked older. The familiar roundel pattern remained but now everything had an almost stony feel. And – surely not – ivy, creepers, vegetation were starting to appear, clinging in long, single strands about her. This was ridiculous.

Quite abruptly, the corridor opened out into a wide area, lush with vegetation, broken columns, an ornamental pond of dark water. At a better moment, Ace might have found all this funny. Now, lost, in semi-darkness and beginning to suspect that she was being led deliberately by an unknown presence, the darkness bore down on her, edging minutely closer.

There was a sudden noise – hissing and snarling – and a flurry

15

in the curtain of ivy and vine beyond the water. She began to edge around this jungle-room, slowly, one hand tracing the roundels in the wall, sweeping through the foliage.

She was taut like a spring, waiting… for… The curtain flashed again and something broke through it directly in front of her. She thrashed out with her hand and touched… fur? That snarl – vicious, feral. A fleeting, cat-like smell. Her foot caught in a root, her ankle twisted; she fell.

The room was silent again. Still. All except… the pool. The water was rippling as if in a breeze. She hauled herself on to its mock-stone edge and leaned out. It was dark. She could see the vaguest of reflections, too broken up by the movement of the water to allow any detail. She moved her head. The reflection moved. She put out a hand, slowly, gently grazing the surface of the water, and felt…

She snatched her hand back. It was unmistakable. Breaking the surface of the pool, she had touched the hand that came up to meet her. It was solid. She had felt for a moment a hard, leathery cushion; cruel claws, opening and closing.

Stumbling, she ran, back the way she had come, away from this crazy garden, gasping and crying.

'*Professor*…!'

The cry echoed around the cavernous rooms of the TARDIS. The Doctor barely heard it. He wasn't even aware that Ace had followed him from the control room. The TARDIS to him seemed unnaturally quiet. Quiet, that is, except for the phantom whisper he could still hear from time to time, as if carried on a breeze.

He was deeper inside the TARDIS than he had been for years. He stood between vast, ancient engines, listening to their deep, gentle hum and trying not to think of the power they contained. This was the very heart of the ship, where dimensions met, space and time, matter and anti-matter, jammed together, held in knife-edge equilibrium by the vast forces of energy Time Lord technology had enslaved. The TARDIS's nexus point. Point zero.

The creature by the sea had unsettled him, caught him off guard. It was as if his enemy knew exactly when and how to catch him off balance. That indicated knowledge of him, and few people knew him that well.

He stared into the pool of potential that was the nexus point, letting his mind drift, trying to calm himself. He jolted suddenly as if an electric shock had passed through him. There was something in there. Something that shouldn't be there. This was where the intruder was hiding.

He reached out with his mind, trying to gauge his enemy, but the energies of the nexus point were too strong and for a second the Doctor reeled, teetering on the brink of the pit.

A bitter wind swirled around the engines and a wave of fear washed over him. He began to back away from the pit. Whatever it was that had invaded his home was strong. Very strong.

'Professor…!'

Now he heard Ace's cry. Desperate and lonely. He had to get back to her. As he turned to leave the nexus point something giggled in the dark.

Chapter Four

'It used our energy field to get here.'

The time rotor was moving again, fast now, and the lights were bright again. Pale, sweating, the Doctor was punching buttons, tapping dials, circling the console like a restless cat. Ace was standing against the wall of the control room, shaking.

'What did?' She had beaten him back to the control room by moments, scared, jumping at nothing. Just some weed floating under the surface of the pond. Reflections couldn't touch you. She tried to pull herself together.

'Did it have anything to do with that creature?'

The Doctor's eyes fell back to the console. He didn't want to think about it. He was being forced into a corner, made to reach conclusions he desperately wanted to avoid. He had no choice now but to brave the flood tide of his own fears, to throw open Ace's book of mysteries.

'*Doctor!*' A new voice rang around the TARDIS. '*Getting a little... introspective, aren't we? Not like you...*' Mocking laughter embellished an iron whisper. '*You know the dangers of the nexus point. It can throw up all sorts of surprises. Drive you insane!*'

The voice was familiar. More than familiar, it pressed hard on the Doctor's nerves, it taunted his memory. He should know it.

'Who are you? Show yourself, intruder!'

'*Don't you recognise me, Doctor? I'm offended.*'

'I won't fight you!'

'*Oh, but you will!*' The voice twisted and cracked. Fury and madness tore through it. '*The great Doctor! Not frightened of anything... except the terrible truth about himself. You* will *fight me, Doctor. You will!*'

The voice was lost in a loud, falling, whistling sound coming down around them. There was a deafening bang. Smoke billowed over them; choking, clogging the taste buds, stinging and blinding them.

Ace was spinning. She could feel something like damp earth and small stones hitting her, spraying against her. She made a grab for what she thought was the Doctor. Her hands closed on air. A moment later she was back on solid ground, as if she had never moved, just opened her eyes. The smoke was thinning away in a sudden humid breeze.

They were outdoors again. Mud and rain-filled holes, gashes in the landscape, stretched in every direction. Ace could just make out large bails of wire stretching across the skyline. The TARDIS console was sitting like a toadstool in the mud, water lapping its edges. The Doctor was hunched over it, poking and prodding, occasionally glancing around at their barren surroundings.

'Doctor, where are we? What's happening?'

'I don't know.' He was crawling around the TARDIS console on all fours, craning his neck to inspect its underside. He was almost gabbling in panic. 'I don't know how we got here and I don't know how to get us out.' His hand disappeared into the guts of the console. It gave a brief stammer – an electronic burble and a few blinking lights – and the Doctor snatched his hand back as if bitten. 'Don't you dare…'

Something overhead whistled, screamed – the same sound as before – cutting across the sky and getting louder. The Doctor sprang to his feet, at last taking in their surroundings properly. Stupid! All the time he'd been tinkering they were in danger. The whistling ended in a loud, dull thump about a hundred yards away, throwing earth and stones into the air like startled birds. They were on a battlefield, and totally without cover. In the distance they could hear the rattle of gunfire.

'Come on!' The Doctor grabbed Ace by the wrist and started pulling her behind him, rapidly up a slope towards the coiled wire that lay between them and the sky.

'That was a mortar, wasn't it? I've never seen one of them go off before.'

'Ace, this isn't a game. We're in the middle of a war.' As they ascended the rise she was scanning the miles of flat desolation, searching out detail in the distance. Occasionally she would stare at the sky, almost as if willing another projectile to come.

Now they were near the cruel barbs, stark against the sky: an immense crown of thorns. The sun, setting in front of them, was raw and bleeding on the wire. Somewhere ahead an order was given. Shouts, then from behind the wire, a 'Push forward!' About thirty figures in mud-soaked khaki, faceless behind gas masks, clambering through their own defences, shambling downhill to a weary and inevitable death. The Doctor froze. His grip on Ace's wrist tightened painfully. She knew they had to get out of the way, but he... not for the first time that day he was staring, lost, into the face of advancing destruction...

It was the masks; the same look of hollow doom as before. The same look that had been in the eyes of the clay creature.

The terrifying, pathetic force was nearly level with them. Ace was struggling, pushing, hitting the paralysed Doctor as the soldiers laboured the last few yards towards them. From the other direction came a burst of machine-gun fire. It was loud, close behind Ace. She felt the first split-second of impact as the bullets pierced her clothing. She felt she was in a goldfish bowl, or back on the lighthouse, sucking in light, sound, smell, from all around her, greedily. She tasted her own flesh. She saw and remembered more in that moment than she ever had before. She was suspended in time...

The soldiers were falling. She could see the impact of bullets, the jerk of bodies then collapsing like straw men. Within a minute they were all dead.

Why was she still standing? She was unhurt... The Doctor was still unmoved. She had stood in the path of oncoming bullets, she knew. She had felt them begin to touch...

'Are you all right, Ace?' The Doctor sounded subdued, numb with shock. He still hadn't moved or released her wrist. The battlefield was silent now. There was no sign of whatever gunner had cut down the hopeless advance. The Doctor was digesting this new scene of destruction. He took a deep breath and knelt down by the nearest corpse. He had to know...

He was shaking. His hands fumbled with the straps on the gas mask. Odd. The corpse before him seemed small; too small to be a soldier. The uniform looked too big, loose and creased and bunched. The Doctor let his eyes flash across the other fallen figures. They all looked too small. Boy soldiers? Finally the straps gave and the Doctor lifted the mask away from the face... He froze. His hands were suddenly useless; he dropped the mask. The face that stared up at him, wide-eyed and stone dead, was that of his young companion. Ace. Her mouth open, her tongue protruding obscenely, spittle drying on her chin.

The Doctor lurched to the next body, clutching and tugging at the mask, prising it away from the head. The same sight greeted him, only...

This one was alive! Desperately he tried to raise her head, to clear her airway. Her breath was so shallow as to be almost non-existent, her eyes were unfocused.

'Ace...'

Her mouth twitched, she looked at the Doctor, seeming to recognise him. She was trying to say something as the life slipped away from her.

'Ace...' the Doctor whispered thickly, hoarsely.

He laid her head down on the broken earth and moved sullenly to the next prone figure. There was little left of the gas mask on this one. It, and the face, had been completely shot away. Or almost completely; enough remained for him to recognise.

Dozens of corpses, all of them identical in life, each uniquely surprised in death, hopelessly unprepared for this moment.

'Dead... Gone... What's the difference?' His words of an hour ago rolled back over him, mocking. Ace absently watched him trudging like a worked-out slave from body to body, uncovering each one, crouching, staring down for a moment before moving on…

He said nothing. She said nothing. From where she stood the bodies looked oddly indistinct, the features didn't seem to register. It was almost as if they were slightly out of focus.

'Doctor…?'

'Stay back, Ace!'

A booming sound filled the air, dragging his attention skyward. It sounded like thunder, directly overhead. But the sky was clear, the air was still and dry.

When, Doctor? When will it happen? When will she die, killed by your meddling? How many others have already died? People who trusted you, travelled with you. People you led like lambs to the slaughter. How many have there been, Doctor? And how many more will there be? How many more of your friends will you sacrifice to your impotent obsessions?

Slowly the Doctor raised his face to the sky, crouched like a baying wolf.

'All right!' he howled. 'I'll fight you! Only leave her alone!'

Instantly the scene vanished. The Doctor and Ace were back in the TARDIS. The mud and tears were gone from their clothes. They were left with the sound of gunfire ringing in their ears.

'What happened?'

'A lesson. A challenge.' The Doctor reached towards Ace. He pulled her tight to him; clung to her, shaking.

'Professor…' she sounded embarrassed, irritated.

'Ace, are you all right?' He relaxed his grip. She pulled away.

'Fine. So, all that… it wasn't real, was it.'

'No… in a sense. In another sense it was all *too* real.'

He turned to the console, rested his hands on its reassuring surface, testing its solidity, its actuality. Apparently satisfied, he let out a long sigh of relief.

'All right,' he breathed. 'We'll play things your way…' He clapped his hands together, making her jump. 'Right. Things to do. There's someone I want you to stay with for a while… you'll find him a bit severe at first, but he'll protect you and take care of you. It's… it's too dangerous for you to travel with me any more.'

'Come off it! You're not going to dump me with some complete stranger?'

'Not a complete stranger, no.' His grasshopper mind was already elsewhere. 'But first there's something I've got to do.'

He dropped to his haunches and peered into the gloomy underside of the TARDIS console. Carefully he removed a panel.

'The telepathic circuit. That's how it got in.'

'What was it, Professor? Did it have anything to do with that thing on the beach?'

'I don't know what it was, Ace.'

That was only half the truth. He let his hand close around the sleek perspex cylinder, perhaps an inch in diameter, three inches in length. This inconsequential-looking piece of circuitry was the thing that linked him to the TARDIS; it was what made them more than just Time Lord and machine. The TARDIS was alive, in a sense. It fed off the Doctor's own mental activity. The Doctor's thoughts, his emotions, his memories charged the console, the machinery which thrust the TARDIS through the space/time continuum, the walls and floor, the very fabric of the ship. He pulled gently on the circuit. It was like reaching into his own body to tear out one of his organs. Closing his eyes, he yanked…

Nothing perceptible happened, but Ace looked around uneasily. It was as if someone had just left the room; as if someone she trusted had suddenly departed, leaving her in a strange place, alone and slightly frightened. The TARDIS was a stranger, now. The Doctor felt it acutely. The ship would still work; it would take them where they had to go, keep them warm and secure, but it was dead. It was just so much souped-up space junk.

He placed the circuit in his pocket, and began punching

co-ordinates into the console.

Ace wanted to shake him, wanted to pin him down, to ask him what the hell was going on, whose had been the voice in the TARDIS, the bodies on the battlefield, what was he so afraid of? As usual she knew he wasn't really talking to her. He was thinking out loud. As usual he would tackle the problem alone and in his way while she just hung on in there.

The Doctor completed the dematerialisation sequence. He felt adrift on the face of a huge and shifting ocean. He needed an anchoring point.

Chapter Five

The cloaked and hooded figure stared into a glass skull, eerily illuminated from within, standing on a long, low stone table. His face was pinched with emotion. Behind him the shadows once more rippled and hissed with hideous, hungry half-life. The man flinched, his eyes darting reluctantly to the seething cloisters, then back again. He could sense the expectation, the demand for nourishment, all around him. He tried to shut it out; he didn't want to lose the intoxicating world – the world of the Doctor's suffering – inside the skull.

'He's coming.' He said it by way of a dismissal. He wanted to be left alone with his tormented, vengeful thoughts. The constant, hungry presence at his back irritated him like the buzzing of a swarm of flies.

'I shall bring him to his knees... to the brink of madness. Then I shall destroy him utterly. Justice...' He brought his palms gently to rest on the crown of the skull.

The constant, subliminal cicada-rattle was getting on his nerves. He pressed his fists into the uneven slab of the table-top. The knuckles whitened. 'I have watched the Doctor. I have prepared. I know the way his mind works. I know exactly what he is thinking even now.' And he hated him for it.

His hands were bleeding. Still he crushed them into the rough stone. Suddenly he lurched from the room, an unseen door opening and closing silently, almost subliminally, about him. He had to be alone. These dark, incorporeal things whose fate was so inextricably caught up with his own had no sense of drama, no sense of irony or justice. They merely scented blood; demanded human life and warmth, ensnared it and sucked it dry. They couldn't reason, couldn't hate, couldn't understand.

He hated. He had to keep control, remain cold, calculating, keeping his hatred from spilling over.

He was in the dark, seething temple again. Alone, this time, inasmuch as he was ever alone. The shadows were, for once, only shadows. He was hungry. He felt a familiar restlessness in the pit of his stomach. The Power was gnawing at him, wanting to be fed. Silently he sat down at the centre of the floor paintings, cross-legged with the pentagram radiating out around him. Softly he closed his eyes, waiting… concentrating…

A tantalising warmth was creeping upward through his body, damp, tingling, thick. The blackness behind his eye was lightening. Shapes were becoming visible: dirty walls, narrow, leaded windows, a cobbled street, a woman's face under a gas-burning street-lamp…

The vision held him. He was tense, his palms were wet, his fists clenched, and he swayed slightly back and forth. A wind started to blow.

The face retreated out of the glow of the lamplight, a wall behind, clothes peeled away, a look of professional lust…

The wind was circling the nave, closing in, getting faster. The dim fires that lit the huge hall flickered, responding to the unearthly breath, reddening and growing. Still in its sitting position, his body started to snake and writhe, his teeth to grind, his head to sway.

Her expression, at first blankly welcoming, was one of uncertainty now. Fear, even. Jumping at shadows? No, my dear, you are beginning to see the true nature of shadows. The darkness is alive. You are going on a journey…

The wind was whipping around him, cruel and unnatural. The braziers burned bright and high, seduced to a frenzy. As if pivoted to the floor, he rocked, buffeted furiously, first in one direction then another, a snarling grimace, a grin of ecstatic agony clawed across his face.

Now she felt pain.

There was a frenzy of blades and flesh, then it was over.

He got up. The wind had extinguished the braziers at last, and then itself died. He was weak, bruised, but breathlessly satisfied. The Power would leave him alone for a while. As he left, the darkness seemed to drink him.

Chapter Six

On that particular day in November 1963, London drew itself close, huddled under a thick, slow-moving, almost Victorian fog. Everything was drained of colour, edges blurred, like a TV picture of the time. It was afternoon and the schools should have been discharging their contents on to the streets. Instead, the streets were deserted. No cars passed, shops were empty, their shutters down, the noise of traffic which is as constant and vital to London as a heartbeat, was nowhere to be heard. Silence.

Sound carries far in a fog; the sound of the TARDIS materialising in Totters Lane must have rolled down most of the streets of Shoreditch, Hoxton and De Beauvoir Town. Not that there was anybody around to hear it.

The Doctor was struggling to contain a churning ball of emotions rising and falling in his chest and stomach. The mix of nostalgia, fear and emptiness had kept him silent and restless, unable to focus his thoughts properly, throughout their journey. He was deliberately flouting the First Law of Time, returning like a lost child to the last period of stability he had known.

'I really tried to make it work here, you know, Ace. Part of the community... I sent Susan to the local school... For six months it was perfect, we were happy. But of course I got restless. I was headstrong in those days... On the weakest excuse I had to ruin it.'

And now he was going back. He just wanted to touch the past, to make sure it was still there. He wanted to gather it up in his arms before it fell apart altogether. An antique black jacket lay untidily across the TARDIS console. Rummaging through the pockets, he produced an old key. His hand hovered for a moment above the door control before coming heavily down on it.

Ace shivered as they stepped out into the damp grey evening. It matched her mood. She remembered the last time she had been here. Daleks, the Hand of Omega... Mike... Then, her trust in the Doctor had been absolute. Now...

She had mentally retreated into a corner, wrapped in her own blanket of fog. She felt distant from the Doctor - isolated - she didn't really understand anything and he had offered little in the way of explanation. He was willing himself into the very state of solitude that he was suddenly finding so hard to face.

'I need a stable base,' he had said. 'Perhaps then I can fight this thing. Right now I feel the ground is being cut out from underneath me.'

And nothing more.

Even through the fog-blanket, Ace recognised their surroundings. They were in an ordinary, slightly dingy London street. On each side of the road was a terrace of small, two-storeyed houses, spilling into larger streets at either end. In fact, the chain of houses on one side stopped short at a pair of large wooden gates and a fence, all about seven feet in height. It was at these gates that the Doctor was banging, pushing, trying to turn his key in the lock. The gates remained steadfastly shut.

'It's impossible. I know this is the right key.'

He now moved along the fence, kicking and pulling at the planks until he found one that moved. He recalled one of them had needed fixing. The gap was far too small for him but Ace might get through there. She walked sullenly forward, feeling as if she was being taken for the first time to see some austere and lionised older relative. She would be looked over, commented on, then ignored in a plethora of 'adult conversation'. She slipped easily through the gap in the fence and unlatched one of the gates, paying no attention to the huge, vague shapes towering around her. The Doctor walked almost reverently into the yard, between pillars and galleries of stacked junk: sinks, basins, corrugated iron and pipes. A wooden canopy afforded some protection for a collection of old furniture, vases and ornaments. The Doctor stood, turning in a slow circle in the middle of this barter paradise. His sense of occasion was gradually giving way to one of unease. Three-quarters of the way round he stopped, then rushed over to a corner of the yard. Was he just too late? No, the junk formed an unbroken wall. It had never been here.

'Ace!' There was a note of urgent authority in his voice that made her hurry over to him. 'The TARDIS isn't here.'

'We left the TARDIS outside.' She checked herself; something in his manner revealed a sudden impatience. Of course he meant the TARDIS of this earlier Doctor, the one they were trying to find, the one she was going to be left with. You'll be all right with him, the Doctor had said, until I come back. He'll look after you. And if I don't come back... He hadn't finished the sentence.

'It should be in this corner. It's never been here. Something is wrong.'

'Doctor...' A noise had made Ace turn towards the gate. Three indistinct figures... four... five... were silhouetted in the fog. More appeared: gaunt, white faces, skin drawn tight over bone. Some wore filthy, torn scraps of clothing, while others were naked. Their dark eyes sunk deep, drowned in the forgotten pools of their sockets. Flaccid, open mouths seemed to breathe a formless, toothless blackness. As they shambled towards the companions, feet dragging in the dust and oil of the yard, Ace knew she was staring at the dead. She turned to the Doctor.

Fixing his eyes ahead of him, he launched himself at a row of tall pipes which covered the front of one of the junk-mountains. The pipes gave way, crashing down on the nearest straggling line of corpse-creatures, followed by the junk that had stood precariously behind.

'The fence is lower at the back. We should be able to get over it.'

Ace had picked up a wooden chair-leg. She stood in front of a stack of stained-glass windows, swinging her weapon in an arc to keep at bay three of their deathly assailants. She heard the Doctor call and, hurling the hefty wooden beam at the nearest attacker, charged at their slow-moving ranks. The thing reeled under the impact of the flying chair-leg. With a sort of deep rasp – almost a snarl – it shot out a bony hand and clamped it around Ace's arm. She was through the undead cluster, but suddenly being dragged back into it. Its touch burned. She felt energy slipping from her, she began to faint. She was dimly aware of a pressure on her other arm. She tried to concentrate. The Doctor was tugging, trying to pull her free. He was wielding a piece of pipe, chopping at the wasted arm which held her. The burning was gone. She was being half-dragged, half-carried over a low pile of timber. He was talking to her but his voice sounded distant.

'Now, Ace, listen to me. You must climb the fence. It's not so high here. I'll help you.'

She pawed and kicked feebly at the wood as the Doctor hoisted her into the air. One arm was over the top, one hung limply down and her legs felt leaden. Holding her arm, the Doctor lifted her feet until she was horizontal, teetering on the top of the fence, then bundled her feet first on to the pavement on the other side. As he scrambled after her, he heard the timber-pile move. He looked back. The yard was still filling with these sad parasites, as if they scented health like starving animals would meat. The closest was barely a foot from him.

Where to go? Not back around to the gate and the TARDIS. That's where they all seemed to be coming from. He had to get away from here. Ace was coming round. They could lose themselves in the streets for a few hours until the cadaverous crowd had disbursed. Harry's cafe was just a few blocks away. At least, it ought to be…

As they stumbled through grey streets, the Doctor still half-carrying Ace, he knew they were becoming increasingly lost. Not only were the dark and fog making everywhere a uniform, flat monochrome, but many of the details he thought he remembered about the area were patently not the same. In fact the whole atmosphere of the place appeared different. At least they weren't being followed. Those things hadn't had the wit to scale the fence or to go around the block. That in itself worried him. What if the attack hadn't been targeted at them? What if it was an entirely random incident; those things indigenous to the area, nightly prowling for food? Too much had changed from the history he knew; a history which no longer seemed to include him.

He was aware of movement up ahead, but not from any sight or sound. Nevertheless, he knew he sensed a presence. He froze. The voice that crackled out of a bull-horn somewhere off in the fog pierced him: 'Halt! Do not move. We are armed and have orders to shoot to kill.' It wasn't the hostility in the words so much as the fact that the speaker sounded scared. Petrified. In that state, he might indeed shoot to kill. Odd; his accent was clearly American.

'We mean you no harm.' The Doctor spoke slowly and softly, cautiously.

'Why have you ignored the curfew?'

'We are strangers here. Visitors. We don't know about any curfew.'

None of this made any sense. The Doctor took a step in the direction of the voice. There was a rich cracking sound, and he felt a bullet whistle past his head. Another followed it.

Silently he slipped a hand over Ace's mouth and, grabbing her arm with his free hand, began to run, dragging her after him. Her legs barely working, they stumbled into a side-road as another rifle retort lacerated the fog. They couldn't run; it was far too dangerous. Tightening once more his grip on Ace's arm, he slipped silently into a sheltered doorway, pulling her after him. Perhaps they could avoid detection in the darkness. Two figures materialised out of the gloom. Both were young, both in the combat uniform of the United States army, both carrying automatic rifles. They paused for a second close to the doorway. One whispered something to another. They moved on.

The Doctor's pent-up breath came out in a rush. He was confused. Nothing was as it should be. He removed his hand from

Ace's mouth, gesturing silence. She was starting to come round. Neither of them felt inclined to leave their place of scant security.

There was a click behind them. The door was slowly opening. They spun round to see a young woman, half-hidden behind the door, gesturing frantically for them to come in. There was little alternative. His arm still around Ace, the Doctor walked gingerly past the woman into an unlit passage. The door clicked shut. Another opened, letting out a feeble light; a shabby living room. They entered. A young man in cardigan and slippers was standing, looking at them, frightened and angry. The woman followed them in. He sat down in a far corner, staring at them. She hovered behind them.

The one remaining frail pocket of hope lurched in the Doctor's breast, and warmth flooded through him. He smiled – a smile of blissful relief, of recognition. Perhaps now he was beginning to reclaim his past, inch by vital inch. 'Hello, Ian...' he said, '... Barbara.'

Part Two

The desert air around Qumran rippled under the blazing sun, the distant waters of the Dead Sea a shimmering flat line in the distance. The two men toiled on, oblivious to the heat, the sweat flicking from their backs as another hole appeared in the hard sand, joining the many other excavations scattered across the road.

'This seems thirsty work. Can I offer you some refreshment?' The two men looked up, surprised as the haze of heat parted like a curtain and a figure approached them down the dirt road, a gourd of water in his outstretched hands.

The two men drank greedily from the offered bottle, glad of respite from their toils.

'Thank you. What is your name, friend? Where are you headed?'

'My name is Joseph, and I have no particular destination in mind. I see where the road takes me.' He nodded at the holes in the road.

'What task is so great that it keeps you out in the desert heat?' One of the men picked up his shovel and resumed digging.

'Our grandfather is said to have buried a great treasure here before he died. My brother and I seek that treasure.'

Joseph nodded slowly. 'I remember your grandfather. I recall that he too took to his digging at the hottest part of the day, though, if my memory serves me correctly, he dug on the other side of the road.'

The two men stared at Joseph. 'You were here when he buried the chest?'

Joseph nodded. He tapped at the desert with his foot. 'Just here.'

'But that was seventy years ago!'

'Was it really that long?'

The two men looked at each other for a moment and then

launched themselves into their new hole with vigour. In minutes one of them struck something hard under the surface.

'It is here! We have found it.'

The two scrabbled in the hot sand and the lid of an ancient chest was slowly revealed. The shovel swung through the air and the old lock shattered. One of the men smiled up at Joseph.

'Thank you, traveller, you will be remembered.'

Joseph smiled solemnly. 'Yes, I expect I will.'

He watched as the lid of the chest was eased back. The rest of the ancient box was rotten and splintered. Coins glinted in the sand beneath. The men were reaching forward when the snake launched itself out of the box, hissing. The two men tumbled backwards, screaming.

Joseph shrugged and re-stoppered the gourd. 'Perhaps the past is sometimes better left buried.' Leaving the two men kicking sand at the angry snake, he resumed his journey down the road.

Chapter Seven

'Are you mad, Barbara?'

'They'd have been killed out there.'

'We don't know who they are…'

This wasn't going to be easy. The Doctor and Ace stood, smiling awkwardly, as the couple slugged it out.

'They seem to know us.'

'That's what worries me.'

A steaming silence descended. Ian Chesterton, old friend, now a frightened man with no memory, was fumbling inside a sideboard. He turned towards the intruders, uneasily clutching a cumbersome army revolver. The Doctor decided it was time to intervene.

'Really, we mean you no harm.'

'How do you know our names?' Ian was brusque, savage.

'Well, you don't know me, at least not yet…' Even if his appearance hadn't changed time and again since he last saw Ian Chesterton and Barbara Wright, they would have been none the wiser. If his calculations were correct they hadn't yet met him.

'Can you tell me what the date is, please?'

'The date?' Ian looked at the little man in front of him, confused.

'It's November 12th,' Barbara cut in.

'1963.'

'Yes, of course,' Ian snapped. 'Now tell us who you are.'

'I am Susan Foreman's grandfather.'

'What?'

'Susan Foreman. She's a pupil of yours. You do both teach at Coal Hill School?'

'Yes. But I haven't any pupil called Susan Foreman.'

'Nor I,' added Barbara.

The Doctor fell silent. Another of the struts of his life gone.

'Now try again, little man. Or I'll throw you back on to the street.'

'Ian, you can't! The curfew!'

'Exactly. They shouldn't have left home in the first place.'

'Yes, about this curfew,' the Doctor's words glided, cautious, curious, over the angry words ricocheting between their hosts. 'What's it all about, exactly?'

'Yes, and why were those two Yank soldiers shooting at us?' Ace was at last starting to take in her surroundings properly. She had kept quiet too long. The baited atmosphere was eating into her patience. She tried to rise from the chair in which the Doctor had dumped her. Too much. She suddenly felt dizzy.

'Are you both mad?'

'Ian, perhaps they haven't heard.' She turned to the intruders. 'The President was killed yesterday.'

'President?'

'Our president. Kennedy.'

'But...'

A brusque motion of the Doctor's hand was sufficient to silence Ace's interjection.

'Really, that's terribly sad. How did it happen?'

'He came to London. First time anyone of any importance has come to the city since the war. He was told of the risks, but he said he wanted to come anyway. He made a speech in the old parliament building in Westminster.'

Ian marched into the corner of the room and switched on the radio.

'Sit down and listen. They've broadcast nothing else all day.'

The Doctor and Ace sat down as the big old set hummed into life. At least that was one thing that hadn't changed: the rigid-backed, Reithian tones of the BBC, or whatever it was called in this bizarre quasi-reality, that steadfast patrician eloquence which had kept the British Empire together, remained undented by whatever bizarre turn of events had overtaken the nation.

'... further reports that looters and gangs are being shot. We

40

repeat, it is essential that you remain indoors. Lock your door and answer it to no one you do not know.'

There was a brief pause, then the voice of another announcer, heavy with grief and dignity, swung in.

'The President had arrived amid massive security. Soldiers, police and FBI agents had been at work in Westminster for weeks preparing for the visit. This was a major political event. No one in the ten-thousand-strong crowd at Westminster, nor anyone listening to the President's words on radio, or watching television back in mainland America, can have failed to be uplifted.'

And the familiar, sincere, almost evangelical tones of the Boston superman, JFK, youngest-ever president of the fifty-one states, burst out into the room.

'Today, the eyes of the world are on Good Old London Town. Now, just as throughout the war, just as so often in the last seventy years, London stands as a monument of suffering and endurance. We are, all of us, citizens of London Town, and throughout the world no man can have a prouder boast than to say, "Maybe It's Because I'm a Londoner."'

Inspired, uplifted, a warm roar rose from the crowd. The grille on the front of the dark wooden box shook as the voice of the announcer smoothly took the helm.

'With the cheers of the public ringing in his ears, the President left the platform. And that was when disaster struck. These are the words of one of the British FBI agents on the scene.'

British FBI agents? Ace looked at the Doctor, puzzled.

'It was unbelievable. These things – these... parasites – unless you've seen them... I never really believed in them before... They came from nowhere. Dozens of them. Bullets didn't stop them. Their touch was enough to... They dropped our men like flies. They cut a path to the President as he was leaving the building, approaching his motorcade, and, literally, cut him to pieces. Their touch seemed to burn him... to cut through him like knives. Horrible... horrible.'

Ian rose once more from his seat and turned the radio off. The sound died slowly.

'So there you are. Now you know.'

Ace was sceptical.

'But, Professor… even I know President Kennedy was –'

'Yes, yes, yes, Ace.' The Doctor cut across her words, waggling his hands at her to be quiet.

The Doctor turned to Ian.

'What exactly are these things?'

'Right, that's it!'

Ian was on his feet again. Barbara tried to calm him.

'Ian, sit down.'

'Can't you see, Barbara? He's either mad or making fools of us!'

'Young man,' the Doctor was talking in a way Ace had never heard before, his voice old with petulant urgency, 'I am sure you appreciate the gravity of this situation. This country – and possibly the whole planet – is facing something entirely outside its experience. I'm here to try to help…'

'Look, whoever you are, we've been facing this, as you put it, for decades. Since before Barbara and I were born. Are you seriously trying to tell us you don't know what's going on? You'd have to have fallen from another planet.'

The Doctor was thoughtful.

'Let's assume for a moment that we did fall from another planet. That we know we are in London in November 1963, and that's all we know. I would like you to fill in the gaps.'

'Barbara…' Ian's patience was all but exhausted, 'you must throw them out!'

'Ian, this is my house, remember.'

With a gasp of exasperation the teacher stalked from the room, shutting the door hard behind him. They heard his footsteps mounting the stairs, and water running.

Barbara turned back to her uninvited guests.

'You really don't know?'

'No. That's why we're asking.' Ace wasn't going to put up with this for much longer.

'All right, Ace.' The Doctor sounded unnaturally calm, like an expert working his way through a ticking bomb, wire by wire.

'Sit down. I'm a history teacher. I'll tell you what I can.

'As far as anyone can work out, this thing started in the late 1880s. Murders. Brutal murders in the East End of London. Prostitutes. They weren't just killed, they were…'

'Butchered. Dismembered.' The Doctor's voice slid in, smoothly, unobtrusively.

'Yes. There was an outcry. The Commissioner of the Metropolitan Police resigned. But it didn't stop there…'

Barbara the teacher was in control now. She told of the rash of brutal murders, mutilations, disembowellings, which had continued to ravage the East End and had spread like a virus through the squalid, tenement veins of outcast London, underclass London, the impoverished skin and bone and thin blood of the Metropolis which surrounded its few soft, fat, well-fed organs.

The public had grown restless. No confidence in the police, one law for the rich, another for the poor. Citizens' militia groups had sprung up, ostensibly to police the streets against the killer, but later becoming increasingly politicised. This in turn had led to conflict with the forces of law and order, complacent in the face of mass murder, galvanised by the spectre of burning palaces and the mob in the streets. The police attempted a crack-down; the self-appointed defenders of life and liberty resisted. Within six months of the first murder, London resembled the Revolutionary Paris of exactly a century before. Barricades were erected and a state of civil war and siege took hold.

'You must understand, Doctor. People were frightened for their lives. They preferred to face the full weight of the law than to be left at the mercy of Jack.'

'Jack the Ripper…?' Ace was finding her feet at last in this twisted history.

'Yes. And what about Jack?' the Doctor half-whispered, not wanting to break Barbara's narrative spell. 'Did the Ripper murders continue?'

'At that precise point? No one's really sure. London was awash with blood. What are a few mutilated corpses when whole districts are being shelled?'

Ace was suddenly itching to speak. 'Professor. None of this happened...'

'Be quiet, Ace. Barbara, please carry on.'

She did. She told of a decade of anarchy and brutality in London, followed by a gradual return to order and a kind of normality. London was rebuilt piece by piece. The spectre of Jack, it seemed, had departed, his appetite for blood finally sated.

And then came the First World War.

'That was the first time anybody actually saw Jack. The British Expeditionary Force at the Battle of Mons. First battle of the war. He was there, hovering over the battlefield like a huge, dark...'

Barbara faltered. The words she sought eluded her.

'Angel?' suggested the Doctor.

'Yes. Like the Angel of Death. Great, hollow, empty eyes, they say...'

The Doctor knew, only too well.

All through the war, Barbara told them, there had been reports and rumours from the trenches, hastily hushed up by the Allied High Command, petrified that the slim morale of the troops would dissipate altogether. Mutilations, Jack's marks, nothing that could be put down to the activities of the enemy. Ghosts which drank blood.

'Then, when the soldiers came home, they brought something back with them. My mother used to say they brought it in their eyes. I never understood what she meant when I was a girl.

'The killings started again, mostly in London, but there were outbreaks all over the country. The police started rounding up a few ex-servicemen who'd cracked out in France. A few were hanged. But the people knew – they sensed – that Jack was back. And this time his power had spread.'

This time the nation, Barbara told them, at first paralysed with fear, had gone mad *en masse*. The Government had withdrawn to Edinburgh, gangs and private armies once again sprang up, fought with each other, fought with the police and the regular army. Religious cranks proclaimed the end of the world, or hailed Jack as the new Messiah who wanted – who commanded – a society purged.

And for the first time the wraiths appeared on the streets. The cold, withered limbs of the Ripper, Jack made flesh, shambling, tormented, night-bound, always hungry.

Barbara looked at the clock. Eleven thirty. In spite of Ian's arguments, she was grateful for the presence of the two strangers. She didn't mind giving a history lesson. Tonight was a tense night and it was helping to pass the time.

'It seems unbelievable now, but when I was a girl my mother used to say that if I was naughty, the bogey-man would get me. That's how long it took to sink in, that there were actual bogey-men on the streets of London. A lot of people still won't believe it; those who haven't seen it for themselves. They blame it all on the gangs or on the preachers or on the breakdown of law and order. But all that came later. First there was Jack.'

The Doctor was gentle, careful. Nearly there now.

'Tell me about the Americans...'

'Well, there was another war.'

Hitler, of course. No such bloody alternative to world history would be complete without him. Just as in the world Ace knew, perhaps as in every possible twist and turn of time, Hitler overran Europe, murdered millions, brought great powers to their knees. Britain stood alone but, despite the Government's flag-waving, its capacity to fight a war was nil. The army was hard put to keep order at home. London languished under martial law. Hitler pounded the capital with bombs. The huge, spectral Jack, all eyes and swastika, was seen, time and again, towering in flame over burning buildings.

And then came the Americans. Overpaid, oversexed and over here. For good. The price of American intervention in the war was de facto control over a Britain strategically vital, but morally and economically bankrupt, and governmentally crippled.

The war ended, Hitler was defeated, the Americans stayed. In a blaze of publicity – Uncle Sam against Jack the Ripper, a propaganda coup for President Truman – the Americans dug in. The Government in Edinburgh found itself effectively redundant, the royal family at Balmoral doubly so. London found itself isolated, ghettoised, and ultimately walled in. Anybody entering or leaving the city had to pass through a checkpoint; nobody got through without the proper authorisation. Any unauthorised persons crossing the 'containment zone' were shot. The Americans had opted for quarantine rather than combat.

'Ian would disagree with me, but President Kennedy was the best thing that could have happened to us. He made Britain the fifty-first state, and actually gave us some kind of status inside the Union. And he came to London. That meant something.'

She wanted it to mean something. The Doctor could see that Barbara, along with Ian and, presumably, the rest of London, were at the end of their tether.

Barbara fell silent. There was no more to say. Ace looked from her to the Doctor, expectantly.

'Professor…'

'Mmm…?'

'What d'you think?'

He was offhand, almost casual-sounding. 'Some kind of gestalt life form, capable of generating and controlling hosts…'

'Like the things which attacked us…'

'Yes… Feeding off life, fear, death… Unpleasant.'

'What about Jack the Ripper?'

'There's a definite link with what you and I, Ace, would call real world events. The real Ripper murders – there were five – did generate a sense of panic and resentment out of all proportion to the actual killings, ghastly though they were, among an already restless population.

'This thing seems to have capitalised on that. It feeds off a bloodbath, then sleeps for a while. The killings stop. Then comes the First World War and the thing wakes again, possibly scenting blood. This time there's no stopping it. And now, as Barbara says, things are completely out of control.'

'So what can we do?' Ace had heard enough history.

The door opened. Ian slipped back into the room. He smiled briefly, awkwardly, sheepishly at the travellers and sat down.

'It's not a question of what we do,' the Doctor said bluntly. 'This is something I have to deal with alone, Ace.'

'You can't leave me here…!'

The Doctor was silent. In truth he didn't know what to do with Ace. He couldn't leave her here, it was true. Not in this cruel, desperate alternative to the sanctuary he had come looking for. But he was afraid for her. He thought of the baby-bodies on the battlefield and shuddered.

'You're going, then.' Nothing in Barbara's voice indicated surprise.

The old Time Lord smiled at her. 'Thank you for your story, Barbara.'

'Thank you for listening.'

'You know, it shouldn't be like this. Something is very wrong with time itself.'

Barbara's eyes flashed between the Doctor and Ace. Both looked entirely serious.

'I know there's no reason you should believe me. You probably think me mad already, but I'm here to try and put things right. If I can do something, when we meet again it will be in very different circumstances, I promise.'

And they would have no memory of this brief, sweet encounter.

For them it wouldn't have happened.

'Doctor, I am coming with you.' Ace sounded defiant.

The Doctor merely looked at her. She was a difficult child, not unlike Susan, who had called him Grandfather, who had been happy here on Earth, in 1963, in a world where Jack the Ripper was merely a historical curio.

They were all surprised by Ian's voice, quiet, almost apologetic.

'She can stay with us.'

Barbara looked shocked, but Ian was not to be put off.

'I know things are no picnic round here, but we've got enough to eat – just – and a roof over our heads.'

Nobody spoke. All eyes were turned towards Ian. Beginning to feel foolish, he blundered on, blushing.

'I know... I know what I said earlier. I was scared. I still am scared. But I was thinking while I was in the bath, suppose you have fallen from another planet? It sounds crazy, but who would have believed a hundred years ago what's happening now? Who would have believed in Jack? We've lived without hope for so long now. Kennedy was our last chance, and he's gone.'

Barbara looked from Ian to Ace to the Doctor.

'Yes. Of course she can stay. But bear in mind the danger. We daren't go out after dark, and now it looks as if we're under threat by day as well, at least as long as this fog lasts.'

The Doctor looked down at his young companion. 'Ace...'

'I'd rather go with you, Professor...'

'All right...' He stretched out his arms, laid a hand on Barbara's shoulder, and one on Ian's. 'Thank you. Both. For saving us on the street, and for your trust. If I can do anything, I will. If it helps, just remember, there are alternatives. Life doesn't have to be like this.'

'What do we do now, Professor?' Ace was yawning as she spoke. It was well past midnight.

'Sleep,' the Doctor replied. 'There's plenty of time until morning...'

Chapter Eight

It was a pale, insipid sun which grappled its way painfully above the rooftops, turning the street a dull orange; a scene viewed through smoke-yellowed glass, unhealthy, diseased. The shroud of the night's fog writhed and coiled in snake-like clusters, scattered as the sun struggled to achieve its zenith, skulked in corners and narrow places, and gradually recombined. Small knots of people bustled back and forth, fooling themselves into some semblance of normality. Shopkeepers unshuttered shops with few goods and fewer window panes. Market stalls, crudely constructed from the debris of years of conflict, took shape on the cracked tarmac, black-market merchandise passing from hand to hand and grey, furtive customers vanishing like the remnants of the fog into the shadows of East London.

Barbara stepped into the street and pulled her coat tight against the cold of this murky November day. Despite the chill, a warm glow nestled inside her, giving a lift to her step and an outlook that was all too rare. As she hurried to the local store to join the daily queue for milk and bread, idly fingering her ration-book, she even toyed with the idea of bartering at one of the rag-tag stalls for a bar of black market chocolate. For the first time since her parents had died she felt as though her life might perhaps encompass some single, slender hope stretching beyond this narrow existence; that the life she and Ian scratched from the grime of the city might one day be as insubstantial as the fog wraiths that slowly dissipated around her as the day grew faintly warmer.

The strange little man who had arrived in fear and bullets had intruded into more than just their home, bringing with him a spark of something difficult to define: something old – ancient – and undeniably good. Even Ian, stubborn and cynical as he was, had woken bright and cheerful, whistling his way through the house, more alive than Barbara had seen him in years.

Her face clouded with sudden uncertainty as the Doctor's face swam more clearly into her daydream. After her impromptu history lesson, he had talked softly and sadly about the London he knew; a London so far removed from Barbara's experience that it scarcely seemed feasible. Despite the confusion and questions and doubts, she and Ian had sat and listened, letting this mysterious magician weave his spell of memories, letting the suspicion and bile of the night wane into early-morning nothingness.

Eventually his young companion had fallen into an exhausted sleep and Ian had carried her into the spare bedroom. The Doctor had smiled at the offer of the sofa, accepted the proffered blanket and turned to the small collection of history books that Barbara kept on a shelf near the radio, muttering that he wasn't tired and might read awhile. Barbara had brought a candle from the kitchen – the power unfailingly went off at some point between ten o'clock and midnight – and bade him goodnight. The Doctor had turned, looked her in the eyes and smiled a smile so full of compassion and sadness that it had brought tears to her eyes. Then he had wished her goodnight and goodbye, and immersed himself in the books.

The rattle of machine-gun fire and the birdlike, childlike scream of a wraith-creature had woken her with a start. It was not yet light. She had lain still for a while, listening, but the quiet of the curfewed night was undisturbed further, save for the slow breathing of Ian at her side. Unable to return to sleep, she had slipped quietly from the covers and crept downstairs to the kitchen meaning to make herself a drink. In the hallway, her eye was caught by a thread of light dancing across the carpet from the lounge door, slightly ajar. Like a child at Christmas, scared, but eager for a glimpse of something supernatural and wonderful, she crossed to the door and pressed her face to the door-frame, one eye shut, the other against the pencil-thin gap.

There was the Doctor, cross-legged among a circle of open books and newspapers, muttering to himself and jotting furiously in a small, leather-bound diary. He was like a shaman in a temple of his own construction, breathlessly voicing the spells that might give him understanding of the mysteries of his unfathomable universe.

The candle on the arm of the chair guttered suddenly and the scene flickered like a bad film. She shivered and pulled back from the doorway. She knew, or would know, or *should* know, this stranger from the fog, but at that moment she also realised that she would never see him again.

She returned to bed and snuggled up to an oblivious Ian, holding in her mind that final image of the Doctor; slowly letting it slip away as she returned to sleep. When she awoke a second time, it was morning. He and his young girl companion had gone, books returned to their shelves, newspapers back in their neat pile in the corner of the room. The only sign that he had ever existed was the stub of a candle in a pool of wax that, despite Ian's protestations, she could not bring herself to remove.

A tide of children surged past her, snatching her from her daydream, screaming and shouting, their game a sick, vivid re-enactment of the events of yesterday: a child president being torn apart by child killers. A rage rose in Barbara. She wanted to seize these children and shake them, tell them that this was not how it should be. This harsh, vile existence was nothing more than a sham, a façade, something that would end, something that they would leave behind as they grew and remember only as a shadowy dream. She knew the reality would more likely be a pile of corpses sucked tinder-dry or scattered in pieces across a blood-brown street. Ring-a-ring-a-roses… Kids knew. Kids always knew.

To be a Londoner gave you two choices: try to shut it out or go with the flow. To live like frightened cattle, every night waiting for death to rap at your window, or to fall into the whirlpool of violence, pitching yourself at everything that moved, at an enemy that grew stronger with every angry thought that flickered through your mind.

The army still maintained that they were in control, but you only had to see the faces of the young servicemen to know the truth.

A shot rang out from across the river. Heads jerked up and the children, their play disturbed by the sobering sounds of a more deadly game, scattered back to safe houses. Two more shots, then silence. Barbara shivered. It was too light for wraiths, the cold night-creatures. The enemy in the daytime streets was far more substantial, though no less terrifying. Jacksprites, they called themselves: youths with torn and bloodied faces, the crude tattoos on their foreheads proclaiming themselves Children of the Ripper. They ran in packs, clusters of scalpel blades taped to their fingers, full of amphetamines, butane and solvents and cheap crack – decades of drug-evolution crammed into a few short street-years – anything to make the world seem bright and bloody.

The shots had come from the south-west, probably attempting to stop a looting raid on one of the West End hospitals as they sought fresh blades and new drugs. Barbara rubbed a clutch of old scars on her forearm. She had more reason than most to fear the Jacksprites. Her last trip West, a year ago now, had nearly cost her her life. An army bullet was all that had prevented her from being so much shredded meat.

Feeling sick and dizzy, she hurried across to the ever-growing queue outside the shop.

Fog and brief, feeble sunshine had given way to clouds in a heavy, sagging sky. The first fat drops of rain began to fall, heavy with soot and grime, diluted acid eroding the substance of London as effectively as the conflict was eroding the souls of its people.

In dead Piccadilly Circus, stopped heart of the metropolis, the rain mingled with the blood of the dead Jacksprite, forming crimson rivulets that swirled and spun through the rubble of the streets, tracing paths like coastlines on some imaginary map. The colour dulled and darkened as it mingled with the dirty sap of the city. The torrent that vanished Thamesward through the drains bore no signs of the drama, the life-loss, that had become so commonplace.

Soldiers pulled the collars of their trench-coats up against the now hammering rain and continued with their grim task of hauling the body into a thick tarpaulin bag, heavy with water. Their job was made more difficult by the lethal blades which protruded from finger-tips and knuckles, hiding in vicious rows behind collars and cuffs and in any crack and crevice in clothing which an enemy might grab onto. They were yellow and filth-encrusted, each blade charged with a potential for death more exquisite and lingering than the slicing, chopping end they promised at first sight. The soldiers manoeuvred the body with care. Too many of them had friends who had been sucked into the MASH unit at Chiswick, their blood contaminated by whatever filth and disease this juvenile carrion crawled through.

All this risk to keep the streets free of bodies, to convince the public that all was well when the public could see all too easily the time-blackened stains soaked into the brickwork. Or stand and watch as soldiers scrubbed tarmac, the foam of the soap on their brushes turning pink as they laboured to remove the permanent stain of death from public places and thence from the public mind.

The group lieutenant, a country boy from Ohio, hurried his squad and the death sack was rolled into the back of a Scammell truck. The rain would go to work on the blood. They had an entire city to patrol before dusk and then, thank God, they would return to the barracks at Clapham and pity the poor bastards who'd pulled night duty. He knew that soon, too soon, the shifts would change and it would be his squad that had to wander the night-choked lanes, waiting for the dark and fog to grow wasted limbs and lurch shrieking into the street-lamps.

When the Americans had first arrived, they had tried to revive London's crippled tube network, but the cool underground tunnels had become a battleground for packs of wild dogs – white, useless eyes and patchy, scabbed and bloody fur – and the homeless of London, naked and crazed, who protected their nests with such ferocity that the troops had withdrawn and sealed up all the station entrances.

The Red Cross still shipped in food parcels for distribution to these city-centre refugees, but the troops piling boxes in the ticket-halls of long empty stations knew that the food was unlikely to reach the tube-lines. If the black marketeers and looters didn't reach it first then the rats would, and not even the dog packs would tackle the rat-tide that turned the boxes into a writhing frenzy of fur and chisel-teeth, their chalk-on-blackboard cries ringing through empty black tunnels and escalators seized and solid. But still the parcels came.

And still on the outskirts of the city, crushed between pestilential street-war and the great white wall which surrounded it like a tourniquet, Londoners stood in long, hopeless lines to collect meagre supplies. Inside the stone and barbed wire and machine-gun barricades, in weary spite of the constant threat of death, life continued.

Some had stayed because they had nowhere else to go, some out of stubborn pride, and some woke each morning with 'Perhaps today will be different' on their lips. Most had merely left it too late to pack their bags and go. And now they could only wait. No one now was allowed to leave the city without proper authorisation. Illegal exoduses met with loud-hailers and machine-gun fire. Applications for exit passes lay in piles, unread, at a dozen military command posts.

Barbara had lingered because of the children, her pupils. Somehow, to flee to the safety of the country when the classrooms were still full seemed unethical, a betrayal of her professional obligations and of the children themselves. So she and the other teachers persevered and presided over a slow deterioration, lack of books, lack of facilities and lack of shelter. How could they expect the kids to sit and learn about Shakespeare or Pythagoras when the world around them was tearing itself to pieces? Was it really so surprising that they had lost so many to the Jacksprites? At least, in a terrible way, what the Children of the Ripper taught their own had some bearing on life as London's people had to live it every day.

It was easier for Barbara than for Ian. She could tell her histories with the few books she had managed to gather and with the knowledge lodged in her memory. The chemistry teacher needed more than papers and memories. He needed laboratory equipment, chemicals, things only the army, the hospitals and the Jacksprites had access to. The long, vain battle to keep alight the candle of knowledge as the cornerstone of civilisation had worn Ian down. Once militant and resourceful, he had slowly surrendered to bitterness and fear. Two years ago he was still prepared to petition their Senator – a man who never got closer to London than Ascot for the racing; a man who was as full of sympathy as he was of obstructiveness – to do something for the children of London. Now it was as much as Ian could do to drag himself out of bed in the mornings. He hadn't attended the leaking, windowless shell they still laughingly referred to as a school for the past four months.

Barbara knew that at the moment, she was living for both of them. It was her optimism, her strength, that was keeping them together; perhaps keeping them alive. Last night she had had an ally. Last night she had seen a light return to Ian's eyes that she had thought long-since extinguished. This morning, for the first time in a year, he had looked at her with the look of a lover.

She took her place at the front of the queue and paid for her daily ration, then sprinted back through the downpour to the small terraced house she and Ian had shared for the last year and a half. Ian was preparing lunch in the kitchen. She gave him a peck on the cheek and took off her soaked raincoat. Ian picked up the coal scuttle and went to coax some life into the fire in the other room. He was whistling *In the Mood*. Barbara followed him. She sat down, leaned back in her chair and smiled as her fingers brushed a puddle of hardened wax on the arm.

Chapter Nine

It is older, now, and fatter; troughing for decade upon decade on the flesh and fear, greed and bloodlust of this rancid peach of a planet, with no sign of its food source ever running dry. It has become almost too easy. Whatever of this conspiracy of appetite and malice was human has long since gone, sucked back into the livid darkness that gave birth to it. All higher functions have gone. It is pure, cold parasite now, light-swallowing, shadow-tentacled, seething, glutting, chattering animal madness. All its senses narrowed, sharpened and focused on its task: feed, survive, grow.

It has spread its dread fingers – the shuffling phantoms of night and fog – so that its grasp covers the city and blots out the sun. It hates light. It lives in a place far from light, corridors now dead and pitch black, climbing walls, wrapping itself around pillars and buttresses, lazing and belching and feeding.

But perhaps the tiniest glimmer of vestigial memory remains. Something pricks at its slumber like a pin, irritating, scratching. It won't go away. It feels no hatred any more, just a desire to scratch back. Slowly it gathers itself, focuses its lazy mind, yawns and stretches…

…and its grey limbs roll out of the fog, another dead-eyed, club-footed assault on the feed-trough, this time rooting for something special.

Something in the wind. A scent, almost, that it has known long before, that for some reason once filled it with rage and sickness. The creature has picked it up again. It has been enough to wake it. It will take little effort to find the source of the scent, to squeeze it, to crush out the life-force which is at once nauseating and irresistible.

This place is so much like all the others, with life stacked in long, low rows like ripe tomatoes. The grey marauders come from all sides, shambling onwards, deadly converging.

Splintering wood, somewhere narrow, damp, where little light can enter. Humans: one male, one female, neither of them the one sought, although the scent of that one is strong here. They shout, they scream, Barbara! Barbara! It is used to their meaningless noises and the aroma of blind panic. It is like seasoning on the meat. One smells of anger, as well as fear. Male. It has a hand-weapon. The bang and bite of hot, angry metal jerks the creature more fully awake. It is nothing, it has happened before. It can afford to lose a few fingers; it has hundreds of them.

It is over quickly. The flesh rent, the life drawn. Sometimes, if the cadavers remain reasonably intact, it might choose to pour a little of itself into them. Just enough that they too might become its fronds and suckers. Not this time. In a frenzy of eating the bodies are ribboned to the bone.

But that singular, tantalising morsel is not here. It has been here but it has eluded the creature's hunters. A low sense of disgruntlement seeps through its thick consciousness. It feels itself groping its way up and out, however briefly, from the sleep it sleeps for years at a time while its autonomic feeding system continues without hindrance.

The city, with its food racked up, shudders. It shifts, noticeably, almost like a tiny earthquake. Waves of new tension, sweet spice, are triggered in the brick-and-concrete cloches. Those humans who are moving stop, point, shout, look up. They look into the face of something huge and dark moving behind the fog, behind the rain, towering over the city. Something shaped by their limited perceptions into almost human form: angelic, demonic, eyes and mouth open, empty, plunging into the same black pit.

They behave as they always do, making a lot of noise, firing loud projectiles which whistle through the air and, finding their target, connect with nothing. As their little glands start pumping, more and more, the aroma threatens to overpower the creature. It convulses with pleasure, and the city shakes again.

But the quarry is gone. The scent, so close, has vanished. The creature feels angry, cheated. It can feed on this rubbish in its sleep. It wanted something special, and its want has been denied. It mews, it snarls, it spits venom over the city in a wide arc…

Chapter Ten

Jed the Idiot Boy, they called him. They always had – in the workhouse – as long as he could remember. He vaguely recalled the workhouse. Through the thin clouds of his pauper's mind he saw long rooms, metal staircases, bare stone and grey paint, not much light. He smelled hard, scrubbed smells, and dirt. He tasted something bland and unvarying. He heard… nothing but tense, ticking silences. That was where they must have started it – Jed the Idiot Boy. They still called him it now. He was thirty-three.

But Jed Barrow saw. Jed Barrow knew. He remembered. He collected sights and sounds as others did acquaintances. Where he could, he collected objects to help him remember. The objects – and the sights, the sounds, the smells – he kept in a special hiding place. Underground. Clever. When he was alone he would go there and sort through the objects, pick up one or another, touch it, feel it, stare at it. The sights and sounds and smells soon followed, crowding into his memory, often unexpectedly hostile, demanding a response, a forfeit, a reason for being summoned from sleep. He would sometimes weep, sometimes even collapse, so intense could these sensations be.

He worked at Christ Church, Spitalfields, tending the grounds, digging graves. Even when he wasn't working he spent most of his time at the church. He was childishly possessive about the tawdry, ill-kempt churchyard, the sad old graves, the mute stone mass of the church itself. The locals were used to seeing him creeping and hiding among the gravestones at all hours. If he saw them, he would whistle or hiss, ludicrously half-concealed behind one of the crooked stones. He played odd, stalking, territorial games. He would mark the entrances to his little kingdom with piss, challenging anybody to cross the gateway, the church doorway, wherever two paths met. He never went inside the church. The Reverend Jefford would never allow him further than the vestry, too wretched to assail the Lord's ears with idiot ravings. Anyway the forbidding weight and simple, stern majesty of the place terrified him. The altar, the cross, had always seemed to accuse him. He remembered from the workhouse lurid tales of Christ's passion. He imagined himself being nailed to a cross. To this cross. It seemed to reach out to him, to cast its dooming shadow across him. He was quite happy with the Reverend's injunction.

The Reverend Jefford was like an extension of the church itself; the wrath of the Almighty (a favourite expression of his) hovered about him like a black halo. Jed avoided the Reverend as much as possible and hid from him whenever duty didn't command his presence. But Jed was clever. Jed knew things that the Reverend Jefford didn't. For one thing, Jed had a key to the crypt. The Reverend didn't know that. Jed liked the crypt, it was cool and quiet, he could get away from the countless distractions and comings and goings and loud and bright things that assaulted his senses up above. It was here he came to take stock, to assimilate the often baffling everyday experiences he hoarded in his attic memory. He kept his collection here, behind some loose bricks in one wall, and here he relived and intoxicated and tortured himself with each recollection.

But recently something had changed: a chill had descended. He felt ill at ease now among the weeds and remembering stones, and especially in the crypt. Shadows were moving around the church, after dark and by day, never distinct. There was a man, he was sure, dressed in black. Jed had seen him pass like a ghost through the crypt, had followed him out into the afternoon smog and the river-fogs of night. Like everything else, Jed kept this to himself. He saw what others missed. He was out, creeping through the streets, while others were fast asleep in their beds or blind drunk in the Angel and Harp in Stoney Lane. Two nights he had followed the shadow. On each occasion he had lost it, but on each of those nights a girl was murdered. He had heard the faint, strangled screams of the second one, from behind the gates of the back yard in Hanbury Street, and he had run. The next day he was back there early. He watched – from hiding, of course – the police find the body, remove it, then scratch around in the dirt, looking frustrated. After they had left, he had gone scavenging to the same spot. He had done better than them, he had found two gold rings. Rings: a pretty treasure. Hidden knowledge: Jed's secret strength. The rings, the incident, the scream were duly filed away for future reference.

When he cared to go there, Jed lived on the edge of Limehouse in a street of once grand houses. They were large, but had long ago given up keeping themselves groomed. They had dropped out of the social round, stopped receiving visitors, no longer bothered to rouse themselves from a stupid, embittered sleep. Like a dying empire, the shell remained defiant but all inside was up for grabs. Jed's great-aunt owned one of these houses. Jane Treddle had lived alone and mad for twenty-five years, seeing nobody but one drab servant girl (the servant girls changed, but always drab) and occasionally her nephew Bartle Treddle, of Treddle's Wharf, Wapping. One day, on a whim, she had sought out her only other living relative, plucked him from St Dunstan's Workhouse and put him to live like a dog at her feet.

Since then, she had studiously ignored his presence. He spent little time at the house. His aunt haunted the place, drifting from room to room, a spectre in black, muttering and cackling to herself, surrounded by the cats that flowed around her legs like a wedding train.

In rare moments of lucidity, she would call Jed to her chambers and ask him to run some errand or other, and most Sundays she would accompany him to the church, nodding and smiling through the Reverend Jefford's threats of Hellfire and Damnation before returning to the sprawling old house in Limehouse, cradling Jed to her chest, cooing softly.

At times like these, Jed would try and avoid her, creeping from the front door to his attic room, kicking at the cats that came too close, huddling on his bed before falling into fitful bursts of sleep, the sound of his aunt's cackling ringing in his ears.

Most days now, Jed left the house at dawn to avoid being seen, picking his way through the carpet of sleeping cats, scurrying out into the fog as soon as the sun had risen.

Jed revelled in the fog. It was his brother, his partner. During his furtive hunts for treasure, it shrouded him like a cloak and he in turn became part of it; insubstantial, background. The sounds of the City carried better too, and the last weeks had brought something new, a taste of something in the air, something that lurked as a constant companion to the frightened look in the eyes of the people of Whitechapel. There were always stories of the murders, of the girls that had been mutilated, butchered by a killer whose name was never far from the lips of gossips and storytellers. A name that left no doubt as to the atrocities that were being committed. The Ripper.

Jed had stopped following the shadow. He was desperate to know what was going on, but frightened of what he might see. Some evenings he had even toyed with the idea of praying in the church, but the dread atmosphere of that cold grey bastion of Christendom always sent him scuttling home.

And then he had met Malacroix. Malacroix the mysterious. Malacroix the magician. Malacroix the mad.

It was a killing that had brought them together. Jed had seen him at Mitre Square, watching with the rest of the crowds as the police had pulled the body of Catherine Eddowes from the street. A short, swarthy man engulfed in an ankle-length coat, Malacroix was unmistakable, his mouth a permanent leer beneath his thick black moustache. Jed knew of him; no one in London could have ignored him. His face loomed from a thousand posters on a thousand walls. The Circus of Jacques Malacroix had been at Stepney for nearly three months now and no one had shown any sign of tiring of it. Malacroix was the consummate showman, the perfect blend of suave charm and mysterious continental danger.

Jed had seen his eyes blaze when the crowd began to mutter and whisper the name of the Ripper. Across the bloodstained yard he had caught Jed's eye and something had passed between circus owner and idiot boy.

Jed had followed him from the murder site through a maze of pea-souper streets, ducking into grey doorways, flitting through the fog like a bat. They came at last to a patch of open ground in Stepney, where the circus was pitched. Jed had watched the circus arrive and set up. He had been mesmerised by the elaborately painted huddle of caravans and the brightly coloured awnings of the seven large tents which stood in a broad horseshoe, and above all by the cages of wild animals, hunched savagely together behind the caravans. He watched the gaudily dressed people who danced and tumbled about their business through the day, and the crowds who poured into the tents by night. He heard the gasps and applause, and longed to know what magic was taking form in the sacred space beyond the canvas. He had never dared approach. The Reverend Jefford had denounced the circus as Lucifer's play-pen. He had watched his second cousin, Bartle Treddle, trying in vain (as usual) to entice his aunt from the house with the offer of a trip to the circus. She had screamed that the circus was full of monsters. And she was right. Jed had seen them. Two identical women, their flesh joined at the waist, a man the size of a babe, a lad whose body ended at the waist, and who bounded about the site on his arms. Jed had turned and fled.

But he had gone back. More than the horror, more than the Reverend Jefford's sermons, the lure of the circus held him fast. Here was something new. And there was something else. There was magic here: a frightening, wild magic here. The twin sirens of his life, his aunt and the Reverend Jefford, could not compete with this.

Now, for the first time, he stepped from the road into the corral of tents, grey and ghostly in the fog.

He had lost the man. Suddenly, he was disorientated by this strange new terrain. He had stumbled against the side of a tent. A slit of darkness opened next to him as the flap was drawn back, and a hand clasped him hard on the shoulder. It was him. The man.

'You have been following me,' the man had said blandly, in a thick foreign accent. *'Pourquoi?'*

'No, sir, not me, swear to God, sir… swear to God…' Jed had babbled.

The man had smiled.

'I have seen you twice, now. On both occasions following a diabolical murder. One could grow… suspicious.'

'No, sir, swear –'

'You watch things,' the man had interrupted. 'You spy, you follow… You steal as well, *peut-être?*'

'Steal… No, sir, never, never…'

'And nobody ever notices you, do they? Nobody ever sees. Ah, but *I* saw… What is your name, boy?'

'Jed, Jed… Jed, sir.'

'I like you, Jed, Jed, Jed,' the man had said. 'I think we shall become great friends.' His smile had broadened, and his grip had tightened, causing Jed to cry out. 'But I will always know when you are lying to me. Do you understand?'

'Yes… yes, sir,' Jed had groaned.

The man had released him, and he had sunk to the floor, clutching at his shoulder.

'From now on, you are my eyes, Jed,' he had said. 'I want to find the man who is stalking our streets at night, this Ripper. I want to know him. I want to look into his soul…'

A gold coin had passed into Jed's hand with the promise of so much more, and he had been told to watch, to listen, and to report to Malacroix in his caravan every night after the circus had closed.

'But remember this, my friend,' he had said to Jed, 'if you ever think to betray me… I have many sets of eyes in this city, and I shall know.'

Jed had felt frightened – he had lost control of his bladder – and strangely exhilarated. In his stunted, animal way he felt on the threshold of a new world. This was the greatest secret of them all: a whole other life which his aunt and the Reverend would know nothing about. He had pitched himself into his task with maniac enthusiasm.

The gold coin had pride of place in his underground store, and every time he brought something of use to Malacroix, his treasure grew.

Another girl had died on the night of their fateful meeting, a prostitute, cut from ear to ear. Jed had listened to the tales and rumours which began to circulate around Whitechapel like a fever, and had brought the news to his new master. He still provided Malacroix with a steady stream of gossip overheard in public houses and scraps from the crime scenes, but he remained silent about the mysterious shadow from the church, too scared to bring the circus owner too close to the Reverend Jefford, who had denounced the circus as the decadent work of Lucifer himself.

On his nightly visits to the circus, Jed would wander through another world of colour and smell. At his first visit, he had stared in awe at the bearskinned strong-man that guarded the door of Malacroix's caravan, and had been led through the circus open-mouthed as he was brought face to face with lions and elephants, with jugglers and trapeze artists – and the freaks.

Even now, the freaks scared him. When he had first seen them he had screamed and run, hiding under one of the colourful circus stalls. Malacroix had laughed – a deep, hissing laugh – and called to one of his minions. 'Ackroyd, go and get the boy out from under there. Introduce him to our twisted friends.'

Ackroyd had pulled the shivering Jed from the mud and sat him down. He had tried to get up again, tried to flee. The giant in the animal-skin had shot out a hand and gripped him by the neck. He had screamed hysterically and continually as the freaks had loped wearily up to him and introduced themselves. Malacroix had laughed heartily.

Tonight, the fog was thick and grey, the smallest of sounds booming in the night air, the city's heartbeat audible through the moist, dank night. Jed was on the banks of the Thames at Shoreditch, scraping through the low-tide mud, distracted from his duties by the promise of more treasures for his store. The coins of Malacroix had already begun to bore him. Jed kept them in a stone jar, completely oblivious to their value. Now crab shells were his fascination, and the Thames was proving generous. Already six lay glistening on the cold grey mud of the riverbank.

A gust of wind, swirling the fog, made Jed look up, but the wharf was deserted, the gas lamps of Whitechapel just pale smudgy glows in the distance. He returned to his scrapings but another gust, more violent this time, made him start.

He clambered to the dockside, gathering the crab shells to his chest, wiping mud on to his jacket. He cocked his head on one side, his keen ears catching the first murmurings of something distant and unfamiliar. The wind grew stronger, the fog whirling and boiling. Leaves and papers began to join in the delicate dance and slowly a noise began to build, a stentorian breathing, like the elephants at the circus.

Jed began to back away as the noise grew and grew, until it became a grinding roar. Leaves and grit stung his face, the wind was impossible. Jed threw himself into a corner and added his own screams to the unearthly alien noise. A harsh blue light swept over him and Jed curled into a ball, his only thought to protect his precious shells.

With unexpected suddenness, the wind and noise stopped and the fog, temporarily banished by the disturbance, closed in again, thick and wet. Jed opened his eyes and stared in astonishment at the tall blue cabinet that stood on the wharf. Here was something new. Something unknown. Malacroix would pay well for this information. Jed's heart leapt. Maybe this time, instead of gold coins, Malacroix would let him take the small monkey skull that sat on his desk. Jed had yearned for the skull ever since his first visit to the showman's caravan.

Jed checked that none of his crab shells had been cracked in his stumblings and carefully stowed them in his mud-stained jacket. He regarded the blue box. It reminded him of the magicians' cabinets that he had seen being loaded in and out of the stage door of the Palace Theatre. But their arrivals had not been accompanied by wind and lightning, only by the wheezing and groaning of the hired stage hands and the goading of the theatre manager, Mr Jago.

Jed made his way from his bolt hole and crossed to the box, pacing around it cautiously. He reached out and touched the rough side and immediately snatched his hand away as if burnt. The box was alive! He reached out to it again, but a noise from within – a series of clicks – sent him scurrying back to the shadows to watch. Watch…

Chapter Eleven

Ace watched as the Doctor paced around the console prodding and pushing at it, peering at small readouts. He had unlocked the outer doors but now he was checking and double checking everything. She chewed at her lip. This was so unlike him. Usually a quick check of the scanner and he was off, out through the doors and away, ready to see what was out there.

He did another circuit of the controls, a big black Victorian coat flapping around him. He had insisted that they went to the TARDIS wardrobe; another rare occurrence. The big overcoat engulfed him, almost touching the floor. He would have looked comedic if not for the bleak, haunted expression on his face.

Ace looked down at her own garments. A long flowing Victorian gown in a deep cream, the dress she had worn the last time they had found themselves in Victorian London. The dress she had worn at Gabriel Chase.

She shuddered.

'Is this dress absolutely necessary, Professor?'

The Doctor didn't look up. 'For once, Ace, don't complain. You can hardly go traipsing around Victorian London in jeans.' His face darkened. 'I don't want to attract any undue attention to ourselves.'

Ace caught his tone and decided not to bother with her usual whinging banter, something that she usually did to wind him up more than anything else. This time things were different. This time was more serious than anything they had ever been through, and that was saying something.

'OK, Doctor.'

He spun and stared at her.

'For once I think I would prefer it if you did refer to me as "Professor". It might help us to remain incognito.'

Ace felt her heart jump. Things really were desperate if he was this scared. Something must have showed on her face. The Doctor gave her a reassuring smile – rare in the last few hours – and tapped her on the nose.

'Don't look so worried. I think that Professor John Smith showing his ward Dorothy the sights of the capital should provide us with the perfect cover to look around. Come on.'

He snatched up his red-handled umbrella and pulled the door lever. The heavy double doors swung inwards with a dull hum, and fog swirled into the console room. Ace pulled a heavy shawl over her shoulders, picked up a large muffler from a chair and followed the Doctor out into the night.

The cold bit into Ace as soon as she stepped from the warmth of the TARDIS. This wasn't like the fog of the 1960s, this was altogether colder, wetter and more malevolent. Ace shivered and pulled her shawl even tighter around herself.

'Why here, Professor? What's so special about a spooky East End wharf?'

The Doctor was wandering towards the Thames. 'I spent the night going through the books that Barbara had. According to her distorted version of history, this is where a sixth Ripper murder – the one that should never have happened – took place.' He tapped at the stone of the wharf with the tip of his umbrella. 'This is where it all starts to go wrong.'

He tensed suddenly.

'There is something here, I can sense it. Something that doesn't belong. Something familiar...'

He frowned.

'Something wrong.'

Ace shivered again, but this time it had nothing to do with the cold. She wandered off towards one of the warehouses, unaware that Jed lurked in the shadows less than fifty yards away. She tried to lighten the mood.

'All these will be flats by the time I'm born.'

There was a grunt from the Doctor, now at the far end of the wharf, staring out over the murk of the Thames.

Ace reached inside her muffler, glad not only of the warmth but the reassuring feel of a can of Nitro-9. Since meeting the Doctor, her reliance on the unstable home-made explosive had waned but, since the beginning of this, since the attack by that creature at the lighthouse, she had felt decidedly undressed without it. Here and now, in unfamiliar and hostile surroundings, and with the Doctor more uneasy than she had ever seen him, she needed some reassurance, some protection.

She hated herself for it – she had thought she had outgrown her dangerous hobby – but at the moment, the cool silver can nestling in the palm of her hand was the only thing she could rely on.

The was a sudden swirl of wind and rustle of leaves. She glanced at the end of the wharf and frowned. The Doctor was gone.

No. There was a huddled shape in the gloom. The Doctor was crouched down over something. Ace smiled. Some clue, no doubt. Something that everyone else would have missed.

'Found something, Professor?'

She began to cross the cobbles, her footfalls echoing eerily around the cavernous warehouses. The huddled shape in the fog didn't reply.

'Professor?'

Still no reply. Ace began to walk faster. 'Doctor…?'

The wind was stronger now, and there was something else, something just on the boundaries of hearing. A sound like voices, muttering, murmuring, chanting.

Ace reached the huddled black shape that was the Doctor. His umbrella lay on the floor beside him. She reached out to touch his back when he suddenly whirled to his feet.

Ace recoiled. The Doctor was smiling, but this was like no smile she had ever seen cross his face before. A leer. Bestial, lecherous. All the signs of gentleness were gone from his face. His eyes blazed with an unfamiliar malice. He had pulled his coat around himself like a cloak. Suddenly the little man that Ace knew

73

seemed to tower over her. She took a step back, her voice wavering. 'Doctor... What's wrong?'

'Wrong?' The Doctor gave a throaty chuckle. 'Poor little Dorothy wants to know what's wrong. Ha ha!' He threw his head back, breathing in the air, breathing in the fog. 'Everything is wrong. Deliciously, gloriously wrong.'

He snatched his gaze back to her face and began to circle around her. 'All this time with me, so trusting, so innocent. All the time blissfully unaware that destiny was to bring you here.'

'But... you said that this is the site of the Ripper murder.' Ace backed away from the circling figure. 'The murder that should never have happened.'

The Doctor's eyes blazed. 'Barbara's books were very graphic about the murder. They say that the expression on her face – what was left of her face – was one of sheer terror. Are you feeling terrified yet, Dorothy?' He spat her name out.

Ace could feel tears beginning to well up. 'Why are you doing this?'

The Doctor ignored her. He began to circle faster, the big black overcoat flapping around him, the fog swirling, the distant chanting growing in pitch. 'They never identified the girl, she was well dressed and no one could work out what a well dressed young lady was doing late at night on a wharf in the East End. None of the prostitutes knew her, no one came forward to identify her remains, the police were at a loss, it was if she had just appeared from nowhere.' The Doctor threw back his coat. Something glinted in the cold light. Ace could see a viciously jagged shard of glass grasped in the Doctor's hand. Blood welled up from cuts in his palms where he gripped it.

'No one will know who you are, no one will mourn you, no one will miss you. Just another mutilated girl, another victim of the Ripper. Another of *my* victims.'

The Doctor lunged.

The attack was sudden and unexpected. Ace crashed to the

floor, the breath punched from her body. The Doctor swooped down on her, the glass blade swishing through the fog. She rolled to one side and she heard glass shatter on stone.

She scrambled to her feet, but the Doctor was already ahead of her, the glass blade now a jagged prong, his blood staining it red. She turned and started to run, to the TARDIS, to some sort of sanctuary, but the Doctor cannoned into her and she tumbled to the cobbled floor again. She twisted on to her back as he crashed on to her, the glass shard only inches from her neck.

She threw her hands up, one of them still inside the muffler, struggling to hold the Doctor back. His face was a mask of hatred, straining to push the blade into her throat. 'Poor Dorothy, I don't think you're in Kansas any more.'

He pushed harder and Ace felt the glass touch her skin.

'Just click your heels together three times and you can go home.'

Her vision was blurred with tears. She could see the face of her friend, her teacher, the only man who had ever let her be what she wanted to be. The Doctor was the only person she had ever let inside her defences, and now he was going to kill her.

Time seemed to slow, she could feel the steady pressure of the blade against her neck, feel her skin beginning to pucker. She thought of all that they had been through, all that he had shown her. The Doctor and Ace, champions of Time and Space, and yet now, with this act, everything that she knew – her future, the future of the entire planet – would begin to unravel. She thought of the haunted, gaunt faces of Ian and Barbara. She thought of the wraiths, and the nightmare that London had become. She thought of everything that would never happen, all the history that would be lost.

All because she had died here and now and the Doctor had gone on killing.

Gone on to become the Ripper.

For ever.

She couldn't let it happen. She owed it to the future. She owed it to the Doctor.

Her hand closed on the can of Nitro as the glass began to puncture her neck.

'I'm sorry, Professor.'

She pulled the pin.

Part Three

In the cold morning light the man staggered over to the window and stared out over the rooftops of Antwerp. He hauled open the window and took a deep breath of air. He shook his head, trying to clear some of the drowsiness he felt. He leant on the window frame, scrutinising the city below, the distant Scheldt, the sounds of workmen on the cathedral. There were fewer leaves on the trees than he remembered. Surely winter could not have fallen so quickly.

Suddenly he noticed his hands. He raised them up to his face. The lines, the scars of time that he knew were gone. These were the hands of a young man.

'Dear God, not again...'

With weary resignation he crossed the room to the mirror that hung near the wash stand, knowing before he looked what he would see in the reflection. The face that he had not seen for seventy years stared back at him again, all the lines of time's passage erased.

He dressed quickly and then gathered every paper, every document that bore the name of John Buttadaeus, placing them in a pile in the centre of the room. Striking a match, he lit the pile and watched as the evidence of his life burned away. When the fire had done its work, he crossed the room and pulled a battered bag from a cupboard, placed it on the bed and began to pack.

Chapter Twelve

As Ace's finger tightened on the pin of the Nitro can, the Doctor's grip relaxed on her for a fraction of a second. In an explosion of movement, she pushed hard against him, forcing him back, the silver can sliding out of her muffler. The Doctor lunged back, snarling. His eyes snapped down to the polished metal. His reflection stared back at him from the brushed steel surface.

The expression on his face changed to one of pure, undiluted anguish and he staggered backwards with a low moan. Ace heard the glass blade shatter on the cobbles as she hauled herself to her feet, drawing in breaths with long, shuddering gasps. With unnatural calm, she re-sheathed the pin into the can of explosive. Only when the cap was back on did her hands start shaking.

The Doctor was standing, staring at the blood dripping from his hands, his face a mask of horror and despair. He kept whispering, over and over, 'I'm sorry. I'm sorry...', his voice a faint croak.

Part of Ace wanted to reach out and touch him, another to run, to get as far away from him as possible. She took a faltering step towards him, but he threw up his bleeding hands and stumbled back away from her.

'No, Ace, run. I can't fight this. It's too strong. You've got to get away from me. Far away.'

Ace hesitated, staring from the Doctor to the TARDIS and back again.

The TARDIS.

Her lifeline.

To leave it, to leave him. Her only way home.

The wind picked up again and the Doctor screamed.

'Go! Go now!'

Ace turned and ran. Into the night. Into her past. Tears and fog stung her eyes as she looked back at the Doctor, the wind tearing at his clothes, his coat billowing around him. The last thing she heard before the fog swallowed him up was a long choking cry of rage and helplessness.

Jed wanted to run, too, but couldn't. He was trapped. Trapped by the wind and the tendrils of fog. By the shadows and demons that cursed and swore at the little man trapped in their grip. He could hear their vicious, sibilant whispering.

'How, Doctor? How did you slip from us?'

'It was planned.'

'It was foretold.'

'Her death to make you one of us.'

'Her death to make us whole.'

'Her death to start and end this.'

A Doctor… He clamped his bloodstained hands to his head and bellowed into the night.

'WHO ARE YOU?'

The wind grew more vicious, swirling around him, tearing at him. It lifted him off his feet, throwing him around like a rag doll. Vague black shapes battered at him. Drops of blood from his hands flicked into the night like berries shaken from a tree.

'We are someone you have always known!'

'Someone you have denied!'

'Someone you have wronged!'

'You will be our puppet.'

'You will be our thing.'

'You will be US!'

'NO!' The Doctor's voice was almost lost in the whirlwind of words, 'I will fight this!'

He scrabbled in the pocket of his billowing coat. His hands closed on something and he roared in pain. Jed's eyes opened wide with awe as the Doctor pulled a small glass cylinder from his pocket. It blazed with a brilliant inner light, illuminating the fog, sending huge skittering shadows over the brick walls of the warehouses. The blood from the Doctor's palms hissed and boiled on its surface. His head jerked back in a soundless scream, he hung in the maelstrom, a dark spot of agony among the brilliance.

Abruptly, he let his hands swing to his sides. His eyes were closed now. His expression one of calm.

The wind lifted him higher, but this time he didn't fight it. The shadows beat at him, bringing up deep welts in his cheeks. The Doctor remained unmoving.

The light in the small glass cylinder began to flicker.

The wind dropped and the Doctor crashed to the cobbles. With a howl of rage, the phantoms were gone.

Jed watched on, terrified, as the little man hauled himself painfully to his feet and staggered to the edge of the wharf. The glittering cylinder, now nothing but a faint erratic glow, arced through the air as the Doctor hurled it into the Thames. He stood for a moment, staring out at the thick tide of the river, then hauled his bloodstained coat close around him and vanished into the swirling night.

Only when he was sure that everything was quiet did Jed crawl from the dark corner that had sheltered him, scared and terrified at the wonders that had unfolded before him. Not even the circus had provided such strangeness.

He crossed the wharf, to the blue cabinet. He could still hear the dull throb from within, feel the vibrations through the air. He didn't like it. He spat at the box and scampered out to the middle of the quay. There on the cobbles was the strangely shaped walking cane that the little man – the Doctor – had been carrying.

Jed reached out gingerly, tapping the cane with his fingertips. There was no vibration here, no throbbing hum. He snatched it up, running his hands over the curved red handle. A trophy of the night, something new for his collection, but… He remembered the cylinder that had blazed with light. That… That would be a prize.

Clutching the Doctor's umbrella to his chest, he crossed to the edge of the wharf and stared down into the dark grey mud. The tide was coming in, fast now, and of that fantastic, brilliant light there was no sign.

No. The Thames could keep its treasure tonight. Tomorrow. Jed nodded to himself. Tomorrow he would return. He reached into his pocket, feeling the crab shells. Suddenly they were dull, ordinary things. He pulled them out and cast them to the floor, grinding them underfoot. He looked off in the direction that the little man had taken. He knew that Malacroix would want him to follow, but the girl... Jed looked at the alleyway that she had fled down. He chewed at his knuckles. The man or the girl. Which would Malacroix want more?

He clasped the umbrella closer to his chest, and was about to set out after the Doctor, when another banshee wail keened through the night. Jed fled for the alleyway, away from the wharf.

The girl. He would follow the girl.

The man watched the image fade in the crystal skull then lashed out, sending it skittering over the stone table. It shattered, shards of glass dancing over the floor like ice crystals, reflecting a million times over the dark cloisters where the shadows boiled and screamed and hissed, drowning out the protests of their only solid flesh.

He held up his hands, pleading, blood dripping from the long deep cuts that marked his palms. The shadows paid him no heed, the noise was piercing, invasive, and he was forced to his knees by its power. With a clap like thunder, the doors to the room crashed shut, and the man was left huddled and trembling in the cavernous gloom. Slowly he rose, his face a mask of pain and hatred, his own shadow pale and insignificant after the blackness of those that he served.

He brought his scarred hands up to his face, clenching them, watching the blood ooze around his knuckles.

'No, Doctor. This is of *my* design, of *my* making and no matter where you run, I *will* break you in mind, body and spirit. And I shall bring what is left to my feet.'

He closed his eyes and a crease crossed his high brow. He whispered under his breath, his lips barely moving.

When he opened his hands, the cuts and the blood were gone.

He turned and swept from the room, his cloak like liquid. Behind him, the shards of glass on the floor began to run like quicksilver, flowing across the marble slabs and up the ornate stone legs of the table, flowing together in an intricate dance until the crystal skull sat once more in its place in the centre of the room, glowering into the gloom.

Ace's headlong run into the night was brought short as she hurtled out of an alleyway and cannoned into a huge figure that suddenly loomed from the mists. Strong arms caught her, lifting her off the ground. She struggled frantically, yelling at the top of her lungs.

'Hold your noise!' A deep male voice boomed from the night.

Ace kicked hard at the man's shins and he dropped her with a curse. She rolled across the cobbles, dropping into a low crouch.

The man was huge and bearded, with a blood-stained apron. She scrabbled around for some sort of weapon.

'What's this?'

Another man emerged from the gloom, clutching a wicked-looking knife. Ace's hand closed around a length of timber and she swung it up in front of her.

'Back off, or I swear I'll do some serious damage.' She could hear the cracks in her voice and tried to brush the tears away with the back of her sleeve.

There was a chuckle from the figure.

'Well, if that don't just take the biscuit.'

The man she had kicked hobbled towards her.

'She may look like a lady but she's the strength of a wildcat.'

'I said back off!'

Ace lashed out with the length of timber, and the other man

laughed. 'And the temper to match it, I'll warrant. Leave her be, Thomas, the lady is fair flustered, and with you dolled up like Leather Apron 'imself it is no wonder that she'll strike out at you.'

The bearded man grunted and hobbled away, while the other man came closer. Ace could see that he too wore an apron drenched in blood. Her eyes never left the blade in his hand.

'Calm down now, Missy, Henry Tomkins'll not be doing you any harm.'

Ace nodded at the knife. 'Just out practising for the serial killers' annual ball, were you?'

The man looked down at the blade. 'Well, I don't know about any fancy ball, but horse-slaughtering is a job same as any other, even if it is one not often discussed in polite conversation.'

Ace relaxed slightly and looked around her. Her headlong flight had led her into a knacker's yard. She could see vague shapes in the gloom and was suddenly glad of the fog's curtain. She lowered her makeshift weapon.

'If you don't mind me saying, Missy, it ain't right for a young lady like yourself to be out unattended. Jolly Jack himself 'as been at work near these parts.'

Ace gave a short barking laugh. 'He's a damn sight nearer than you'd think.'

Henry frowned. 'You've seen him, ain't you? You've seen the Ripper!' He looked at the bloodstains on the front of her dress. 'By the saints, he's tried for you, ain't he?'

He turned and bellowed into the fog, 'James! Charles! Stir yourselves!' A collection of men and boys began to crowd around Ace. Henry took one of the boys by the arm. 'There's a constable who comes near to these parts on the hour. Find him and bring him back here. Hurry now!' The boy hurried off through a set of double gates.

Henry turned back to Ace. 'Now then, Missy, where did you see him?'

Ace shook her head. 'A warehouse, back there. But it wasn't the

Ripper.' Her eyes were filling with tears again. 'It couldn't have been... It was the Doctor...'

'Aye. They say he's a medical man.'

Around her, people were milling around frantically as news of the Ripper galvanised them into action. Ace held her head in despair. The last thing she wanted at the moment was to get into lengthy discussions with the authorities. Especially Victorian authorities. She tried to pull her dress into some kind of order. She looked a shambles: her dress was torn and stained with blood and dirt. She grasped her can of explosive, still hidden within her muffler. If the police got hold of that...

As Henry passed her, still marshalling his army, she caught his arm. 'Is there anywhere near here I can stay for the night?'

Henry scratched at his head. 'I'm not sure if I know of anywhere that is suitable for a lady... Besides, the constable will be here shortly, he's bound to be wanting to talk to you, and...'

'Henry,' Ace stopped him. 'I just need somewhere to get out of this fog, and to change. I can come back. Please...'

Henry looked at her for a moment, his face stern, suspicious, then he turned and pulled open the heavy gates. He pointed to where a brown glow lit up the fog. 'That there is the Whitechapel Road, Missy. You'll have no trouble finding a lodging house from there.'

'Thank you.'

'When you're done, ask anyone to direct you to the yard of Harrison, Barber and Co. Most folks are acquainted with our whereabouts.'

Ace shuffled guiltily, then pulled her shawl tight around her shoulders and vanished into the night.

Ace stumbled up towards the lights of Whitechapel like a zombie, still reeling from the shock of the Doctor's attack. She emerged on to a street bustling with life. It took her by surprise; she had not expected so many people.

Stallholders struggled with faded awnings, some finishing for the night, some getting ready for the morning. Horses clattered to and fro. Prostitutes, shabby and old, stalked their clients, cooing; their tongues poking from venous lips. The air was thick with sulphurous fog and the stench of sewage. Ace almost gagged. It was all so different from the London that she was familiar with. Scant days ago, she and the Doctor had walked through the blitz-torn East End of the 1940s and she had felt utterly at home. This London was more alien to her than any far-flung world that she had ever journeyed to, and she was totally out of her depth. She suddenly realised how dependent she was on the Doctor, and how utterly lost she was without him.

She was swept into the crowd, dizzy and confused. She knew that she had to find shelter, but where to start…?

'I'll get my money and no mistake, you be holding that bed for me.'

Ace turned. A woman in her late thirties staggered from a doorway. She caught Ace by the shoulder, steadying herself. The smell of gin hung around her grotesque painted face. 'What d'you reckon to my fine bonnet, then?' The woman tipped the hat back on her head and struck a tottering pose. 'No trouble finding my doss looking this fine, eh? Worth more than fourpence?'

She eyed Ace up and down, swaying slightly. 'Well, strike me dead, a lady…' she said, and fingered the material of Ace's dress.

With a cackle, she vanished into the night. Ace stared at the doorway she had emerged from. Taking a deep breath, she entered the dingy doorway.

The hallway was dim, lit by a single candle. Sheets, yellow and stained, hung from the ceiling. Ace could hear movement in distant rooms above, the creaks of floorboards. She closed her eyes and held her breath, trying to shut out the smell.

She followed the sound of rough male voices into a smoke-thick kitchen at the end of the passage. Half a dozen men sat hunched around a table, playing cards and drinking heavily. One turned and squeezed her arm roughly, slurring something unintelligible as she asked for a room.

'All right, Tom,' another drawled, pulling him back by the shoulder.

The man called Tom lashed drunkenly out with his drinking-pot, spilling gin over the table and catching the other man hard across the face. The other man swore and pulled a knife from his jacket. The two stood, swaying, staring murderously at each other. The rest of the company had fallen silent. Eventually Tom spat on the floor and sank back into his seat. The other man, skinny, sallow, unshaven, limped across to Ace, a measly, ingratiating smile playing across his face.

'I'm after a room,' said Ace, trying to sound more confident than she felt.

The man gave a low, drunken bow. His fellow card-players laughed raucously.

'Well now,' he said, 'per'aps we can do business, my dear. Thomas!' He bellowed the name into the rear of the house, before promising Ace a whole bed to herself as if this was paradise. He wouldn't dream of taking payment in advance. Not from a lady. Which was a good thing, because Ace was completely skint. Apart from the clothes she stood up in and a can of Nitro-9, she had nothing.

There was a scuffling, and a young boy – dirty, and so thin that it made Ace wince – shambled into the kitchen. He clutched the remains of a mouldy loaf that he tore at with his teeth.

'What is it?' He barely got the words out through the mouthful, before Barney cuffed him hard round the ear.

'Show some respect! We got a lady stayin' with us. Now go an' get the top room ready. Off with you!'

He clouted the lad again, and the lad scrambled up the stairs.

Barney caught Ace by the arm. 'It's a double bed, my dear' – was that a wink? – 'so I'm going to 'ave to charge you eightpence.'

She couldn't decide quite what was in his voice. Was he just a smarmy creep, or was there an oily insinuation in his fawning?

'A candle, my dear,' he drawled, peeling a greasy, misshapen nub of wax from the tabletop, lighting it with an unsteady hand and pressing it into her palm. Ace flinched at his touch. 'To light you to bed. You want anythin' in the night, my dear, you come down an' see me. Barney's the name.'

He club-footedly ushered Ace to the foot of the stairs and she began to climb them, shuddering at the noises emanating from each room that she passed. The stairs emerged on to a rickety landing. A single door led into a long, hot room which stank of unwashed bodies. By the light of her candle she could see, propped up against the wall like sacks, a row of bedraggled women. They were held there like so much shabby washing by a length of clothes-line drawn between two hooks. The women were hanging forward over this wire, trying to sleep.

The boy, Thomas, was waiting for her in the darkness. He drew back a shabby curtain to reveal an alcove, practically filled by a dirty-looking bed.

'This 'ere's the room,' he said. And without waiting for a response, he scampered back down the stairs.

Ace closed the door. The 'room' was empty, apart from the mound of the cloth mattress. A cracked and dirty skylight was set into the sloping roof. Ace rubbed at the cracked glass with her sleeve. London stretched out before her, swathed in its blanket of night and fog, the gas lamps giving everything a yellow glow. She craned her neck, looking for something familiar. She could see nothing she recognised. She gave a hollow laugh. Back home, back in the twentieth century, she had watched groups of holidaymakers pay to be given tours around 'Jack the Ripper's London', and here she was, stuck in the middle of it.

'And I didn't bring my damn camera.'

Ace slumped down on the mattress, setting the candle down on the floor. She eased off her shoes. The mattress was hard and prickly, and she could hear rats scampering in the walls. Her eyelids were heavy and she desperately wanted to sleep, but every time she began to nod off, the Doctor's face loomed before her, twisted with hatred, startling her back into consciousness.

The stub of the candle suddenly spluttered and went out. The sudden dark was strangely soothing. The sounds of the street rung around her. Exhausted and frightened, Ace finally surrendered to the demands of her protesting body, and slept.

Chapter Thirteen

The rattle of hooves on cobbles broke the still of the night. A hansom cab and a rough workman's cart clattered to a halt at the front of the wharfside buildings. Malacroix stepped from the cab, the lumbering shape of De Vries the strong-man at his shoulder. He strode down the narrow alleyway and out on to the wharf itself. De Vries gestured at the men on the cart to follow and shuffled after the circus owner.

Malacroix was circling a tall blue box, the gold tip of his cane tapping on the cobbles. He finished his circuit and stood, staring up at it. He stroked his moustache thoughtfully. 'Now then, my young Jed, what have you found?'

De Vries shuffled uncomfortably.

'What the devil is wrong with you, De Vries? You're as skittish as a pony!'

The strong-man pointed up at the sign at the top of the TARDIS. Malacroix followed his gaze.

'Ah! Police. Yes, our young friend has a most remarkable talent for sniffing out the most entertaining of curiosities, but he is rather lacking in the more elementary social skills. Reading is a gift that I may have to impart to my young charge at some later date. The sooner he can read, the sooner he can learn to be more discretionary with the treats that he brings me.'

Malacroix stepped close to the battered blue box. 'I don't think we have anything to worry about from our uniformed friends. I rather wager that the sign is merely to throw us off our guard, a deception to keep prying noses out, but I am not so easily dissuaded.' He pulled off one of his delicate calfskin gloves and placed his pale palm against the wet woodwork. The vibration trembled though his veins. Malacroix's eyes closed in ecstasy, his voice dropping to a hoarse whisper.

'Ah, but my young Jed, this time you have brought me the most exquisite of prizes. Come, De Vries…'

He grasped the huge man by the arm, pulling him closer, forcing his hand alongside his own.

'Come, man, do you feel it? Power!'

The strong-man snatched his hand away, stepping back, shaking his head.

Malacroix threw back his head and roared with laughter. 'The great De Vries, scared by a wooden box. Every night you face the lions, you can bend iron with your bare hands, and yet this simple contraption scares you!'

He turned back to his prize. 'It is power, and I must learn its secrets.' He stepped back, pulling his glove back on. He called to the men lurking in the shadows. 'Bring the wagon!'

With a clatter of hooves and wooden wheels the low cart trundled on to the cobbles of the wharf, the horses nervous and jumpy, their driver keeping them tightly reined. It backed up hard against the TARDIS and Malacroix looked expectantly over at the strong-man.

'Now, Mr De Vries, you are not here merely for your pleasing countenance. I have brought you tonight to make use of your particular skills. The box, *s'il vous plaît*.'

De Vries shrugged off his heavy cloak, passing it to one of the circus hands. He squared up to the TARDIS, his breathing becoming deeper, his chest expanding wider with each breath. He reached down and grasped the base of the tall cabinet, his fingers sliding on the wet woodwork.

He crouched for a moment, almost like a man at prayer, then with a guttural roar he lifted. His feet dug into the cobbles. Muscles bulged in his back, his shirt stretched almost to breaking. Veins stood out like rope on his arms. Air hissed from his nostrils as inch by inch the TARDIS toppled backwards, until with the crunch of protesting timbers and whinnying from the horses, it lay on the back of the wagon.

Men swarmed over it, covering it with tarpaulins and lashing it down with ropes. De Vries struggled back into his heavy cloak aware of the admiring eyes of his employer on his back. The sound of applause made him turn.

'Bravo, Mr De Vries, bravo.' The soft clap of Malacroix's leather-clad hands echoed around the yard. 'Now come.'

He spun on his heel and strode back towards the waiting cab, his voice echoing through the night's fog. 'We have much to do.'

Light was only just beginning to glimmer over the rooftops of London when Jed appeared once more among the dark and decaying brickwork of the wharf, picking his way down to the thick mud of the riverbank.

The Thames, brown and sluggish, had exposed its usual array of treasures, but Jed only had one particular treasure in mind. His night had been haunted by the mysterious blue box and its occupants, by the shimmering cylinder that had arced into the mud. Every chink of light that had broken the blackness of his room had reminded him of that blazing, beautiful brilliance and he had lain unsleeping, restless, waiting for the first light of dawn, for the time when the dark grey banks of the Thames would be uncovered again, glistening and smooth, ready for him.

Now he waded, knee high in the thick ooze, his unfailing memory taking him to the place where he had seen the cylinder vanish. His hands raked through the mud – long gouging trails – a methodical pattern, slowly erased as the cold slime slid back into place behind him. There was no panic to his movements, no rush. These were not the flounderings of a madman. Jed's quest was all-consuming, it blotted out everything else. All that was on his mind was the light. The beautiful light.

His grasping hands sank deeper and deeper. The mud was up to his chest now, sucking at his clothing. The rising sun glinted off the wet surface, turning the banks of the river into plains of burnished gold. Jed could hear his prize. Hear it calling to him. It was close now, So very, very close.

The mud before him glowed gently. His hands closed on something small and glassy, and with a cry he dragged it from the cold shroud of the river. He rubbed at it with his sleeve, washing it clean with spit. The little cylinder gleamed in the sunlight. Jed held it aloft, threw his head back and laughed.

Back in the cool crypt of the church, Jed pulled away the loose bricks that concealed his collection. He reached into the hole, pulling at a small cloth bundle. Squatting down behind one of the huge stone tombs, the mud cracking and flaking from his clothes as it dried, Jed laid his treasures out in front of him: the rings, the coins that Malacroix had given him, a gold tooth that he had pulled from one of the graves in the churchyard; mementoes from his scavenging nights.

When everything was out in a pattern on the cold stone floor, he reached inside his jacket and pulled out the cylinder, placing it in the centre of the collection. Then he sat back, rocking backwards and forwards on his heels, a vacant smile on his face.

He had scuttled through the city with his prize clasped close to his chest, weaving his way through the crowds, snarling and cursing at everyone who came near him. The golden light of morning had faded swiftly, the fog rising from the Thames like a ghost, blanketing the city in its moist veil once more.

He had crept into the churchyard, sniffing the air, desperate not to be seen. Pulling the key to the crypt from around his neck, he had slunk along the wall of the church, unlocked the side door, and vanished into the gloom.

The cylinder was still pulsing softly, not the blazing scalding light of the previous night, but a warm, comforting glow. Jed began to feel drowsy, hypnotised by the flickering light. Shapes seemed to appear inside the cylinder, moving. He stared into it.

Jed suddenly found himself somewhere else. He stared about him in panic. It was like London, like the streets that he knew, but different. Strange machines littered the roads and there was a low mournful wail far in the distance, rising and falling. There was something else. Above the wail, getting louder: a drone, like a wasp. Jed strained to see through the cloying grey skies. Suddenly the world around him erupted into a cacophony of noise and flame. Explosions tore buildings apart, brick and metal whistled past him, tore through him. Through the smoke a figure appeared, a shambling giant wrapped in tarpaulins. Jed could see the scabrous metal face of the monster. It threw its head back and let out a terrifying anguished roar.

Jed curled himself into a ball, tucked his head in his hands and screamed and screamed.

With terrifying suddenness, the noise stopped. He was lying on the flagstone floor of the crypt, the cylinder pulsing softly before him.

Shaking, Jed got to his feet. He scrabbled for the rough cloth bag that had held his treasures and threw it over the light.

Another terrifying bellow made Jed start, but this roar was from a far more familiar monster. The Reverend Jefford was looking for him. Jed bundled his collection together, pushing everything back into the rough hole in the wall. He picked up the cylinder in its hessian shroud, and hesitated. There was another bellow from the church. Jed pushed the bundle inside his jacket, eased the bricks back into place and hurried out of the crypt.

Chapter Fourteen

The dream rocked the peace of Ace's night. She was back in the TARDIS, back in the cloisters, back where she had encountered that... thing. That thing that was destined always to be part of her.

She'd always had her violent side. Always barely under control, barely restrained. Gabriel Chase had proved that, when she'd expressed her anger by burning the place to the ground. Back then she'd vented all her aggression and frustration at any figure of authority that came in her way. The police, her probation officer, her mother.

The Cheetah planet - months back, now - had proved how dangerous those emotions could be. It had nearly changed her for ever, into a predator, a wild thing, and it scared her that she had almost let it happen, almost given in to her darker side. The Doctor had brought her back.

What was it he'd said?

If we fight like animals, we die like animals.

And there is an animal in everyone, sometimes just under the surface, under the water. In her dream, she reached out to the dark cloister pool and touched the claws that came up to meet her...

Ace jolted awake. Through the curtained partition she could hear the mumbling and snoring of the women asleep against the wall next door. She was lucky; she had a bed, albeit filthy and uncomfortable.

She had lain awake for hours, listening to the dull roar of voices from the kitchen, gradually dying away, leaving only the sounds of her fellow sleepers.

Several times in the night she thought she could hear the creak of quiet, irregular footsteps beyond the curtain. She was sure the fabric had moved slightly in the darkness.

Her nerves were playing tricks on her. She could almost hear movements outside the little window of her alcove. Shuffling, tapping…

She must have fallen asleep somewhere towards dawn, because she was suddenly aware of Barney's voice shouting beyond the curtain. Damn! She'd wanted to be out of here before he came for his money. She remembered his readiness last night to pull a knife… She peeped through one of the curtain's many holes.

'Come on, girls,' Barney drawled, 'out you goes.' He unhooked one end of the clothes-line and let it be snatched from his hands as the straggly row of women, most still asleep, fell forward, starting and swearing.

There was nothing Ace could do. She darted back into the bed. Barney swung club-footedly around and twitched back the curtain.

'Mornin', my dear,' he weaselled, leaning over her, smiling. His breath stank. 'Uncle Barney's come for 'is blunt.'

'What?'

'Money, my dear.'

'I…' She'd have to try and bluff it out. 'I have decided to stay a few more days,' she said in the haughtiest voice she could muster. 'I'll pay you at the end of that time.'

Barney looked closely at her, his half-smile never leaving his face. 'All right,' he said. 'I'm glad you're stayin'. Brightens the place up, 'tractive gel like you.'

He stepped slowly back and, with a bow – Ace couldn't tell whether or not he was mocking her – he stepped back outside the curtain.

She dressed, carefully smoothing the creases from her clothes. Her ladylike appearance was all she had until she could find out what was happening. Find the Doctor…

She slipped down the stairs and through the kitchen, picking her way carefully around the snoring, stinking bodies of the gamblers of the night before, and stepped out into the haze of the London morning.

* * *

The city was already wide awake. Ace passed south across busy Commercial Road, down Berner Street towards where she thought the river ought to be. She scoured the horizon for Tower Bridge. It was nowhere to be seen. Had it been built yet? Or was this yet another twist of history? The city looked strange to Ace. Unreal, almost. Of course, there would still be plenty of streets like this in her day, but somehow, devoid of motor traffic and the signs and symbols of the late twentieth century, Ace could not help but feel as if she was walking through a very good film set. She thought of all the crappy Jack the Ripper movies she had seen on TV in the early hours of the morning, and laughed bitterly to herself. In the distance – wholly unobstructed by office blocks – she could see the Tower of London. It looked quite unchanged; its ancient stonework somehow seemed to Ace more real – and more modern – than anything else around her.

She reached the wharves and began looking for the TARDIS. She was sure this was where they had landed. The TARDIS, though, was nowhere to be seen.

What was happening? Had he fled, leaving her behind? She would never believe him capable of that. Her thoughts flew back to the previous night. Before then, she would never have believed him capable of...

She must be mistaken. This must be the wrong wharf. They all looked so alike. She began following the course of the river, searching with increasing desperation for the police box.

After nearly two hours she conceded defeat. The TARDIS was gone. She was stranded. Whatever might have become of the Doctor, she was alone now, cold, and desperately hungry. She began picking her way back into Whitechapel. She had to get some food, somehow.

The streets were bustling, and the crowd thickened around her as she walked. Ragged, dirty children ran about her swirling skirt, hands out, begging in loud, persistent voices. She suddenly found herself in a street of costermongers' barrows. Shabby, second-hand clothing being pawed over by eager hands, a knife-grinder, a lad selling matches. A fruit stall. She moved to the blind side of the fruit vendor and slipped a couple of apples into her wrap. He spun around, about to shout at her. Seeing her, he stopped.

'Oh, I beg your pardon, miss,' he said. 'I thought someone was pinchin' from me stall.'

Ace smiled nervously and moved away into the crowd. She ate the apples quickly. They did little to dampen her hunger. Further down the road a man was selling fat penny-pies. Once again Ace strolled casually up to the stall and waited until the coster's back was turned. She wished these begging kids would leave her alone...

She grabbed a pie and thrust it out of sight beneath her wrap. Again she tried to sink back into the crowd.

'Oi, mister!' a young voice at her elbow cried out. 'That lady just pinched one of your pies!'

With an oath, Ace pushed the urchin to one side and ran into the road. She could hear the pie-seller shouting at her back. She turned round to see him, fat and panting, his fist in the air. There were already yards between them. To his rear, the shoal of little beggars helped themselves from his stall. Ace ducked into a side road: a narrow alley, empty of people. She crouched in a doorway and devoured the meat pie in two or three ferocious mouthfuls.

The alley opened on to another, quieter road. Looking around her, she saw a faded board. Harrison, Barber & Co. The horse-slaughterers' yard. The man she had met last night, Henry, was the only person she knew in London. Perhaps he would help her. She was about to move forward when she felt a hand on her shoulder.

'A moment of your time, miss.'

She spun around. A policeman. She braced herself to run.

'I have been informed that a young lady answering to your description might be able to furnish us with certain particulars regarding the fiend what's been murdering these girls. Now would that young lady happen to be yourself, miss?'

Run? Where could she run to?

'Perhaps you'd be so kind as to accompany me to the station, miss.'

The time plodded forward with leaden, echoing ticks. According to the clock on the wall, Ace had waited nearly three hours in the police station. Someone special wanted to question her. An inspector from Scotland Yard. The desk sergeant, solemn behind his drooping moustache, wrote steadily and without cease in a ledger, pausing only to give Ace the occasional impassive glance.

Henry had sold her out to the police. She couldn't help feeling betrayed. Hunted. Now she felt caged.

She could stand no more. Her heart was racing. Her hunger was back, nagging and gnawing at her. She jumped to her feet.

'All right, mush,' she shouted, 'where's this bloke who wants to see me? 'Cos if he doesn't come soon I'm out of here.'

'Sit down, miss,' the sergeant said with weary indulgence. 'He won't be long now…' He returned to his ledger and resumed his slow scratching.

A man bustled in and the sergeant rose.

'Is this her?' the newcomer asked.

'Yes, sir,' the sergeant replied.

'Good,' said the man. 'Come with me, miss.'

He was wearing a tweed suit and a bowler hat. Ace followed his stocky figure down a corridor and into an office.

'Sit down, miss,' he said, sinking into a chair himself. Ace sat across a desk from him.

'I apologise for the delay,' the man said. 'Yard business. Now… We have information that you might have witnessed an event last night pertaining to the recent killings. Is this so?'

Ace said nothing. She had a natural aversion to policemen of any century.

'Indeed, from what I hear, you might have narrowly avoided being one of Jolly Jack's victims. Is this so?'

Still Ace remained silent. What could she say? She couldn't grass on the Doctor… The inspector was looking at her curiously.

'We don't get many of your sort round these parts,' he said. 'That's how we picked you up so easily. What are you? A runaway? These are bad parts to run to.'

'No,' said Ace. 'I'm not a runaway.'

'All right,' the inspector said, 'then we'll start off with your address.'

'I'm… living in a lodging house on the Whitechapel Road. I don't know the number. A man called Barney runs it.'

'Sounds nice…' murmured the inspector, scribbling on a sheet of paper. 'We'll check up on that. Now, last night…'

'I didn't see anything, really.'

He put his pen down.

'Young lady, this fiend has killed four women. Last night, perhaps, he nearly made it five. If you know something about him you'd best say so sharpish, miss. If you know who he is –'

'I saw something,' Ace blurted out. 'But it wasn't the Ripper. I mean… It couldn't have been.'

'Let us be the judge of that,' the inspector said gently. 'Can you give us a description?'

What should she do? The man was right: if – and the very thought brought her to the brink of tears – if the Doctor was who they were saying he was, then she ought to tell what she knew. If the killings were to be stopped. And if he wasn't, he might be in trouble. She couldn't find him, but the police might. Still, to actually put into words… to grass on him…

'He's called the Doctor,' she said. 'I… don't know his real name.'

By the time Ace left the station she had given the inspector a full description of the suspect and of his most recent whereabouts. She felt drained. Empty. It was dark outside; the darkness of the evening clung around her in cold, wet strands.

She was still hungry. The hunger which had dogged her all day was painful now. The costers in the market were closing down their stalls. Many had piled their unsold wares by the side of the road. The smell of bread rose from a stack of baskets. It was almost overpowering to Ace. She could only think of her hunger. Why was she so hungry...? With the briefest flicker of conscience she bounded forward and threw back the lid of the topmost basket.

'Oi!' the vendor shouted, seeing her. Ignoring him, she grabbed a pair of loaves and ran, her teeth already tearing at a thick crust.

She ran until she was breathless, and the loaves finished. Feeling slightly better, she slowed to a walk. The day's work was over and the city of night was awakening. She wandered the gloomy streets, peering into windows. A pub, crowded and noisy; thin singing from the towering white church which loomed over Red Lion Street. Women – mostly old women – walking up and down in front of walls or standing in doorways, waiting...

At the end of the street, a man loomed out of the gaslight shadows directly behind one of the women. Ace ran forward. The woman twisted around. The man brought his hand up to her face. Ace opened her mouth to shout. They were smiling at each other. They exchanged a few words and disappeared into an alley.

Why was she so jumpy? She felt as if she was speeding. The very fabric of the city seemed to needle at her consciousness. The sounds, the smells...

She could smell blood.

As strongly as if it were under her nose, she could smell blood. Sniffing, she followed the scent. She could practically *see* it, hanging in the air. She followed it down the street and into a narrow, lightless gash in the brickwork which a faded sign announced as Miller's Court. She could see a cluster of people at the far end of the street, peering over something, talking animatedly across one another.

A minute sound made her turn. In the shadows, a hunched

figure was crouched. Her stomach lurched. She stepped forward.

'Doctor…' she said.

She stopped. Was it him? He seemed smaller… twisted, somehow… his features twisted with hatred and horrible exhilaration. He let out a giggle… and suddenly sprang forward. He was carrying something – a walking cane – he swung it sharply upward. It whistled past her head. She ducked to avoid the blow. Her bastard shoe twisted on the damp, cobbled ground and she fell. The figure scuttled away into the darkness.

A figure appeared above her, and helped her to her feet. She'd fallen hard. Maybe sprained her ankle.

'Are you all right, young lady?' the figure asked. A vicar.

'That man…' she whispered.

'Man?' the vicar queried. 'I saw no one…'

He was gone. Had it been the Doctor? It had looked like him. Something like him… It was so hard to tell in the dark.

It couldn't have been… That look in his eyes… Worse than the malice, worse than the appalling glee… a look totally lacking in recognition. He hadn't known her.

'Allow me to introduce myself,' the vicar said. 'The Reverend Samuel Jefford, at your service. I am the vicar of Christ Church.'

Ace didn't reply. She was still staring into the darkness after her attacker.

'I say,' the vicar said, looking past her towards the far end of the narrow cut, 'what do you suppose is going on down there?'

The commotion among the little crowd was growing. Somewhere, a police whistle sounded.

'Oh, my dear Lord,' the vicar whispered. 'Please God, don't let it be another one…'

Ace wanted no more to do with the police that day. Suddenly she had felt sick. Dizzy. She had limped away into the darkness as the vicar had hurried to join the mortified crowd.

She found her way back to the lodging house on Whitechapel

Road. There was nowhere else to go. Barney was alone in the kitchen as she entered, and drunk.

'My dear…' he oozed, 'join me for a small night-cap, why don't you?'

'No… thanks,' Ace muttered. She pulled herself wearily up the stairs.

'Good night, then,' Barney called after her. 'Pleasant dreams…'

The women were already slumped against the wall, leaning forward on their clothes-line, snoring and muttering. Ace stepped behind the curtain into her alcove. A street lamp burned outside her window, filling the narrow space with a pale light. She began to undress.

Almost immediately, she heard Barney's irregular tread on the floorboards beyond the curtain. She could see his outline against the curtain. She could hear his wheezing breath…

'My dear…'

He twitched the curtain back and peered around it.

'Are you decent in there?' he asked, staring straight at her.

He limped forward.

'It's time you an' me had a little talk,' he said. 'You ain't got the blunt for this bed, 'ave you?'

'You what?' Ace drew back against the wall.

'The money. You can't pay Uncle Barney for the bed, can you?'

His face was right next to hers. His breath stank of gin.

'But we won't let a little thing like that worry us, now will we? I mean, I wouldn't dream o' sendin' a pretty young woman like you out there with ol' Jack prowling the streets with 'is cuttin'-knife, now would I? You're much better off in 'ere with Uncle Barney…'

He pushed himself forward, his hands tightly gripping her shoulders, his thin, stubbly lips grazing her neck.

Pushing him away with one hand, Ace lashed at his face with the other. Barney staggered back with a scream, half-tripping over the bed, and clutching at his cheek. Three long, deep cuts gashed the skin, welling with blood.

She couldn't have done that… her nails were bitten to nothing.

'Bitch…' Barney hissed. 'No bitch does that to me…'

He pulled his knife from his pocket and limped forward, grinning evilly.

'No… bitch… does… that… to…'

Ace wasn't listening. Her heart was racing again. She could hear her pulse pounding in her ears. Without thinking, she jumped forward, springing off the bed, and launched herself at Barney's throat. Her hands connected and he staggered back with a cry, tearing down the curtain as he fell. She was on top of him, her fingers tight about his windpipe.

One of the clothes-line women screamed. Ace looked frantically along the line. 'Go on!' a drunken voice slurred. 'Show 'im what for!'

Her eyes stopped on the little window, only feet away from her. There was a face… there was a face looking in through the window. Staring. For a moment their eyes had connected, then the face had vanished.

They were on the first floor… The strangeness of the vision seemed to jolt her. There was blood on her hands, and on Barney's throat, and a look of terror in his eyes.

She had to get out of here. Once again she felt trapped by the stinking walls around her. Hastily gathering her few things together, she ran from the room, down the stairs and out into the darkness.

Chapter Fifteen

The Cirque Jacques Malacroix was silent but for the caged restlessness of the big cats. Jed scuttled around the shadowy huddle of caravans, breathless, drooling slightly. There was still a light coming from Malacroix's van. The maestro was inside, reading from a book.

Jed paused to get his breath back, to try and think what he would say to Malacroix. His thoughts were jumbled and strange nowadays. Ever since the light… At the back of his mind, he could see the glowing cylinder all the time now.

He had been following the girl, on and off, for days. He had tracked her from alleyway to alleyway, always keeping just out of her sight. He had nearly been seen on a couple of occasions, but Jed knew the streets and alleyways of Whitechapel better than anyone, knew all the hiding places… He had observed her exchange with the horse-slaughterer, and followed her to the lodging house on Whitechapel Road. He had seen her candle appear in the little upstairs window and had climbed on to the roof of the outhouse below. He had watched her undress…

The following day he had been waiting for her, watching, as she scoured the Thames wharves for the blue box which now sat in the mud of the circus next to his master's caravan. The following night he had been waiting for her return, back on the slate roof as she had made her way to bed. He had seen the man with the limp coming for her, pressing himself against her, and then he had seen…

He had tumbled from his perch and run all the way here, to Stepney, to this mystical patch of dry dirt with its bright awnings.

The circus was quiet when Jed stumbled into its precincts. Peter Ackroyd, circus-hand and freak-keeper, was sitting under the night-sky with his misshapen charges. Pansy, one of the Siamese twins, was strumming at a Spanish guitar, while her sister Poppy fingered chords on the fretboard.

This was *their* time. The gawping crowds, the cussing men and fainting women, had gone home to tell their families about the abominations they had witnessed in the freak-tent. The streets surrounding the waste ground were empty now of the children who scampered close and howled abuse at them during the day. Malacroix, their master, had retired to his caravan in the company of De Vries, the strong-man. By night they could come out and play, like the myth-creatures they were.

Even among this most isolated cluster of souls, the night's talk had been of Jack the Ripper. Ackroyd had listened to stories from all sides of the capital, accusing tongues with theories of the Ripper being a medical man, a Jew, a member of Parliament, even the Devil himself. That night, outside the freak-tent, he had heard the most absurd rumour of them all. A man had declared to his wife that it would not have surprised him if one of these monstrosities turned out to be the killer. Ackroyd now told the tale to his friends.

'Who?' laughed Saul, whose body ended at the waist. 'Me?'

'Or me?' added Tiny Ron the midget, barely three feet tall.

'It was her,' said Poppy, elbowing her twin. 'I was there. I saw her.'

They laughed and were happy under the stars. Then Jed appeared.

Ackroyd's face immediately clouded. There was something about Jed which made him feel uneasy. Jed was both a pitiful and somehow revolting character. He seemed isolated; alone in a way that even the freaks were not. They had their brotherhood, they had each other, and Ackroyd himself. Jed seemed forever to be on the outside, hiding from the world, watching, scavenging among the experiences of other people.

Ackroyd was always apprehensive when he saw another mortal being drawn like a fly into Malacroix's webs of intrigue and obsession. Ackroyd knew only too well the influence that Malacroix could bring to bear on the weak-willed. Once in the ringmaster's clutches, nobody ever broke free. Malacroix always found ways of binding people to him. But what could he possibly want with this skulking imbecile?

Jed was obviously in a state of high agitation as he stumbled up the steps of the huge, scarlet and gold caravan that stood at the far end of the circus site and hammered on the door. The top half of the door opened and De Vries, bare-chested and huge, leaned out to see who it was.

'Malacra...' Jed stammered. 'Mal... Malacra.'

The mute strong-man looked impassively at the idiot boy, then idly jabbed a tree-trunk arm forward, catching him in the chest and sending him tumbling back down the steps. Jed immediately picked himself up and assaulted the steps again. Again De Vries sent him tumbling.

'Doesn't work, really,' said one of the clowns, ambling over to Ackroyd and the watching freaks. 'Lacks comic pathos.'

Jed sat dumbly on the ground, his hands clutching at the thin sprinkling of grass that grew through the hard dust. Ackroyd rose to his feet and went over to him.

'Is everything all right, Jed?' he said, placing a hand on his shoulder. Jed flinched and pulled free, mumbling to himself.

The door of the caravan opened. Malacroix stood in the doorway, a cigarette and holder jutting from beneath his moustache.

'Ah, Jed, *mon cher*,' he purred. 'Come in, come in.'

Jed picked himself up and entered the caravan, still mumbling. De Vries emerged and stood like a sentry at the top of the steps, arms folded. Malacroix closed the door.

Ackroyd pulled his jacket straight and mounted the steps. De Vries glanced down at him.

'I need to speak to Malacroix.'

De Vries merely unfolded his arms.

'I won't disturb him for long…'

Ackroyd tried to slip past the strong-man, but a huge hand grasped him by the collar and for a second he hung, dangling in the air. Then, with a flick of his wrist, the giant sent Ackroyd tumbling into the mud. The young keeper pulled himself to his feet, trying to regain some dignity as he crossed back over to the now silent circle of freaks, his mind racing. What was going on between Malacroix and Jed? What plans did the circus owner have in mind for the boy? Ackroyd glanced over at the tall blue box that had been brought in the other night.

'Something is amiss,' he said quietly to himself. 'Something is definitely amiss.'

The caravan of Malacroix was as mysterious and exotic as its occupant. Trinkets from the four corners of the world filled every corner, creating a world in miniature that Jed never tired of. The rough wooden walls were adorned with heavy drapes and curtains, and with fading posters proclaiming the past glories of the circus of Jacques Malacroix. The floors were awash with carpets of exotic design, from India and Asia, Egypt and China. Jed felt his feet sink into the deep pile as he stepped further into the permanent semi-gloom. The air was thick with incense and tobacco smoke, delicate blue-grey plumes curling their way towards the curved ceiling, with its elaborate paintings of stars and comets.

Ornate boxes lined the walls, their tops scattered with heavy, ancient books. Books were a mystery to Jed. He had tried to look at the books at the church, the hymn books, the huge jewelled Bible that stood on the lectern, but the Reverend Jefford had caught him and beat him from the church, screaming at him for his unworthiness.

Books were powerful, mysterious things, and that Malacroix had so many of them meant he had to be a powerful man indeed.

'Now then, young Jed, the sun only just up and you here again?'

Malacroix's voice boomed from the far end of the caravan, Jed could see him, a vague, smoky silhouette behind the huge roll top desk that was the centre of everything to do with the circus. Jed crept forward, head bowed. The desk was awash with newspapers and periodicals, all of them with stories of the murders that had been taking place around Whitechapel, with stories of the Ripper.

A crude map had been drawn in Malacroix's spidery hand on a sheet of parchment, a ragged cross where each of the murders had taken place. A huge bottle of black ink stood unstoppered, the pens standing upright in the monkey skull that Jed coveted so much. Malacroix had been working through the night, but Jed could see no sign of exhaustion in his face. The circus owner's eyes blazed with fierce intelligence, the deep black of his suit reflecting the dozens of candles that burned around the room. The only colour came from the blood red cravat that wound around his throat, and the silver pin that held it there. Jed shuffled uncomfortably, aware as always of the shabbiness of his own jacket.

Malacroix folded the map and thrust it into one of the desk's cavernous drawers.

'A pattern will emerge, Jed, mark my words, and when it does, with your undoubtable skill we shall have him.' Malacroix rose and clasped Jed's shoulder with a black-gloved hand.

'Think. The Ripper, here, in the Circus of Jacques Malacroix!' His eyes narrowed and the grip on Jed's shoulder became painful.

'All over the globe they will have heard of him, and he will be here, the greatest, most depraved of freaks, part of my own personal collection.'

He released Jed and sank into a huge leather armchair, clamping his cigar between his teeth. He stared deep into Jed's eyes.

'Now, what brings you to my caravan so early, boy? Another prize so soon? Another box of delights?'

Malacroix listened as Jed recounted in his broken English his trailing of the girl. Her search for the box, her eventual return to the lodging house, the man with the limp, the fight. The way the girl had suddenly appeared to Jed, the sudden savagery of her attack, the thing which, just for a moment, the girl had appeared to become. Something savage, clawed, not human.

Malacroix leaned forward in his chair, his face eager and attentive.

He grasped Jed's knee.

'Again! Tell me again what this creature looked like!'

'Like our lions, Sir! I swear! Like our lions but with spots on its skin.'

Malacroix crossed the caravan to one of his chests and pulled open a leatherbound volume. He spread it out on the desk before Jed, his finger stabbing down on one of the delicate engravings.

'Is this what you saw, boy?'

Jed looked at the savage creature on the page before him. There was what he had seen at the lodging house. They knew! The books knew! He looked up at Malacroix in awe.

'You're absolutely sure?' the ringmaster said slowly.

'Swear-to-God, sir... swear-to-God, swear-to-God, swear-to-'

'Yes, yes, all right,' Malacroix snapped. 'A cheetah...' He breathed the words like cigar smoke.

'A cheetah girl.' Jed could see the determination in his eyes. 'This fair city is being most generous with her gifts.'

The painted door opened and in a flurry of movement, Malacroix swept from the caravan, buttoning his cape. The strong-man outside the door looked down expectantly at his employer. Malacroix's face was wild with excitement.

'Gather up the men, Mr De Vries, and the nets, we're going on a little hunt!' Brandishing that curious red-handled umbrella, Malacroix ushered Jed down the steps. Ackroyd watched him with mounting anxiety as he pulled on his top hat and pointed the umbrella directly at him.

'Get another cage prepared, Ackroyd! A new attraction is

coming to town.'

With a sharp laugh, he vanished out of the circus gates, Jed under his wing. Moments later, De Vries and a gang of burly circus workers followed the circus owner out into the brightening morning.

Ackroyd felt a tap on his knee. 'What is happening? Where are Jed and Malacroix going?'

He looked down to see Tiny Ron, and crouched so that their heads were level. 'I wish I knew, Ron, and that's the truth, but we've been asked to prepare a new cage, so I gather that our numbers are to grow.'

Ron shook his head. 'What manner of beast has Malacroix found now?'

Ackroyd stared out past the circus gates. 'I wish I knew, Ron. By God, I wish I knew.'

Chapter Sixteen

'So I told 'im – I said – I pays the Ol' Nichol mob, I said. If you're movin' in on top o' them, they'll 'ave somethin' to say about it, and no mistake.'

'You told 'im what for, did yer, Barney? You told them circus freaks.'

There was unkind laughter around the pub. The man called Barney shook his head vigorously. 'An' Malacroix, 'e jus' laughs. But it weren't no joke, I tell you,' he said. 'It's 'ad me rattled all day, thinkin' about it. That Malacroix – there's somethin' Devilish about 'im… It wouldn't surprise me if 'e weren't the Ripper 'isself.'

''E did it again last night,' someone else cut in. 'Killed a gel in Miller's Court. Policeman reckoned it 'ad been done by the devil or by a wild animal, not a man.'

There was a concerned muttering.

''Tain't Malacroix, though,' another voice said. 'Ain't you 'eard? 'E's offered a reward for anyone what can catch the Ripper. Says 'e wants to put it in 'is show.'

'What did 'e want with you anyways, Barney? Did 'e want you for 'is freak show, or what?'

More laughter.

''Tweren't me 'e were after,' said Barney. 'A gel what was stayin' with me. A mad girl. I reckon she must 'ave been one of 'is freaks… She give 'im the slip, though. An' good riddance to 'er an' all.'

He rubbed his throat slowly with his hand. Deep, ragged cuts were visible beneath a dirty neckerchief.

'I'm wi' Barney,' someone said. 'I don' like that Malacroix, nor 'is monsters. 'Tain't natural. Them freaks is like to murder us in our beds.'

'Ah, the Ol' Nichol mob'll take care o' that Frenchman if 'e steps out o' line.'

'The Ol' Nichol mob leaves Malacroix alone,' said Barney bitterly. 'They's just as scared of 'im as every other bugger seems to be. You remember what 'e did to the Jewboys las' year? They was pushin' in on 'is rackets…'

There was a murmur of recognition.

'They even reckon it was 'im that burned that synagogue out…'

'Nah…' somebody said.

'Yes –' a new voice cut in. An old voice. A man sitting alone at a table, watching the throng. His accent was not English. German, perhaps. A hint of the Orient… There was a sudden, respectful hush in the pub. 'That was Malacroix. He was behind the desecration.'

''Ere, I 'eard what 'appened to one cove what come up against 'im,' said a woman in a conspiratorial whisper. 'This were a few years back, when 'is circus was 'ereabouts. A man got into a quarrel with 'im, so they say — a Yorkshireman what 'ad moved down 'ere – over some chickens. This man reckoned one o' Malacroix's animals took some of 'is chickens out of 'is yard in the night. Anyway. Malacroix is as nice as pie about it, an' pays the man the value o' the chickens, only a day or so later, the man vanishes clean off the face o' the Earth. The circus moves on, an' six months later this man's brother, what lives back up in Yorkshire, is visitin' the circus an' 'e wanders into the freak show, an' what does 'e see there but 'is brother; no arms an' legs, jus' stumps, covered in feathers an' squattin' in a pit, squawkin' like a chicken an' flappin' what's left of 'is arms.'

The conversation rose again and became indistinct, many voices talking at once; a mixture of awe and incredulous laughter. The attention of the man sitting alone in the corner wandered to the yellow-stained window. He smiled at the reflected dancing candle-light. He didn't know these people, but he found their chatter soothing, like birdsong, or the slow lowing of contented cattle. Absently, he reached into a pocket of his jacket and took out a pack of playing cards, which he shuffled quickly and deftly.

"Ere we go, Gloria,' a voice called. "E's doin' it again…'

A crowd immediately started to gather around the man. He ignored them. He laid the cards out in four neat fans on the table in front of him, then flicked each of the fans over to reveal the jumble of suits and numbers in each hand. He gathered up the cards and shuffled them again, letting them cataract through the air from hand to hand, then once more laid out his four fans. He turned each of them over. Diamonds, spades, clubs, hearts. Each in perfect numerical order.

His audience clapped and murmured approval.

The landlady was pushing through the crowd.

"Ere, Gloria, where d'you find 'im?' someone shouted at her.

"E jus' turned up a couple o' nights ago. Din'tcha, Johnny.' She slapped a pint pot down in front of him. 'I think 'e's feeble-minded,' she said. 'Never says nothin' to no one. Not a dicky-bird. 'E's good with the cards, though, I'll give 'im that.'

"E's probably somethin' to do wi' that blasted circus,' Barney spat. 'Bloody freak.'

'Ah, leave 'im alone,' said the landlady. 'There's no 'arm in 'im. Yer jus' a lost soul, ain'tcha, Johnny.'

The man smiled absently at her and raised the pot to his lips. She was kind to him. A beer or two as the evening wore on, and a shilling for lodgings at the end of the night. Apparently her customers found him entertaining.

But he was looking for something in the cards.

He began rapidly sorting through the pack, extracting cards seemingly at random. He balanced eight on their edges in a square, faces outwards.

"Ere 'e goes,' whispered the landlady. 'It's good, this.'

A hush descended on the watching crowd. The man barely registered it. He was working with agitated fingers now, selecting colours and numbers, building flimsy platforms, walls, coaxing the tenuous structure, level upon level, rising from the rickety pub table.

117

He had to work quickly. It was coming back. The soothing murmur of drunken voices had acquired a new tone. A buzzing which hurt his head. The chitinous rattle of something insectoid, something alien. Every so often he would catch a look in the eyes of one of these people which disturbed him: hollow, hungry, hopeless. Hope drowned by despair. The buzzing got louder and more painful. There – out of the corner of his eye – a glimpse of one of these 'people' as they truly were: dark, shuddering, rattling things, faces wrapped in dirty bindings, bodies crawling with minute, black, many-legged parasites. He kept his eyes fixed on the cards... concentrate...

'Get 'im another beer,' one of the things buzzed.

He glanced up. The pub was beginning to grow darker. The shadows creeping inwards, swamping everything. The darkness seemed to amplify the clickings and scamperings of the things around him. He clamped his hands over his ears... It did no good. A light began to shine in the dark.

There – picked out in the middle of this alien huddle, almost luminous in the dark – a woman. A mask of white paint and lipstick, a dress of rags and bandages. He had never seen her before... It was as if she had been singled out by the greasy yellow light. It cast deep shadows over her filthy dress, deep living shadows that disguised her real features, disguised her eyes. But he knew what he would see in those eyes. She would be just like the others.

He dropped a card he was placing. His hand went to the pocket of his coat and closed on something thin and cold and metallic. He clutched the thing tight in his fist.

The room was drenched in her sick-light. The woman – the thing masquerading as a woman – tottered through the door on to the dark street beyond.

He made to rise, to withdraw his hand from his pocket, but felt a sudden pressure on his wrist, holding him down. A man was sitting next to him, staring into his eyes. A real man, not some demon in disguise. He was short and old. A white beard clung about his wrinkled face. His eyes were deep and kind. They stared, urgent and unblinking.

'My name is Joseph Liebermann,' he said. That voice again, old, East European. 'Concentrate on my name. Concentrate on me.'

The man at the table began to tremble, to shake violently. Joseph Liebermann held his wrist tightly in his hand, held his eyes with his gaze. The man slumped forward, scattering the house of cards.

The crowd murmured its disappointment and turned its attention to other matters.

They were just people again. Ordinary people.

Chapter Seventeen

Ace awoke to warmth and the last sound she expected to hear: the happy laughter of children. She was in a broad bed in a small, neat room. The day was bright and the sun high.

She had dreamed of the cat-creature again…

A woman she didn't recognise was standing over her, smiling. Through a doorway without a door, in the wall behind her, she could see four or five children running about while another, older, woman flapped her arms and tried to quiet them.

'How d'you feel, my dear?' the woman asked.

'Where am I?' replied Ace, disorientated. 'Who are you?'

The woman turned her head towards the door. 'Henry,' she called loudly, 'she's awake.'

She turned her gaze back to Ace. 'I'm Martha Tomkins,' she said. 'Henry's wife.'

Ace was still puzzled.

'Henry Tomkins, the horse-slaughterer,' the woman went on. 'I'm his wife.'

Ace looked around uneasily, and made to rise from the bed. Henry had grassed her up to the police. Thanks to him she'd given them a description of the Doctor.

'Henry…' the woman called again. She sounded nervous. The big silhouette of the horse-slaughterer suddenly filled the doorway. Self-consciously he knocked on the doorframe.

Ace smiled at him. 'Can you tell me where I am?' she asked.

'You're at the yard,' Henry replied, keeping his eyes fixed on the floor.

'Come in,' said Ace. 'I can hardly hear you from there.'

'Oh, miss,' said his wife, 'it's hardly proper, you being in bed and all…'

'Don't be daft,' said Ace. 'Come in.'

He took a self-conscious step forward.

'How did I get here?' asked Ace. 'I can't remember anything…'

'You've been feverish,' said Martha.

'I found you yesterday morning,' said Henry. 'Down in the yard, among all the carcasses. In a dead faint, you were. The missus has tended you since then.'

The couple exchanged a quick glance. That look of partially concealed nervousness again.

'I washed your dress, miss,' Martha said. 'It had got a bit messy down there. I got out most of the –' she seemed to have trouble finding the word – 'marks…'

'Marks?'

'It was quite messy down there. Blood…'

For the first time, Ace noticed the faint sheen of red covering her hands, thickening at her bitten-away nails.

'Is there anything to eat?' she asked. She was suddenly starving again.

Another hasty glance between her hosts. 'I've some soup on,' said Martha, and withdrew to the outer room, shooing children from her path.

The rough-and-tumble of kids suddenly spilled through the doorway. A boy of about eight and two girls, a little younger, were suddenly dancing about the bed. A harsh word from their father sent them packing.

'Sorry about that,' he said. 'Miss… I'm sorry, I don't know your name…'

'Ace,' said Ace.

'Beg pardon…'

'Dorothy,' she said with reluctance.

'Miss Dorothy, forgive my asking, but… where d'you come from?'

'Perivale,' replied Ace.

'Country girl, eh?' said Henry.

'No…'

'Look, miss, not meaning to be rude or anything, but… shouldn't

122

you go back there? I mean… this ain't a nice part of town for a lady to be stuck in.'

'I… don't know anyone in Perivale now.'

'So how do you come to be in Whitechapel?'

'I'm looking for someone…' said Ace.

Martha returned, carrying a steaming bowl of broth.

'Where are you staying, love?' she asked.

'I was staying in a lodging house on the Whitechapel Road,' said Ace. 'But I can't go back there. I don't have any money to pay for the bed.'

Henry and Martha exchanged another of their silent glances. Ace ate with abandon. When she finally put down her spoon and drained the last of the soup from the lip of the bowl, Henry was holding out some coins to her.

'It ain't much,' he said. 'If I was you I'd get yourself hired out as a servant. There's an office on the Commercial Road, always on the lookout for healthy girls. It'd be a steady wage and a roof over your head.'

Ace read the look in his eyes; the tone of his voice. He wanted her to go away. They both did. The nervous tension flickering between them screamed for her to leave.

An hour later, Henry Tomkins and his wife watched their guest depart down the rickety wooden steps into the yard, past the lean-to where he had found her unconscious the previous morning, where the horse-carcasses hung, out into the busy road beyond.

'We didn't ought to have let her go,' Martha said. 'Not after the way you found her. She could still be feverish.'

Henry shot a glance at their children. 'I told you what I saw, woman,' he said.

His wife nodded solemnly.

'We can't risk it. Not with the little ones. I still say we ought to have talked to the law again.'

He shuddered at the memory of the sight he had seen among his carcasses the previous morning. For a moment, he had thought the Ripper had attacked again. The girl lay there insensible, blood smeared up her dress, clotting around her mouth, caked thick upon her hands. Thin strands of meat hanging from her jaws, caught in between her teeth. And one of his hanging carcasses, great gouges of meat torn from it, stripped almost to the bone.

'Name.'

'What?'

Dandruff fell lazily from his dark, greasy locks on to the desk he sat behind.

'Yer name. What is it?'

'Oh… Dorothy. Dorothy Gale.'

'Position sought.'

He had a thin face, red with acne; a pinched look, a skeletal body in a too-small suit. He could scarcely have been any older than Ace.

'What?'

A choked, chortling noise came from his companion, sitting on a tall stool in the corner of the room and cramming a Chelsea bun into his overflowing mouth. The thin youth threw a look at his fat colleague.

'What is it you do?' he said to Ace in an exasperated tone. 'What experience 'ave you 'ad? Yer work.'

'Oh… I was a burger flipper for a bit.'

'A what?'

'I worked in McDonald's. You know? The fast-food restaurant.'

'A restaurant.'

'Yeah. Sort of.'

'A waitress.'

'Yeah. If you like.'

'We don't supply restaurants. Only private 'ouses. What experience 'ave you 'ad in that line?'

Ace shrugged. 'I did a bit of work experience in an old folks' home when I was in school. Wheeling mad old ladies round, that sort of thing...'

He looked again at his colleague, now wiping crumbs from his fat lips. 'Mad old ladies...'

Fatty slipped from his stool and waddled up to Ace. He gripped her arm and squeezed it hard. 'She looks strong,' he said. 'And she acts tough enough. She might do. God knows, we've tried everyone else on our books...'

The thin youth was writing on a piece of paper. He handed it to Ace.

'Go to this address,' he said. 'You'll be working for a Miss Jane Treddle. You'll be a maid-of-all-work. The wage is twelve guineas per annum. You will receive a uniform, and bed and board. Good day to you.'

He brought his hand down on a bell which sat on his desk and his fat colleague held open the street door with a greasy smile.

Thirty minutes later, Ace found herself once again among the Thameside wharves, perhaps half a mile from the point where the TARDIS had landed. Her destination was a row of big, drab houses which butted on to Treddle's Wharf. This was to be her new home. She had been disappointed by the Tomkins' obvious reluctance to let her stay under their roof. She didn't know what to expect here, or indeed why she was here, except for the fact that she had nowhere else to go.

The sound of the knocker against the big, peeling front door seemed to reverberate within. Heavy footsteps approached, and the door creaked open.

'May I help you, miss?'

A short, thick-set man wearing a worried, hopelessly middle-aged expression stood at the door.

'I've come about the job,' said Ace. 'Are you the butler?'

'The butler...' He drew himself to his full, inadequate height. 'I am Bartle Treddle, the nephew of the lady of the house.'

'So is there a job going here, or what?'

'I beg your pardon…'

'The servant's job.'

'The job… What employer, may I ask, taught you that it was proper for members of the servant class to call at the main door of a house as if they were dropping in for tea?'

'Look –' Ace was in no mood for this – 'is there a job going here or isn't there?'

The man seemed to deflate.

'Come in,' he said. 'You have spirit, it would seem, and that is the prime requisite of this position. You will do. Come with me.'

He ushered her up the big, bare staircase, then up a smaller one to the attic floor of the house, to a small room under the eaves with a tiny skylight window set over a narrow bed.

'This will be your room,' he said. 'Although in truth you will have the run of the upper storeys, should you wish to use them. My aunt never rises beyond the ground floor and there's no one else in the house… most of the time. It is my aunt – Miss Jane Treddle – for whom you will be working. You will cook and serve her meals, and clean if you have time, although in truth dirt seems invisible to my aunt. You will find her… a singular character, and not the easiest of employers. Eccentric, you might say.'

Barking mad, thought Ace.

'I shall call in from time to time, and you might encounter my unfortunate cousin, once removed. His wits – if ever he had any – are quite fled, and you should simply ignore him… Now, here is your uniform. Please put it on and make yourself known to my aunt. You will find her somewhere on the ground floor. Just follow the cats.' He took a silver watch from his pocket. 'I must take my leave of you. Business demands my presence at the wharf.'

He bustled out of the room and hurried heavily down the uncarpeted stairs. Ace looked with distaste at the black dress and white apron and cap which lay draped across a chair-back.

126

Reluctantly, she slipped from her dress and into her uniform. It wasn't too bad a fit. She plodded reluctantly down the stairs to the ground floor.

The winding passageways were largely unlit. Down here they stank of cats. 'Hello,' she called.

She could hear the sound of a piano being played badly – excruciatingly – somewhere deep in the house. She followed the sound to a pair of double doors, slightly open. The room beyond was huge, and lit with shafts of narrow daylight cutting through dust. The bulk of the daylight was shut out by heavy, closed curtains. Only the many holes in the drapes admitted any light at all.

'Hello…' Ace said again.

The piano – really, it sounded as if it was being hammered by a five-year-old child – suddenly fell quiet.

'Who is there?' a dry voice croaked. 'Have you come to murder me?'

Ace's eyes were becoming used to the gloom. In a corner, at a piano, sat an old woman – an ancient woman, skeleton-thin and almost completely bald.

'I'm the new servant,' Ace said, stepping forward. Then she stopped. At the woman's feet, something seethed. A mass of dark shadows hissed and writhed. They were cats, Ace suddenly realised. A dozen or more cats surrounding the woman's long, tattered dress. At her approach they drew back. They were all staring up at Ace, their backs arched, their hackles raised, mouths drawn back over tiny teeth, spitting their hatred at her.

'Hah!' the old woman exclaimed. 'My cats detest you. A promising start. No doubt I shall detest you too, before very long, and you will detest me. It is the way of the world. Now, where is my luncheon?'

'Your what?'

'I luncheon at one-thirty. It is now nearly three o'clock. You think because I'm old, I'm dull-witted. Let me assure you that I am not. And another thing –' she suddenly lurched from her seat towards Ace and gripped her neck in the claw-like fingers of both hands – 'I'm not as weak and feeble as I look, either.'

Her fingers pressed hard into Ace's windpipe. Ace jumped back, trying to pull free. The woman clung on. Ace jerked her off her feet. She weighed practically nothing. Ace was flinging her about like a rag-doll, and still she clung on, cackling and choking. Howling cats darted underfoot as they danced.

'Get off me!' spluttered Ace, tripping over a cat and slamming into a corner of the room. The woman released her grip and stood, breathless, in front of her.

'So now you know,' the woman wheezed. 'Bring me my luncheon.'

This was insane. What was she doing here? Waiting for the Doctor to find her...

Even if he did – even if he cared any more about finding her – what would he try to do to her? How *could* it be the Doctor? All his selflessness, his bravery, his moral sense – his... goodness – was it all just over-compensation for an equally black, murderous side hidden until now? Everything seemed upside down. The Doctor had killed the girl in Miller's Court, and he had tried to kill her.

The full weight of the loss, of the betrayal, fell upon her. She began to cry bitterly.

This kitchen was hopeless. She couldn't see a thing she recognised.

Slowly mastering her tears, she set about opening cupboards, flinging their doors wide. She was starving again.

A larder. Her eyes flashed over the food. Several uncooked joints of meat, a plate of cold cuts, cheese, baskets of vegetables on the floor. She sunk her fingers into the plate of cold meat and stuffed great handfuls into her mouth.

* * *

She spent the day ignoring the old woman. Let the old cow scream for her. Let her starve. Ace wasn't going near her again. She set to exploring the house. The woman's injunction had given Ace a plan: there must be some money stashed somewhere in the house.

The still, empty passages seemed to wind on for ever. In the silence, every footstep seemed to echo. Even her breath seemed to blow back at her. Avoiding the ground floor, she wandered from room to empty room. Some still contained carpets and furniture; most were bare of both.

One room she entered contained scores of sumptuous gowns, many torn, many flung to the floor in an untidy carpet which caught around her feet. A large dressing-table was covered in spilt face-powder and discarded brooches and necklaces. One old dress was draped across the dressing-table mirror. Ace brushed it to one side. The mirror beneath was cracked into dozens of irregular shards. Her broken reflection stared out at her. She flung the gown back across the glass and left the room.

She was sure she could hear movement in the silent corridors. A footstep disappearing around a corner ahead of her. She was so sure that once she called out. There was no reply, barring a faint echo of her own voice.

Jumping at shadows. The house was growing gloomy as the evening advanced. She found a nub of candle and lit it. The shadows danced about her.

There was no money here, and the house was starting to spook her. She returned to her attic room. The best thing she could do now was to try and sleep. Tomorrow she would act.

Chapter Eighteen

Johnny (at least the landlady of the Angel and Harp called him that, and as far as he knew he had no other name) was sitting at his customary corner table in the pub. He was calm, and sat quietly, watching the amiable bustle of the drinkers, who at this point in the evening were well-oiled and blithely ignoring him. He had arrived late and many had already left. The evening was winding down.

Absently, he rubbed his fingers together. They were sticky.

He noticed several tight huddles of men, whispering conspiratorially. Every so often a group would disappear through a door in the back wall.

Somebody tumbled into a chair beside him.

''Ullo, mate,' the man said. 'Barney's the name.'

There were sniggers from the three men standing behind him. Johnny said nothing.

'We saw you with the cards last night. Right good, you was.'

The man appeared to be waiting for some sort of reply. When he got none, he continued. 'Now, me an' me mates was wonderin', seein' as 'ow you provided such a top-notch entertainment for us last night, whether we mightn't return the favour, so to speak.'

Still Johnny was silent.

'Now it so 'appens there is a little somethin' occurrin' 'ere tonight what jus' might tickle yer fancy.'

The sniggers became open guffaws.

'Will you be our guest, so to speak?'

Johnny allowed himself to be drawn to his feet.

'That's it,' the man said. 'You jus' stick with yer Uncle Barney.'

He followed the man, who limped on a club foot, through the narrow door in the back wall and down a short passage. Another door led into a large and brightly lit room, crowded with men. A wooden-walled pen dominated the centre of the room. Men drank and smoked and exchanged pound notes, talking loudly all the time.

A man was barking over the crowd. Suddenly a hush fell. Two men stood outside the pen, opposite one another. Each was holding a metal cage. There was frantic movement within each cage. A signal was given and each man lowered his cage into the pen and opened the door. From each emerged a black bird.

Johnny drew back from the pen.

''S all right,' chortled Barney. 'They's only chickens.' He patted Johnny on the sleeve of his dark overcoat, then withdrew his hand quickly. The coat was stiff, crusted with something dark.

The birds circled each other, restless, alert, jabbing lightly at the air with their beaks. Suddenly both flew forward, talons extended. On each of their feet was a metal spur: a spike, sharp and vicious. They came together, wings flapping frantically, feet flailing the air, gouging at each other. Feathers and blood exploded upward. Beaks snapped. The claws flew and flew.

Cheers and groans went up from the crowd as one bird skewered the other through the throat. Propelling it to the ground, the bird brought its beak down hard into its victim's black bead eye. The losing bird howled, and so did the crowd. The victor tore its spike free of the other's throat in a great gush of blood. The bird keeled over on to the blood-dark wooden floor, twitched slightly, and died to the loud appreciation of the crowd.

The barker was in full voice again. More money exchanged hands. The winning bird was lassoed by the neck and hauled back into its cage, the other scooped from the ring and dumped in a sack. Two more birds were placed in the ring.

The atmosphere mesmerised Johnny. The shadows were back – those creeping animal shadows. They clung about the windows, nestled in corners. They splashed from the wounds of the birds.

The birds tore at each other. Somewhere at the back of the hall, a street-door opened and someone rushed in. A murmur started, spread and grew.

'The Peelers reckon they know what the Ripper looks like.'

Gradually the crowd's attention was drawn from the fighting-pen. The birds finished their battle. The winner was caged, the loser bagged. Two new birds were placed in the ring. The barker tried in vain to recapture the crowd's attention.

'Someone reckons they saw 'im. Little cove. Long, dark coat.'

Watching the birds, the shadows from the birds, Johnny scarcely noticed the crowd drawing apart around him. Barney was staring at him, something between a smile and a snarl on his lips. He put his hand to his face. Suddenly he limped forward and gripped Johnny's coat.

'Well, this is a fine thing,' he said to the crowd. ''Is coat's covered in blood. Dried blood.'

The crowd had fallen silent. Now they roared. They surged forward, grabbing at the coat, grabbing at Johnny, pushing and pulling him. He fell to the floor. Something clattered from his pocket to the floor. A pair of dessert spoons. 'Did yer see that?' someone shouted. 'That was 'is knife!' They kicked and clawed. His head began to buzz. The words of his tormentors became a hysterical, chitinous rattle. They were old. They were dead. Blood-light oozed from their filthy rags and bandages.

He felt hands gripping his lapels and lifting him to his feet. He struggled to recognise the human mask which hung from the seething alien life-mass beneath. Barney...

'So you're the Ripper, eh? Well, my friend, we're goin' to give you a very big taste o' yer own medicine. You'll know what rippin' means after you've made the acquaintance o' the fightin' cocks.'

The crowd was bellowing again. Barney heaved Johnny forward and pitched him over the wooden wall into the pen where he floundered like a fish. The birds ceased circling each other and approached him, jabbing the air with their beaks.

'They loves the smell of blood,' Barney yelled. 'It drives 'em mad.'

The birds lunged. Wings beat at Johnny's face. Spiked feet flashed in front of him. With a cry he flung his overcoat across his face. A spur ripped into the thick cloth. Another slashed his hand.

Around the pen he could just about make out men holding cages, opening them, emptying birds into the ring. Wings beat the air about him. Beaks and claws raked at his arms and legs. Feathers caught in his throat. The noise... the smell... The coat was in shreds. A bird flew into his face, its claws open.

Part Four

He pulled down the wrap that covered his face and stared up at the distant Matterhorn. The trek across the glacier had taken longer than expected, and the storm that had been so distant now loomed ominously over the mountain peak. The last time that he had been here the roads had still been passable.

He stared around at the vast expanse of nothing that had once been a city, bustling with life. Traders, merchants – all of them confident that the trappings of civilisation would keep the elements at bay.

He had warned them not to be complacent. Warned them that nature was a fickle mistress, poised to show how transient civilisation could be.

The second time he had visited the city, it was already showing signs of its demise. Buildings had toppled into disrepair, fields had been neglected. Cracks in the civilised veneer.

Now he scoured the ice for any sign that the city had ever existed, but nothing broke the flat featureless white, not a stone, not a branch. The only sign that man existed was the trail of footprints that marked his own painful progress from the valley below.

A sudden flurry of icy wind scattered powdery snow into his footprints, already starting to erase the marks of his intrusion. Ahead of him was nothing, no path, no indication of where he should go next.

For the first time in centuries, he wept.

Chapter Nineteen

He was aware of a woman's voice, sharp and loud. The bird at his face was kicked hard to one side. Other feet kicked at the birds around him. Gloria, the landlady, and an old man Johnny only half-recognised, were flapping at the birds with long coats, shouting and kicking.

'Will none of you 'elp me?' Gloria shouted to the crowd. 'Are you all cowards?'

Reluctantly, men began to climb over the sides of the pen, wrapping their coats around their hands, moving inward, slowly corralling the birds.

Gloria helped Johnny to his feet. ''Ow could you do this?' she demanded to the crowd.

''E's the Ripper!' someone shouted.

'Balls!' shouted Gloria. 'My poor lost Johnny, the Ripper? Why, any of you can see there's not an ounce of harm in 'im!'

'Ask 'im!' somebody else shouted.

'Well…?' Gloria demanded. She was staring into his eyes.

'I…' He struggled to speak. Speech was so hard… 'I don't… know…' he said.

The crowd was beginning to shout again. The old man waved his hands in the air. 'This man is coming with me!' he shouted. 'He is unwell.'

'You stay out o' this, Liebermann!' retorted Barney. ''E's Jack, no doubt about it. 'Is coat's covered in blood.'

'He is coming with me!' the old man repeated. With one arm about Johnny's shoulders, he plunged into the crowd. Reluctantly they parted before him. Barney made to intercept them, but Gloria stepped into his path. 'You come through me, Barney Slipman,' she said in low voice. Barney took a step forward, then stopped, spitting at the ground.

'What, is 'e one o' your lot, then?' Barney shouted after them.

'Some's said as 'ow the Jews is be'ind it…'

The old man half-carried Johnny through the pub and out into the street. He hailed a hansom and gave the driver an address in Bethnal Green.

'Now, my good fellow,' he said to Johnny, 'where are you hurt?'

His hands were bleeding. He could feel warm blood on his legs and his face was scratched.

'Can you talk?' the old man asked. That soothing German lilt again.

'Who are you?' Johnny said in a quiet voice.

'My name is Joseph Liebermann,' the old man replied. 'I introduced myself to you last night. And you are…'

'Johnny.'

'Just Johnny?'

'That is all I know,' Johnny replied. 'Did I really do what they said I did?' His voice dropped to a whisper. 'Am I the Ripper…?'

The old man nodded. 'I fear so,' he said. 'I have been observing you for some time.' He fingered the blood on Johnny's overcoat. 'Perhaps I should have acted sooner…'

'Why didn't you tell the police?' Johnny demanded. 'Why did you save me from those men?'

The old man sighed. 'I am a Jew,' he said. 'I know what it is like to be alone against the crowd. I have also known what it is like to be a part of that crowd. I would endure stoning before I would be part of such a crowd again.'

He was silent for a while.

'Besides,' he said, 'I was curious. You did not seem to fit. I… thought perhaps I recognised something in you. What are you doing in this part of London?'

'I don't know,' said Johnny. 'Waiting…'

'Ah, then perhaps that is what I recognised,' said the old man. 'I too am waiting.'

'What are you waiting for?' Johnny asked.

The old man smiled to himself. 'Perhaps I am not so unlike the poor people who live in these quarters. I am waiting for a miracle… And you? What is it you await?'

'I don't know,' said Johnny. 'Something terrible…'

Their journey ended at a small house in a quiet, tree-lined street. The old man ushered Johnny through his front door.

Clocks lined the walls of the narrow passageway. Clocks dominated the room at its far end. Clocks of all shapes and sizes, watches, some only half-made, backs open, cogs and springs splayed out across the workbench beneath, hands frozen.

'Welcome to my home,' said Joseph Liebermann. 'You must forgive the mess. It is so rare I entertain guests.'

Johnny ignored him. He was moving from clock to clock, smoothing polished cases, opening glass face-covers, moving hands. He fished in the pocket of his jacket and, taking out a tiny jeweller's screwdriver, began gently probing a clock's delicate inner workings.

'You understand clocks?' asked Joseph Liebermann.

'Yes… oh, yes,' said Johnny.

'You too are perhaps a clockmaker?' Liebermann asked.

Johnny turned his attention back to the old man. 'I don't know,' he said. 'I really don't know. I remember so little…'

The old man sighed. 'To be free of memory…' he mused. 'I have such a long, long memory.'

'I seem to remember things, sometimes,' Johnny said. 'Things that are just out of sight, just around the corner. Awful things… Things which do not… belong here. Things which do not seem to belong in this world at all…'

'Yesterday evening, in the pub…' Liebermann was staring hard at him. 'The cards. Those were not merely tricks, were they? The house of cards you were building… I noticed the numbers. I confess I could not divine their precise significance, but I understand enough to know what you were doing.'

'Yes…'

'You were attempting to construct a matrix.'

'Yes…'

'Why?'

Johnny looked down at his filthy, still-sticky hands. He shook his head. 'I… I don't know…' he said again.

He slumped into a chair. Liebermann got to his feet. 'But, my friend,' he said, 'you must forgive my mean hospitality. You are injured, and doubtless tired. And I confess that I, too, have a few cuts that ought to be bound. Those wretched birds…'

Johnny bathed, and then allowed the old man to bind the cuts on his arms and legs. Liebermann gave him fresh clothes: a sober, black suit, very fine and very old, and the two men supped together on chicken soup.

'I have made my home in these parts for many years, now,' Liebermann said. 'You must not judge the people too harshly in their treatment of you. They are all outcasts too, in their way. They are not evil men, they are merely men born of the city, shaped by the circumstances in which they live. It is futile to blame men for their deeds. Will you take some wine with me?'

He poured a heavy, red vintage into two thick glasses, and sipped. 'We Jews believe in the Quaballah,' he said. 'It is a part of Quaballistic teaching that the material world is a result of the constant contest between the realms of light and darkness. God and the Devil. The one cannot exist without the other, and all of us contain, in fluctuating measure, the two states.' He smiled slightly. 'The Quaballah also teaches that God's creation was only achieved after several unsuccessful attempts. I tend to think that the East End of London is such a failed attempt. It is a world which breeds crime and contempt. Here, as everywhere, men's lives are shaped for them. The streets of Whitechapel bore them, and the same streets bend their lives out of shape with poverty and drink and vice. These streets, too, are a sort of matrix, if you will…'

He poured himself another glass.

'The Quaballah is a tree of life,' he said. 'A mystical path we cannot see, so omnipresent is it, and yet one which we can but follow. Our paths intertwine in unimaginable ways. And sometimes we do unimaginable things.'

He was looking hard at Johnny.

'Life is diseased here,' he said. 'I cannot know what tortured images fill your mind, or why you acted as you did tonight and on other nights, but I believe that you are no more than one of this world's diseased limbs. In truth, I had been expecting Jack or his like for some years. You were inevitable, my friend. If not you, then another. This city is the Ripper.'

He put down his glass. 'But I see that my words trouble you. Come, it is late. I shall prepare a bed for you. You shall sleep, and then in the morning we shall begin repairing some clocks.'

Chapter Twenty

Ace jerked awake. She'd definitely heard something. Something breathing, something moving. She slowed her own breathing, straining to hear over the sounds of the city and the lapping of the Thames. It must be nearly dawn... She lay for several minutes, not moving, listening.

A scuffling from somewhere beyond her door brought her jerking upright. There was something... something in the house with her. Surely it would be light soon. She decided it was time to move.

She returned to the disused dressing-room and searched among the long-discarded clothes. The dress she had taken from the TARDIS was looking shabby now, in spite of Martha Tomkins's best efforts. She hated the maid's uniform she had been given. The one thing that had stood her in good stead so far was the notion that she was a lady. She selected one of the best-preserved of what presumably, long ago, had been the old woman's clothes, and put it on. From her attic room she'd salvaged her fur wrap, shawl and muffler. They were grimy, but the nights were cold. Her muffler still concealed its deadly payload of Nitro-9, and around this she stuffed handfuls of the brooches, necklaces and rings. She could search for ever for money in this place; she ought to be able to pawn this stuff for a fair amount of money. Give herself something to live on until she (or the police) could find the Doctor. Finally, grinning to herself, she pinned a bonnet to her head with a long hatpin. Might as well do this right.

She stepped out on to the still-dark landing and groped her way to the stair-top.

'So you thought you could cheat me, did you?' The old witch, her voice dry and freezing. 'I suppose they told you I never come upstairs. Well, there's a lot my nephew doesn't know about me. I suppose they told you I was mad... Well, maybe I am!'

Ace was aware of a sudden breeze disturbing the dark, dusty stillness, and something flying at her. The hag was on her once again, hissing and cackling, bony talons, sharp nails digging into her bruised neck. Ace toppled backwards. She felt the banister crack beneath her weight. The floor vanished beneath her feet and she toppled down the stairs, the old woman still clinging to her. The muffler bounced heavily down beside Ace, shedding jewels. If the Nitro-9 went up...

She managed to break the old witch's grip as they fell, but now the woman had hold of the front of Ace's dress, snatching at her bonnet.

'I know how to fix scheming little she-cats like you,' the old woman hissed. Her hand flashed forward. In the last of the moonlight Ace saw the vicious glint of her hatpin. She howled with pain and anger as it plunged into her arm.

For a frozen moment the two women lay at the bottom of the stairs, motionless. In that moment, Ace saw the old woman's expression change from one of mad triumph to one of momentary confusion, nausea, fear. It was the same play she had seen on the face of Barney just before she had fled the lodging-house.

Her blood felt hot. The pain in her arm had become an almost pleasurable burning. She licked the blood from her skin. Then she brought her hand hard across the old woman's face, opening her brittle skin, scattering her thin blood.

The old woman fell backward with a scream. Ace sprang to her feet and bore down on her, grinning malevolently.

A sudden sound made her freeze. Peering out from behind the grandmother clock which stood in the stairwell was a man... a boy... No, a man... but with the air of a boy. His eyes were wide and wondering, his fingers played about his lips, his hair was a dishevelled mess. He was staring at Ace. His appearance acted on her like a sharp, cold wind. Shaking her head to clear it, she picked up her muffler and ran to the huge front door, opened it

144

and vanished through it.

Jed Barrow crept out of the shadows and stood motionless, looking down at his great-aunt as she bled on to the broad, tiled floor. She extended a trembling hand towards him. He looked at her, then at the open front door. Her mouth moved to say something. He couldn't make out the words.

In truth, his mind was elsewhere. The girl... the girl he had followed and lost. Here, in his great-aunt's house. Jed had no notion of coincidence: to his fevered brain, everything was significant; everything fatally tied to everything else. He had caught sight of her last night. He had spied on her as she had gone in and out of rooms, returned time and time again to the kitchen to gorge herself at the larder, finally retreated to the attic room like all the girls did.

He hadn't known what to do. His first instinct had been to run and tell Malacroix. He knew he should... But this was his great-aunt's house. She never admitted strangers, and to bring Malacroix here... His aunt beat him often, for the smallest transgressions of her unwritten house rules. She choked and scratched him, burned him with fire-irons... Malacroix and his great-aunt. He had twitched and paced all night, furtively gazing into the beguiling light of his glass treasure, wrestling with his conscience, paralysed between these two giant wills.

Now he was in no doubt what he must do. He'd seen it again! Just for a second, in her eyes. The cat...

With a final glance at the old woman lying at his feet, he hurried through the front door, closing it behind him.

It was bitterly cold. London was still mostly asleep. Ace had run half-blind from the house, in the direction of the river. Already the memory of what she had just done was blurring. Had she killed her? She could see fear in the old woman's face, and then nothing. What was happening to her thoughts? Why was it so difficult to remember? She stopped, breathless, beneath a sign which swayed and creaked slightly in the pre-dawn wind. Treddle's Wharf. Warehouse buildings stood in shadow on either side of her. In front of her the river lapped dully. She leaned over the choppy grey murk, and wished she were home.

A footstep. There *was* something following her. Her eyes darted around the dim yard. She pulled the Nitro-9 from inside her muffler and stalked across the cobbles, holding the can out in front of her. She had to stifle a laugh. Like a vampire hunter with a crucifix!

The clink of bricks spun her around. There. A dark shape darting through the shadows of the wharfside buildings.

'Hey!' She ran over to one of the shattered windows and peered in. 'Hey! Who are you?'

Nothing. No reply.

Ace slipped into the dark of the warehouse. Even after the low light of the November dawn, she still had trouble adjusting to the gloom. Shafts of dusty yellow light from dozens of broken windows pierced the blackness like swords. She stepped forward gingerly. Something brushed past her legs and she jumped back with a cry, snatching out at the shape, missing.

'Come on out! I know you're there.' Her voice boomed around the huge brick edifice, the echoes thrown back at her. Mocking. Taunting.

Steeling herself, she started forward again, moving further into the warehouse. Squinting, she tried to make out shapes. Every step had her catching her foot or the hem of her dress. Rats scampered away from her as she made her unsteady way deeper and deeper into the huge Victorian building. Her voice dropped to a whisper.

'You've been there for days. Following me. Watching me.'

Something skittered to her left. She whirled.

'Always on the edge of my sight. Always when I least expect you.'

She strained to see, strained to hear.

'Always seeming to know where I'm going, what I'm thinking. Who are you?'

There was a low growl from the blackness. She was being hunted. Played with.

'What are you?'

Ace barely had time to register a pair of eyes in the dark before something came at her. Fast. She hurled herself to one side, lashing out at her attacker.

Her hand brushed through matted fur. She felt her breath catch in her throat.

Her dream.

The creature slammed into her again, sending her tumbling over the piles of shattered bricks. She felt the can of Nitro slip from her grasp. She scrabbled desperately for it, and in that moment her attacker was on her.

The thing snarled and spat. Ace struck out blindly at it, her fists connecting with muscle and fur. She twisted herself to one side as claws raked the dirt. She grasped the creature's throat, holding it back. Her mind raced. She knew what this thing had to be, but it was impossible. It shouldn't be here. It *couldn't* be here. She had to know. She had to see.

With a supreme effort she rolled to one side, pulling the creature into one of the shafts of light.

She stared up in horror. It *was* a cheetah person, but unlike any of the creatures that she had met on that doomed planet. There, the creatures had been noble and elegant, carrying their savagery with pride. This was merely bestial, driven by nothing other than hunger. Its fur was matted and scabbed, the claws broken and torn. Saliva dripped from yellowing fangs.

Ace waited for the killing blow, but it never came. She looked up. The Cheetah was scrutinising her, its head on one side, puzzlement on its face. Ace stared up into the slitted yellow eyes above her, and choked back a cry.

It was like looking in a distorting mirror.

Through the grime, through the expression of bestial hunger, she could see herself. Some sick twisted alternative of the creature that she had so nearly become.

She began to scream and punch, beating the creature from her with a rain of blows, driving it back with her anger. The creature vanished with a terrible cry and Ace stumbled to her feet.

She stared around the dark warehouse, desperately searching for her hunter. It all made sense. Her paranoia, her feeling of something stalking her that knew her every move, her every thought. It was bestial... it was her.

A wind swirled dust through the warehouse, making the beams of weak sunlight flicker. Ace heard a faint mocking laugh, a whisper of voices. The voices that she had heard in the TARDIS. The voices that she had heard when the Doctor attacked her.

'No.' Her voice was shaking with rage. 'Not me.'

She had spent too long being the pawn of other people. Too long holding back because of what that might mean to other people.

This time it was a problem that she could deal with herself.

This time the problem was hers and hers alone.

Her hand groped in the grit of the warehouse floor and clamped on the smooth shape of her Nitro can.

'Not this time.' Her voice was vicious.

She popped the cap and pulled out the pin. She bellowed into the huge warehouse.

'I'm not going to play your sick games!'

She hurled the can into the gloom, and began to run, counting down under her breath. 'Four...'

The door loomed, a bright rectangle in the dark.

'Three...'

She stumbled, barely holding her footing.

'Two...'

She was out into the morning, her heart pounding, the warehouse looming over her shoulder.

'One...'

The ground came up to meet her and she covered her head with her arms as the explosive went off.

Chapter Twenty-One

Jed knew the wharf well. He had crept into one of the neighbouring buildings, scampering up the stairs to the first floor, crouching by one of the shattered windows where he could watch. He attempted to muffle the light from his beautiful glass cylinder in his cupped hands, anxious that he shouldn't be seen, but unable to leave this, the greatest of his treasures, behind in the safety of the crypt.

He had watched from his vantage point as Ace padded around the deserted wharf, calling to someone unseen. He had hurried back to the ground, intending to follow her into the cavernous warehouse.

As he approached, something had made him stop, an animal instinct, something that made the hairs on the back of his neck rise. He had crept over to one of the tall windows and peered into the gloom. Nothing. He had moved to another window. From inside he could hear the sound of something breathing, and there was a smell – like the lions' cage at the circus. Jed craned his neck to see… and something lithe and savage had swept past, its yellow, slitted eyes raking over him. With a cry, Jed had stumbled backwards, crashing to the earth, whimpering. He was scrabbling back to the safety of his hiding place when the girl came tumbling out of the warehouse door.

Seconds later, Jed's world turned upside down as the blast hit him.

The noise was deafening: a thunderous clap that echoed across the Thames, sending seagulls screeching into the dawn sky. Bricks showered down around him like raindrops. He could hear them splashing into the muddy waters of the river. There was the noise of shattering glass as the projectiles bounced off the other warehouses and Jed curled into a ball, desperate to protect his glowing treasure. Over the noise of the explosion and his own screams, Jed thought he could hear the roar of an animal.

The noise stopped and Jed crawled to his feet, brushing aside broken bricks, and coughing as the clouds of dust caught at his throat. The warehouse was half gone, nothing more now than a collection of ragged brick walls silhouetted against the rising sun. As he watched, one of those walls collapsed, sending another plume of dust skyward.

Jed looked around for the girl. He couldn't see her. The wharf was a mess of broken bricks and cracked cobbles. He began to pick his faltering way over the piles of rubble, the seagulls screeching their protest above him. He picked half-heartedly at the brick piles. If she was under all this…

A noise from his left made him start. It was the girl, lying half-buried under a pile of timbers. Jed crept over to her. She was lying on her back, her dress torn and dirty, but Jed could see the steady rise and fall of her pale bruised throat. She was alive.

He stood, regarding her, unsure what to do now that she was here before him. What would Malacroix want? Jed tapped his teeth with his fingers. There was a brooch on her breast, a delicate design of silver and jewels. Something he could give Malacroix as proof she existed. He reached forward, but hesitated. The brooch belonged to his great-aunt, he was sure. He never touched her things, partly out of fear, partly out of disgust. To Jed, everything in that house was tainted with madness and decay. His fingers hovered uncertainly over the brooch.

The girl groaned and stirred and Jed snatched his hand back. She was waking. If he didn't move soon… He reached out again. And her eyes suddenly snapped open. Jed screamed.

Her eyes were slitted and yellow, like a cat's.

He scrambled backwards, tripping and stumbling. The seagulls screamed in alarm. In the distance, Jed could hear voices, the shrill of police whistles. He could hear the girl calling after him. Without pausing to look back, he hurled himself at the beckoning mouth of the alleyway and vanished into the ever-increasing morning bustle of Shoreditch.

Ace's head was ringing. The Doctor was probably right. She should improve her safety distances. She forced her eyes open – staring straight into the terrified face of a grubby street urchin. Ace was startled, but nowhere near as terrified as the man looking down at her.

He backed away from her, screaming. Ace called after him but he was gone, vanished into the early morning mist.

She struggled to her feet, brushing the fragments of brick from her ruined dress. 'What the hell got into him?'

She looked over at the ruined warehouse and nodded with grim satisfaction.

'Got you.'

Another notch on her gun-barrel.

She suddenly heard the sound of police whistles.

'Damn.'

She took a step and winced. One of her shoes had come off. She glanced down to her feet, to the rubble and glass. There was the shoe, poking out from under a pile of half-bricks. She bent down to retrieve it and caught sight of her reflection on a piece of broken glass.

Two slitted cat-like eyes stared back at her.

'No!'

She smashed at the glass with her shoe.

'NO!'

The whistles were louder now. Ace slipped on the shoe and with panic growing every second, raced for the safety and gloom of the remaining warehouse.

She barely made it to the door of the building before the first figure appeared on the far side of the wharf, stopping in astonishment at the sight of the demolished building. More and more people crowded on to the quayside, pointing and shouting, before a handful of policemen started to try and bring some order to the growing crowd.

She could see her reflection in the broken window pane. The yellow eyes stared back at her. Ace ground her fists into her sockets.

'No. I can control this.'

She thought of the scabrous animal face of the creature in the warehouse.

'I'm not like that... thing.'

The familiar mocking laugh rang out through the echoing warehouse. Ace spun.

'I told you that I wouldn't play your sick games, and I meant it!'

She forced her gaze back to the window, to those eyes.

'I *will* control this.'

She closed her eyes, breathing deeply, trying to shut out the mocking whispers that swirled around her, the sounds of the crowds outside growing ever nearer.

She tried to think of what the Doctor would do, of how he would respond. She thought back to everything good that had passed between them, to quieter moments in their manic two-step through time. She brought the words that she had remembered earlier to her lips.

'If we fight like animals, we die like animals.'

When she looked in the glass again, her eyes were normal.

She shouted into the empty room in triumph, 'See! I'm stronger than you! I can fight you!'

The phantoms grew louder, hissing their disappointment.

'Scream all you want! I'm not such an easy target!'

There was a shout from outside. One of the policemen had heard her and was making his way across the shambles of the wharf. Ace dashed across the room to another door. It was stiff with disuse but she was determined. With a groan of protest, it slid open and Ace squeezed through and out into the street beyond. By the time the policeman had made his way to the doorway of the warehouse, Ace was long gone.

154

Chapter Twenty-Two

Ackroyd sipped at his tin mug of tea and watched as the circus slowly came alive under the rising November sun. Barely dawn, and already everything was a bustle. It was rare that the circus was quiet, even in the dead of night there was the steady breathing of the animals, the occasional roar from the big cats as some unwary East End dog came too close to the cages.

All over the site, showmen were uncovering stalls, getting ready for the steady influx of curious Londoners, coming out despite the bitter weather and the whispered rumours of the Ripper.

Ackroyd looked up, puzzled at a shouted curse from the circus hands on the far side of the yard. Jed came thundering into the midst of them, pushing people and animals aside in his haste. Ackroyd watched as Jed shook himself free of protesting hands and struggled his way through the mud and straw to Malacroix's scarlet and gold caravan.

De Vries, the strong-man, stood, swathed in his huge bearskin cloak, outside the door. Jed stumbled over to him. Ackroyd could hear him shouting something quite incoherent.

De Vries regarded Jed for a moment, then pushed the door open. Jed slipped into the caravan.

The rain caught Ace by surprise and she ducked into a deep doorway. She hunched down, turning against the wall, pulling what was left of her shawl over her head to try and get some protection. She pulled out the cake that she had stolen, tearing at it with her teeth. She grimaced. 'Where's Mr Kipling when you need him?'

She huddled in the doorway, the sound of the rain calming her. The last few days had been a whirl of strange emotions, bizarre feelings. It was like she was living life through someone else's body, or rather that someone else was making her body do what *they* wanted. She tried to pick out details from the murk of her memory, but everything was churned and confused.

Her ears pricked up at the sound of footsteps at the end of the street. Cautiously, she peered round the doorway. A group of men were clustered in the shelter of a shop-front. Several of them were holding nets. Ace frowned. Something was going on.

There was a noise from the other end of the street. More men. More nets. Ace placed the remains of the cake down on the step. She didn't like this. There was a side alley barely ten feet away, but if she didn't move soon, the men would be level with it and she would be trapped. She tried to calm herself. She didn't even know that they were after her.

She strained to hear above the sound of water rushing into gutters. The muffled voices were hard to make out, but two words suddenly made Ace tense: cheetah girl.

She cursed under her breath. 'It never rains, but it pours.' The men were almost level with the alleyway. It was now or never.

She gathered herself in the doorway, took a deep breath, and exploded out into the rain.

She could hear the startled cries of the men, and the splash of their feet in puddles behind her as they started their pursuit. The rain was streaming off her, stinging her eyes. She skidded into a square, losing her footing and crashing into a wall. One of her pursuers was almost on her. Damn, he was fast. He loomed over her, a wiry, evil-looking man. A gnarled hand reached down and hauled her to her feet.

'I've got 'er! I've got 'er!'

'In your dreams, Linford!' Ace struck out. Her fist connected with the little man's jaw and he dropped like a stone. She whirled, nursing her bleeding knuckles and flicking her wet hair from her eyes. The square was gloomy and squalid, with no indication of which way would lead out. With the rest of the baying gang almost upon her, Ace made her choice and darted off to her right.

The alleyway was narrow and dark, the chill rain barely making it through the tangle of roofs and gutters. The walls began to close in on her, dark brick rising higher and higher. Ace began to panic – if this was a dead end…

A man with a barrow piled high with sacks loomed in her path. Ace cannoned into him, sending him sprawling. She clambered over the barrow, spinning it so that the alley was blocked, frantically pulling sacks off, pushing them to the floor. A hand suddenly caught her, reaching out over the barrow, pulling her shawl tight around her neck. Ace twisted, caught hold of the grimy hand and bit hard.

There was a yell of pain and she was free again, racing ever deeper into the squalor of the East End. She turned again, the tangle of houses becoming ever tighter. She could hear people shouting at her from windows and doorways, hear her attackers in the distance. A dog suddenly lunged at her, snapping at her ankles, Ace kicked at it savagely, sending it yelping back the way it had come. Everything seemed to be against her. Her breath was burning in her throat and she could feel tears welling. She wiped them away angrily. Light suddenly loomed ahead of her and with renewed vigour Ace sprinted for it. With a gasp of relief, she was out of the network of alleyways. She could see St Paul's looming through the rain. She could get her bearings from there.

There was suddenly a blow that punched the breath from her body and she felt herself being lifted into the air, held upside-down by massive arms. She tried to fight, but it was a struggle just to draw breath. Through streaming tears she could see a dark figure before her.

'Well, well. Our little hell-cat. Gently now, De Vries, we don't want her damaged.'

She tried to twist to see her captors properly, but the blood was pounding in her head, rainwater was running into her nose. She coughed and spluttered. She could hear running feet, see more figures surrounding her.

'Bring the nets.'

Rough rope nets surrounded her and she was hoisted roughly on to the shoulders of several of the men. Her head was beginning to swim. She caught a glimpse of the giant that had caught her, then the dark figure drifted into her line of sight. He was nothing more than a shadow beneath the umbrella that he held; an umbrella with a curiously curved red handle.

Ace slumped. It was the Doctor's umbrella. It was over. He had caught her. She had lost. In total despair, she stopped fighting and let unconsciousness take her.

She awoke warm and dry and sore to her bones. She lay for a moment, trying to remember what had happened to her. Then the memories of the last few hours came flooding back. Slowly, she forced her eyes open. Her head was still swimming. Thin straw carpeted the floor. She was covered in a heavy blanket. Where the hell was she?

She reached out blindly and her hand connected with strong metal bars. She was in a cage! She pulled the blanket back and clambered to her feet, swaying unsteadily. The cage was just high enough for her to stand up in. Ace grasped the bars and peered out into the darkness. She was surrounded by tents and could see half a dozen similar cages nearby. There was movement in the one next to her.

'Hey! Hey, where am I?'

She rattled the bars noisily. There was a roar and something huge lunged through the air. Ace fell backwards, scrabbling through the straw. The lion stared at her, snarling angrily, then it turned and slunk back into the shadows of its own cage.

There was a chuckle from the gloom. 'They seem to have taken to you already.'

Ace could see vague figures in the shadows, swathed in smoke.

A man stepped into a pool of light. He was dressed completely in black, a huge cigar clamped in between his teeth. He leaned casually on an umbrella. Ace felt her breath catch in her throat as she caught a glimpse of the familiar red question-mark handle.

'Who are you?'

'Monsieur Jacques Malacroix at your service, mademoiselle.' The man gave a short bow. 'No doubt you have heard of me.'

'Sorry, sunshine, doesn't mean a dicky bird,'

'And I thought that the entire world knew of the Circus of Malacroix.' He shrugged. 'No matter.'

A smaller figure scuttled around his legs: a mouldy collection of rags. Ace dimly recognised the face. A strange man-boy, curiously unsettling to look at. At the old woman's house, perhaps? Why could she remember so little of her short time there? The man-boy scampering around the impresario, like a dog around its master.

The Frenchman began a slow circle of the cage. Ace never took her eyes off him.

'Why are you keeping me cooped up in here?'

'We must look after our new guest.'

'Guest?' Ace snorted. 'I don't think much of the accommodation.' There was a snarl from the next cage. 'Or the other residents.'

Malacroix came close, scrutinising her through the bars. 'You really are exquisite.' He stared at her, a dreamy expression in his eyes. Ace began to feel uncomfortable. She nodded at the umbrella.

'Where did you get that?'

Malacroix started, woken from his daydream. He brought the umbrella up to his face, staring at the handle. 'This? Oh, Jed here acquired it for me.' He patted his imbecile pet on the head. 'My little magpie.'

'Steals a lot of things for you, does he?'

'Steals?' Malacroix tutted. 'No, no. *Acquires* is far more apt a term. Jed has a particular talent for bringing me curiosities for my collection. Objects of great value. Don't you, Jed?'

Jed smiled, showing a crooked row of yellow teeth. 'Watched you... Watched you, I have. Watched you since you arrived. Oh, yes, oh, yes…' He scampered to the far side of the tent. 'Saw you arrive, in this…'

Ace followed his gaze. Standing behind the cages was the TARDIS. She slumped back into the straw. No wonder she couldn't find it. All that time searching… pointless.

She stared at Malacroix with weary eyes.

'What have you done with the Doctor?'

'The Doctor?'

'The man I was with…'

'Ah.' Malacroix leaned close, his face pressed against the bars, his eyes blazing. 'Ah, yes. He nearly got you, didn't he. A few more seconds and another pretty face would have borne the scars of the Ripper.'

'He's not the Ripper.' Ace's voice was low and menacing.

'Jed has been searching for him, but without success. He seems the most elusive of men, this Ripper of yours.'

'I said he's not the Ripper!' Ace hoped she sounded more certain than she felt.

'And when I find him, he will be the greatest attraction in the Circus of Jacques Malacroix! '

'No!'

Ace slashed out at the circus owner, her nails raking across his face. Malacroix snatched his face back from the bars, clasping his hand to his cheek. He brought his hand away, staring at the blood. He pulled a handkerchief from his pocket and dabbed at the cuts. 'De Vries is always telling me that I'm careless around the big cats.'

Ace stared at him in horror.

'You can't know…'

'Oh, but I can, my dear.'

Malacroix snapped his fingers and Jed scrambled over, a tin bucket in his grasp.

'Jed, tell me what you see.'

The boy looked puzzled.

'In the cage. Tell me what you see!'

'A girl, Mr Malacra. 'Tis a young girl.'

'The girl you saw at the wharf?'

Jed nodded.

'The cheetah girl?'

'Yes, yes, swear to God, swear to God…'

'Very good, Jed. Now leave the bucket and go.'

Jed hurried out gratefully. Malacroix turned back to Ace.

'You see, my dear, I know all about your very special talents, but you are of no use to me until others can see you as you really are.'

His voice was hypnotic. Ace was shaking.

'You're mad.'

Malacroix pulled a hunk of dripping meat from the bucket. All around Ace could hear the lions pacing in their cages, smelling the blood.

Malacroix smiled at her. 'You have a simple choice, my young freak. In the absence of the Ripper, you will fulfil an admirable role as my star attraction. Change into your true form for me –' he hurled the meat into one of the cages – 'or starve.'

He turned and strode out of the tent. Ace could hear the lions tearing at the meat, the roars as they fought each other. She curled herself into a ball in the straw, pulling the blanket over her head, trying to shut out the noise, and her own hunger.

'Where are you, Doctor? Where the hell are you?'

Chapter Twenty-Three

Time was everywhere in the house, yet there seemed to be no sense of its passing. The constant ticking of a hundred or more timepieces soothed Johnny. He saw nothing but round, ordered, calm clock-faces, and the bright eyes of the little white-bearded man.

Johnny worked quietly alongside Liebermann, taking apart an elegant old clock, its innards badly damaged.

'This was made by a great master,' Liebermann said. 'Antoni Patek of Warsaw. It is very old, and there are no spare parts, so it is necessary to remake them.' Working with the tiniest saws and files, the old man was fashioning new cogs from thin, fine plates of metal. Johnny fitted them deftly on to their tiny axles. It was a complex task, and the business took many hours.

'I learned the art of clock-making in Paris,' Liebermann said. 'It is one of a number of useful skills I have acquired as I have travelled through this troubled world. Vienna, Prague…'

The old man seemed quite transported by his reminiscences. Then abruptly, he checked himself. '*Mein Gott*… but I am a monster. Here I talk of memories to a man who has had his past taken from him. I beg you, forgive me…'

'I killed them…' said Johnny quietly. 'I know that, somewhere deep inside me. And yet I can remember nothing.'

'I have read of diseases of the mind,' Liebermann replied, 'where a man's higher self – his rational will – becomes somehow detached. Submerged. And other urges, which seem to dwell quite outside himself, take command of his faculties. As far as he is concerned he becomes as a lifeless thing. A puppet, if you will, animated – or so he believes – by the will of another. My people have the legend of the golem. A creature of clay, made to walk by the powers of sorcery, staring out from soulless, insentient eyes – a man made in mockery of the life God breathed into Adam.'

A creature of clay... staring out from soulless, insentient eyes... Why did the image frighten Johnny so?

Absorbed by his theme, Liebermann appeared not to notice. 'The creature exists as a slave to the man who created him. Perhaps to have such a brain-fever is to experience that sense of non-life.' His smiled darkly. 'But then,' he said, 'as I said last night, we are all puppets. Perhaps we are all golem.'

Several times as they worked, Johnny noticed the old man become very still and stare at him, unblinking, for whole minutes.

'You know,' Liebermann said eventually, 'you remind me of a man I once met. It was many years ago, long before you were born, and far away from this place. He was a traveller, as I was myself in those days, although his path was stranger even than mine. You do not resemble him physically, and yet still I am reminded...'

He shook his head slowly and continued with his task.

Sitting on the straw of her cage, knees drawn up, Ace watched the circus morning unfold before her. Clowns and acrobats tumbling, burly roadie-types lugging equipment in and out of the big, bright tents. Freaks – Ace felt something strange thrill through her body at the sight of these weird things crawling or limping about the site. All morning, other men – outsiders, furtive men – crossed the site to and from Malacroix's caravan.

No one spoke to her. They barely even looked at her, except for the odd sneaked glance as they went about their business. Only Jed looked openly at her. He was crouched in the shadow of one of the tents, alternately staring at Ace and peering into a ragged cloth bag which he clutched tight to his chest.

No... someone else was looking. A young man, little older than Ace, who looked at her with concerned eyes as he went about his work, and immediately lowered his eyes when she returned his gaze. After a while he walked across to the cage.

'Are you all right?' he asked in a low voice.

'Great,' said Ace. 'You should try living in a cage yourself.'

He lowered his head. 'I'm sorry,' he said.

'Look,' said Ace, urgently, 'you seem all right. Can you get me out of here?'

He shook his head. 'I'm sorry,' he said again. 'We're not even allowed to talk to you.'

'Please…'

'Even if I could get the key from Malacroix… No, I'm sorry. You see, he would punish others for my disobedience.' He cast his eyes to where a huddle of freaks was standing, surreptitiously looking at them and whispering.

'OK,' said Ace, 'OK. Can you at least tell me what he's going to do to me? I mean… he's mad, isn't he?'

'Perhaps he is,' the lad replied, 'but he's not foolish. Anything but. As for what he wants to do with you… I imagine he will put you in the ring. If it's true what he says you can do…'

Ace didn't reply.

'Hello,' said a curious, quiet voice. 'This is a rum do…'

A little man – a midget – had left the group of freaks and was standing next to the young man.

'She looks normal,' the newcomer said. He pushed his hand through the bars. 'I'm Tiny Ron,' he said.

'Ace.' She shook the miniature hand. He nudged his friend in the knee.

'Oh… My name is Peter Ackroyd.'

'Welcome,' said Tiny Ron with a short, solemn bow.

There were low, muttering voices. The other freaks were gradually drawing up to the cage.

'These are our friends,' the midget said, and introduced them, one by one. Pansy and Poppy Bellamy, Carlos the lion-tamer, Saul, whose body ended at the waist and who balanced on one arm to shake Ace's hand. She felt the same strange frisson as before when she touched them, but their welcome was warm, and sincere.

There was a shout, in French. Malacroix was striding across to the cage, walking-cane in hand. 'Be patient, be patient, my little mishaps of nature,' he boomed, clanging his stick against the bars. His tone was avuncular, but Ace could see the freaks shrink back as he swung the ebony cane. 'Soon she will amaze us all, but for now, let us work. We have a show tonight!'

Ackroyd's eyes flashed between his employer's and hers. Ace pressed herself against the bars. 'Can you get me some food?' she mouthed.

The freaks melted away into the thin morning smog. Ackroyd, too. Ace slumped against the back wall of her prison.

'You know,' said Malacroix, 'three months ago they, like you, I kept in cages. Monsieur Ackroyd persuaded me that, in these philanthropic times, it was… misleading. So I got for them all caravans.' He sighed. 'I think perhaps I might put them back in cages.'

A shadow fell over Ace. De Vries was hauling a huge length of canvas over the roof of her cage. It hung down to the ground, and utterly blocked out the light.

'Once you have done the small thing I have asked of you,' said the vanishing Malacroix, 'then you may be merry with my other monsters, but first you have to earn your place among them. Until then, you will speak to no one but me. I shall ensure it.'

The last crack of light vanished.

Ace couldn't tell how much time she passed in the darkness, before the canvas twitched and Peter Ackroyd's head appeared beneath it. It was nearly dark outside. Ackroyd slipped a loaf through the bars. He tipped a plate of cold meat on to the floor.

'Sorry about that, miss,' he said. 'The plate's too big to get through.'

Ace picked up the thick chunks of meat with both hands and stuffed them into her mouth. The bread quickly followed.

'I couldn't come sooner,' he said. 'Malacroix was watching me. He's gone to prepare for the show now.'

There was a low, expectant murmur in the air, and the muffled roar of many hundred feet crossing the dirt.

'The punters are arriving,' said Ackroyd. 'I'd best be quick.'

'I hate circuses,' said Ace quietly.

Ackroyd lowered his gaze.

'Why do you stay here?' demanded Ace. 'Your boss is a nutter.' She shook her head. 'I'm beginning to think everyone in this century's insane.'

'It is true, we live in sorely troubled times,' said Ackroyd. 'The circus is no worse than many places. Better than some. It's safe, provided you don't cross Malacroix.'

'I hate the way he talks to the freaks,' said Ace. 'Can I call them freaks?'

'Oh, yes,' said Ackroyd. 'They are freaks. What else would you call them?'

'It's so fake,' she continued. 'He sounds so… friendly, when you can tell they're terrified of him.'

'He feeds them, and keeps them warm,' said Ackroyd. 'I do what I can for them… And where else would they go?'

'You could go,' insisted Ace.

Ackroyd shook his head. 'I will not leave them,' he said. 'Besides, there's no welcome for me out there. I…' He paused. 'I must go. The circus is opening. I will return later.'

The sky darkened and the show sprang into life. Ackroyd saw Malacroix taking his place outside the freak-tent. 'Ladies and gentlemen,' the impresario bellowed, 'behind these canvas walls lies a great secret. Something which will amaze and astound you. It is a collection of horrors – yes! But it is more than that… Inside this… chamber of horrors… lies proof that the almighty God laughs at we poor mortals and uses us for sport. I am about to reveal to you God's most neglected miracles. God's jokes!'

He pulled back the canvas and the crowd which had gathered shuffled slowly into the tent. This was Malacroix's warm-up to his performance in the main tent later tonight.

Ackroyd joined the back of the group and entered the tent. His friends were in their customary positions, each on his or her little stage. Saul gambolled about on his hands to the shrieks of the women. Carlos the lion-tamer practised with his whip, whirling it around his head. Pansy and Poppy played patriotic airs on their guitar.

'I spoke of miracles,' Malacroix continued. 'In ancient times such abominations would have been worshipped as gods. Heathens... barbarians... Jews would bow down and sacrifice to them. Perhaps we too should fall down in awe at their feet, for what better proof is there of the infinite, grotesque wonder of creation? The followers of Monsieur Darwin would dismiss them as nature's blunders, but almighty God does not make mistakes. They are his playthings... and now they are ours. Feast your eyes on their ugliness, and thank God you were born whole!'

Later, Malacroix would lead his friends in procession around the main tent, while the audience would yell and jeer from their seats, but for now the crowd, brought so close to the horrors, passed by mostly in shocked silence.

Does God make mistakes? To Peter Ackroyd, little in the world seemed planned. The world was all chaos and confusion, misunderstanding and mistrust. The circus was no different to anywhere else...

He left the crowd to feast on his friends and stepped back outside the tent.

Jed was crouching outside the flap of the tent. He would not dare enter, Ackroyd knew – he was still terrified of the freaks. His eye was pressed to the mouth of a cloth bag which he kept tightly clasped in his hands. Ackroyd had noticed him doing this on many occasions. Whatever was in the bag quite fascinated the imbecile.

He always hid the bag when Malacroix was around.

Ackroyd moved to talk to him, but Jed looked up like a startled animal and crawled away under one of the caravans.

'Monsieur Ackroyd.'

He jumped. Malacroix was standing behind him.

'Tonight,' said the ringmaster, 'I want you with me.'

The canvas was slightly dislodged where Peter had moved it, and Ace, by placing her cheek to the floor, could peer out at the circus ground. She watched the crowds flowing to and fro, and through the sharp gashes of light from the tent flaps, she glimpsed the spectacle within.

There was a clanging, and Ace's cage lurched. The cage next to hers, and others beyond that, were being towed to the back of the big top. The animals inside were restless; the cats stalked and growled, the elephants snorted and stamped.

She could see the idiot from the old bag's house – what was his name? Jed? – skulking and sneaking about as usual. As she looked, Peter emerged from one of the tents and went up to him. Jed hid under a caravan. Then Malacroix appeared, and led Peter into the big top. Jed scampered further away, squatting with his back to Ace, just a few feet from her cage. He was looking into that bag again...

A harsh light seemed to lance from the bag's tight mouth. He opened it a little wider, flinching and covering his eyes as he did so. Ace's stomach lurched. There – inside the bag – was the TARDIS's telepathic circuit. It couldn't be anything else...

A sudden noise seemed to startle Jed. He crushed the bag closed and scuttled away into the darkness. Ace's mind was racing. She had to make use of this, somehow... She had to get hold of the circuit.

Her hunger forgotten for the moment, she stared helplessly at the comforting blue shape of the TARDIS. All she could do for the moment was wait...

It was not until the show was approaching its close that her ordeal was lifted. Tiny Ron peered over the lip of the cage.

'Pssst!' he hissed.

Ace dropped to her haunches. The midget was wearing a bright crimson tunic and pantaloons, like something out of *The Arabian Nights*, topped with a Tommy Cooper-style fez. He pushed a bottle of water through the bars.

'Peter couldn't come,' he whispered. 'Malacroix's watching him. Keeping him close. He managed to tip me the wink.'

Ace pulled greedily at the water bottle.

'Thanks,' she gasped. 'Ron, I need you to do me a favour. That moron who's always hanging about, he's got something belonging to a friend of mine. It's very important. I need to get it off him. Can you... help me? He keeps it in a bag...'

'I've seen it,' said Tiny Ron.

'Can you get it off him?'

'Oh, aye, I should think so,' said the little man. ''E's not that sharp, after all... I'll see what I can do. I'd better go now, the big parade'll be starting soon. I got to ride round on one of the elephants. Dressed up like this... Ah, well...' He shrugged. 'That's the life.'

Ace watched him depart in the direction of the big top. She scanned the site through her narrow aperture. Jed was nowhere to be seen.

The big top show meant little to Ackroyd. He could see beyond the greasepaint. He could see the wires and the safety harnesses. He watched as the Tumbling Boleros, a family of acrobats and footpads, thrilled the crowd. The clowns – killers to a man – larked and fell and kicked one another in the trousers. Some of the circus-folk were better than others, but all were ultimately in thrall to Malacroix.

The big cats came in. What secrets of theirs did Malacroix hold, Ackroyd wondered.

The show progressed from marvel to marvel, building to its grand climax. This was the gathering of all the performers; the star-turns, the jugglers and fire-eaters from the smaller tents, even the freaks, would parade around the ring with plumed horses and somersaulting monkeys, the elephants towing the caged lions. It was a spectacle, he had to admit, but to him it was a spectacle of human bondage. Not for the first time, the smell of the oil-lamps and the sawdust and sweat made him feel sick.

Chapter Twenty-Four

The church was full, for once, and the Reverend Jefford could not resist making the most of the occasion.

'The Sins of the Cities of the Plain!' he thundered. 'The Judgement of the Lord is being visited on this cesspool of vice! Let every one of us reflect upon the fate of this poor wretch and examine our own hearts. For sin is its own seed-bed. Sin breeds sin, like a plague of locusts. Sin insinuates itself everywhere and destroys everything!'

They were burying the victim-before-last of the Whitechapel murderer, the Ripper. The police hadn't held on to the body for long. The story was too familiar to tell them anything new, and a sense of defeat and lethargy was creeping into their work. Lethargy was one of the Reverend Jefford's bugbears. Lack of moral fibre. If even the forces of law and order were falling to the sapping disease which, day by day, seemed to suck the life out of Whitechapel...

He had seen his flock dwindle to almost nothing in the past months. It took a sensation like this to bring them back. They stood and sat at the wrong times; they knew neither the words nor the tunes of the hymns, and none of the responses. The Reverend Jefford saw it as a challenge, and he always rose to the occasion.

The coffin was taken outside to the little churchyard. Jed was present, for once, standing with his spade held in both hands by the side of the open grave. The onlookers crowded around the hole, trampling on graves and clambering over gravestones to get a view as the coffin was lowered. The preacher scanned the crowd. Half of Whitechapel seemed to be here: women he knew to be whores, local tradesmen, many of whom had closed their shops to come, a few respectable, philanthropic women, wringing their hands, a clutch of scribbling journalists. The Frenchman from the circus was present, gazing intently around, smiling slightly. The preacher noticed Jed. He was agitated, trying to arrest the attention of the Frenchman. Jefford scowled. He knew Jed was spending time at the circus, and he had roasted the fool for it. Perhaps a more pointed lesson was called for.

His eyes strayed to the door of the crypt. An indistinct figure appeared to be standing there – little more than a shadow – but somehow the Reverend Jefford felt his blood chill. He blinked. The figure was gone. It hadn't moved; it had just seemed to melt into the old door.

He shook his head and tried to remember his place in the ritual. The mood of the crowd had changed; it was as if they all sensed the same sudden chill in their souls. He rushed through the words. The burial ended, and the crowd dispersed. He noticed the Frenchman talking to an old Jew who was standing next to a little man in a long, black coat. Jed seemed desperate to approach the Frenchman.

'Jed…' Jefford growled, 'don't hang about, lad; get filling in the grave.' He watched him shovelling earth on top of the coffin, craning after the vanishing onlookers. He watched him until the Frenchman had departed, then turned his attention to the crypt. The door, as he thought, was locked. He fished for the key. The door opened easily – that was strange, for he had not been down there in nearly a year, and the church had had no verger for most of that time.

He stepped inside. Immediately shadows surrounded him. The temperature dropped away to a damp, penetrating cold. His footsteps echoed. His knuckles white upon his Bible, he groped his way between the ancient stone sarcophagi.

He sensed a movement. He turned. There was nothing there.

He turned back.

His breath caught. A figure was standing directly in front of him. A frail shaft of light caught his face. His face… he had too many faces, diaphanous, insubstantial, ghost-faces – some young, some old, all gaunt and hollow-eyed – which seemed to bob and flow in the ether, waxing and waning like candlelight.

The Reverend Jefford felt himself falling, crashing to the damp flagstones of the vault.

And I saw a beast rise up out of the sea, and the beast had seven heads and ten horns...

He struggled to master his fear. The figure was gone, swallowed by the darkness.

The Reverend Jefford scrabbled to find his feet and lurched through the door to the outside, slamming it behind him.

Ten minutes later, in the vestry, he was still shaking. A heavy knock on the door made his heart lurch.

'Reverend Jefford...'

The door opened and a police constable entered, apologising for the intrusion.

'I am sorry to inform you, Reverend,' he said, 'but one of your flock was found dead this morning. Miss Jane Treddle, spinster o' this parish.'

'Miss Treddle... oh, I am sorry,' the preacher replied, attempting to sound clerical. 'She was a pillar of the church.'

'She'd been dead a couple o' days, judging by the state of 'er,' the policeman continued. 'Murdered, I'm sorry to 'ave to say, sir. Found at the foot of the stairs with 'er throat ripped open. We're looking for Jed Barrow, 'er idiot nephew, sir. I understand 'e works 'ere as a gravedigger.'

The Reverend Jefford peered past the policeman, out into the churchyard. The grave was unfilled. Jed was gone.

'That's right,' said the Reverend, 'although he has been but little in evidence digging graves here of late. I have barely clapped eyes on the fool. I fear his mind is growing yet worse. But surely you do not think...'

'We are also looking for a servant girl, sir, who seems to 'ave made 'erself a bit scarce,' the policeman replied. 'It may be that they was in on it together. We are not at present lookin' for anyone else.'

Joseph Liebermann watched his new friend picking apart an intricate clock and trying rapidly to reassemble it. Those hands, normally so steady and so deft, were shaking. Springs and cogs went everywhere.

'My friend,' Liebermann said, 'I fear I have done you harm, though my intention was wholly otherwise. I hoped that the funeral might set something in motion in your mind, but I had no wish to cause you this sort of distress. Sit, I beg you.'

Johnny allowed the old man to ease him down into a chair.

'Do you wish to talk about it?' the old man asked gently.

Johnny shook his head. What was there to talk about? What could he say? How could he describe the raw, creeping fear he had felt in the churchyard? They had stood at the far edge of the crowd so as not to draw attention to themselves – Johnny remembered the cock-pit well enough – and watched the wooden box being lowered into the earth. That was when the voices had started: an urgent whispering in his head, hysterical whispering, whispering so loud he had feared it would burst his eardrums. And then the whispering had become as nothing; a plaintive squeak, driven before a great roaring wave, a moving wall of cold, pure malevolence, bearing down on him.

He had been aware of his elderly friend talking to someone. A Frenchman who had placed his hand impudently on Liebermann's shoulder and blown cigar smoke in his face. He had tried to concentrate on what the Frenchman was saying; to blot out the cacophony behind his ears. 'The Jews will be blamed for this,' he had said. 'Whether they did it or no. It must always be so.' He had glanced briefly back at the grave. 'Well, Uncle, I had not thought to see you again in this part of the city. You should have left after our last meeting.' He had patted Liebermann on the shoulder. 'Already they say it was the Jews. It makes them feel better, to think of it thus. Rest assured, old man, the people will be purged of their evil.'

He had patted Liebermann on the shoulder in a manner of mock affection, and left.

Johnny had seen the Frenchman's back swim into an inky nothingness. The voices had closed in again. He had been aware of nothing more until the cool stillness of Liebermann's house.

What could he say to the old man? He rose from the seat and returned his fevered attention to the clock.

'Work, if it helps you,' Liebermann said gently. 'Work is a good way to calm a troubled soul... Although, since you have been helping me, there are so few clocks now to mend. And so we may be idle in the day.' He chuckled hopefully. 'You and I, together we manage to cheat time, yes?'

Chapter Twenty-Five

Ace had awoken to her second day of captivity early. She could not remember falling asleep. The circus ground seemed to be quiet for such a short time between the departure of the punters and the beginning of the new day's labours. Malacroix had stood on the steps of his caravan, stretching and surveying his kingdom. He had said something to De Vries, and strolled out of the ground. The next thing she had seen was the back of the strong-man's bearskin. He was standing right in front of her spy-hole. He was standing guard.

'Oi... Whasyername... De Vries!' she whispered.

The giant didn't move.

'Come on, Arnie...' she said. 'Give me a break here. Napoleon's not around...'

Still he didn't move. With an oath, she turned around and tried to get back to sleep.

She was woken some time after by a furtive hissing sound. Peter Ackroyd's head was sticking up under the canvas. He was pushing food through the bars.

'Where's De Vries?' asked Ace.

'Call of nature,' Ackroyd grinned. Ace shot a quick, embarrassed glance towards the back corner of her cage. 'Eat, now.'

'Have you seen Tiny Ron?' demanded Ace between mouthfuls.

'No...' said Ackroyd. 'Why?'

'No reason,' said Ace. 'Where was your boss going this morning?'

'A funeral,' said Ackroyd. 'One of the Ripper's girls.'

'Why is he so obsessed with Jack the Ripper?' asked Ace.

'Why is everybody obsessed with Jack the Ripper?' Ackroyd replied. 'Malacroix says he wants to exhibit him, to show him to the world.'

'That's what's so mad about this whole thing,' sighed Ace. 'We came here to save the future and I'm stuck in the Christmas panto from hell.'

Ackroyd looked confused.

'I mean... I've seen some really nasty circuses in my time, believe me, and... well, this *is* just a circus, after all...'

'You don't understand at all,' said Ackroyd. 'You don't understand the circus and you don't understand Malacroix. The circus travels about the country like... like an assize. Collecting tribute. Crooked money, protection money. You've seen the men coming and going from Malacroix's caravan. They're nothing to do with the circus. Malacroix has men in every town we visit. Not many men – just a few – but it's enough, he says. You don't need big numbers to keep folk scared. I've often heard him say it's not how many men you've got, it's what they're prepared to do. How far they're prepared to go. Look at the Ripper. Look at what one man's doing to London. It's no wonder Malacroix's so infatuated with him.'

'And how far is Malacroix prepared to go?' Ace asked.

'You remember the anti-Jew riots in Bethnal Green last year?'

'Yes,' she lied.

'All those people killed... It started off as a gang thing. The Jews against Malacroix. He turned it into a bloody pogrom. There was dozens killed. Innocent people. All over a bit of turf.'

Ace swallowed dryly.

Ackroyd peered around the canvas. 'De Vries is coming back,' he said. 'I'll try to see you later.'

She watched him slip away between the cages.

Why hadn't she told him? He seemed... too... upright, somehow. His face was open and angelic, just growing into manhood. His hair was straight and blond, falling in great sheaves about his eyes. His eyes were lake-blue.

He looked like a bloody boy-scout. That was why she hadn't told him. He just might not approve of the theft. She scanned the sight for Tiny Ron, and saw, instead, Malacroix returning across the dirt.

He strolled straight to Ace's dark prison. Through her crack she saw him pause, snatch some meat from the bucket of a passing keeper on his way to the cat pens, and pull the canvas back from the bars.

'And how is my little cheetah girl today?' he beamed. 'Hungry? Hungry enough to kill?'

'To kill you maybe, mate,' Ace spat. 'When are you going to let me out of here?'

'You know the answer to that, *cherie*,' Malacroix oozed. 'But I shall encourage you... I shall let you have the light back. A gesture... You see, I have been to church this morning. I am full of Christian charity.'

He fixed her with cold eyes.

'You *will* change for me,' he said.

Jed clutched his precious bag to his chest as he ran. He saw Malacroix, talking to the girl, and stopped some way off, slumping awkwardly on to all fours. He would not get close to the cage when she was looking at him. The previous night he had lifted the canvas and watched her while she slept. Like so much of the world, and especially the fairground, she both tantalised and terrified him.

He was aching to speak to Malacroix. He contented himself with a peep inside the bag. What visions would the strange light bring? Strange skies, many moons...

As ever, he closed the bag quickly. Malacroix was walking towards him. He thrust the bag behind the wheel of a caravan and got to his feet. He stepped forward and tried to speak, but the words caught and jumbled in his mouth, and wouldn't come out. And now Malacroix was speaking to him. He received the words in his usual, vacant manner. Something about his aunt being dead. He pictured his aunt, sitting in her chair in the semi-darkness in a room that stank of cats, rocking and cackling. He pictured her lying on the floor, blood coming from her neck, hand raised, trembling, towards him. He tried to picture her dead. He couldn't.

In his mind's eye she just appeared to be sleeping. Dead – actually *gone* – he couldn't raise any image at all.

He put it out of his mind. Malacroix was patting him on the shoulder. He pinched Jed's cheek, then turned towards his big caravan.

It was then that Jed, squatting in the dry mud, reaching for his treasure, found that it was gone. The bag was gone… His mouth opened. All those tangled words resolved themselves into a wailing, a roaring of pain and lack of understanding.

His eyes swept back and forth across the site. Circus hands stopped what they were doing. Malacroix turned. The midget kept on walking…

Tiny Ron nearly completed his mission. Ace had watched him skirting the idiot boy as he hid the circuit and talked to Malacroix, moving in under the row of caravans, slipping away with the bag. It was only when he had broken cover to reach Ace's cage that the alarm was sounded. Jed had started bellowing inhumanly, Ron had glanced behind him, and increased his speed. Jed had pointed at him, and howled.

The next thing Ace saw was De Vries, appearing from nowhere in response to a sharp command from Malacroix, picking the midget up by his collar and suspending him in the air, legs kicking and dangling. Malacroix snatched the bag from Ron's fist. Jed hovered, cringing, in front of Malacroix, his hands imploring.

Malacroix's eyes played between Tiny Ron, Jed, and Ace, watching expectantly. He looked at the closed bag. A smile spread across his face.

He dangled the bag in front of Jed's face. Jed sprang forward with a glad whimper – and Malacroix snatched the bag away from him. Jed fell forward into the dirt. Malacroix ignored him, put the bag inside his coat pocket and turned back to Tiny Ron, still dangling from De Vries's fist.

'And as the midget seems so keen to be a thief, he can be treated like one. He can share our new friend's captivity.' He produced a ring of keys from his pocket and opened Ace's cage. De Vries threw the little man in next to her. 'Watch her at all times, Ron,' Malacroix sneered, already walking away. 'She is wild. She might eat a little morsel like you for breakfast.'

A policeman was loitering outside Malacroix's caravan. 'I shall return,' the Frenchman said, and strode away.

The captive pair sat in silence until they were alone.

'Sorry, miss,' Ron said.

'That's all right,' said Ace flatly. 'You tried.'

Ron ran his hands across the cold bars. 'You know,' he said, 'for a while I really didn't think I'd ever see the inside of a cage again.'

'Malacroix said he used to keep you caged up,' said Ace.

'He's a clever one,' said Ron. 'Fair enough, he took us out of the cages. We're more comfortable now, but have you seen our caravans? Bars on the windows... Doors locked at night...'

'You could still escape...' Ace urged.

Tiny Ron shook his head. 'Malacroix knows we can't go anywhere,' he said. 'The bars are just to humiliate us. We are freaks. The circus is all we know. Where else should we go?'

The door of Malacroix's caravan opened, and the policeman emerged. He was approaching the cage. He was carrying a pair of clumpy-looking handcuffs. Manacles.

De Vries was behind him. He opened the cage with Malacroix's key, and stepped inside.

'Miss Dorothy Gale?' he said to Ace.

'Who told you my name?' she demanded.

'You left it at a servants' hiring office,' the policeman replied. 'They gave you a position.'

Ace said nothing.

'Dorothy Gale,' the policeman repeated, 'I am here to arrest you for the murder of Miss Jane Treddle, spinster.' He clamped a manacle around her wrist. She tried to pull away. He seized her other wrist and locked it into the device.

'I should come quietly if I was you, miss.'

'Where are you taking me?' Ace shouted.

'To the police station,' said the policeman. 'Then you'll be up before the magistrate and charged. Then it's off to Newgate for you, until you can be tried and executed.'

'*What?*' Ace cried.

'Oh, yes,' said the policeman. 'Judges hate cases like this. Servants killing their masters. Juries, too.' He tugged at the manacle and began dragging her towards the door of the cage.

'You'll hang for this, I promise you.'

Part Five

The little girl stood on the Rialto Bridge, letting her tears drop into the waters of the Grand Canal as they meandered past the façades of Venice and out into the Basin of San Marco. The sun was high and warm but she paid it no heed, concentrating instead on the delicate patterns in the softly shifting water.

A shadow fell across her and she looked up eagerly, but the man looming over her was no one she recognised. Her eager face dropped to a frown once more and she turned her attention back to the water.

'Is something wrong?' The man crouched beside her. 'You look sad.'

The girl nodded. 'I had a friend. His name was Salathiel. He was old and kind. He made me boats out of paper, but now he's dead.'

'Dead?'

The man sounded surprised. 'Are you sure he's not just gone away?'

'Dead. Gone. What's the difference? I'll never see him again.'

'Oh...'

The little girl turned to him. 'People are saying horrible things about him. They are saying that he must have done something terrible because he went away without saying goodbye to anyone.'

The man smiled. 'Sometimes people say horrible things because they don't understand. I'm sure your friend had a good reason for not saying goodbye. Trust your memories of him.'

'I don't know.' The girl slumped back on her haunches and rested her chin in her hands. 'I will miss him.'

The man stood. 'I must go now too, I have a long journey ahead of me. I hope you will learn to forgive your friend for leaving you.'

He placed something on the floor and began to walk off. The little girl looked down. A small origami boat lay on the floor next to her. Jumping up, she shouted after the man. 'What's your name?'

He didn't stop, but called back over his shoulder: 'I haven't decided yet.'

Chapter Twenty-Six

'He was here... He was here...' The shadow-whispers bubbled and mocked behind the pale, cowled man as he worked. All through the dark complex they gathered and mocked. The beast-power that drove him on – that all the time threatened to overwhelm his purpose with their appetites – now seemed to taunt him. Their appetites... more and more he felt them becoming his appetites. He had to bring this to a conclusion soon.

He had been here... The Doctor.

He had been so close...

Clay was clumped under his nails. He was working with barely restrained fury. Eleven clay figures, barely humanoid, crudely fashioned, stood in a row against the wall. He gouged out the last of the clay from a twelfth figure, then scooped all twelve up in the folds of his habit and glided out into the great, vaulted corridor which led windingly, terrifyingly, to the nave of the great cathedral.

When he at last emerged into the towering space, he had to cover his ears to drown out the animal mutterings. His clay figures clattered to the floor. Mastering himself, he set them in a circle where lines and angles met and intersected.

He began his summoning-song. Slowly, his wraith-coven coalesced from the shadows. He sensed them struggling against him. He sensed his animal ally, whispering and rasping in the echoing vaults, lurking everywhere in the darkness, pushing the coven forward. He savoured the pitiful moans of the wraiths as they closed about the clay figures, as they were stretched like the lengthening shadows they were, as they were sucked into the clay.

One by one, the figures vanished.

The pea-soup fog rolled along the river and across East London that afternoon. It was the worst people could remember. And with the fog came something else; something which might have been the embodiment of the net of fears that choked Whitechapel and its environs. Shambling phantoms of fear. Crude, heavy imitations of men, men with great holes for eyes, grey skin glistening like clay, almost invisible behind the fog, looming out of nowhere. Searching…

One marched in a straight line, out of an alley and into Berners Street. It crashed through the front door of a tenement block and marched past the terrified occupants, its head scanning the narrow space. It didn't stop; it marched forward, splintering another closed door, casually upsetting a large Welsh dresser, punching and stomping its way through an external wall, out into an alley and away into the smog.

One passed south towards the river and through the Billingsgate fish market, ploughing into stalls, demolishing them, not even breaking its stride, its head turning all the time from side to side. The day's catch was scattered and trampled under huge clay feet. Market-traders and porters shouted. Their shouts died, strangled in their throats, at the sight of the clay giant. One angrily punched the hulking figure, only to collapse to the ground clutching his hand in agony. The giant stomped on, heedless of the feeble assault, tramping back into the mist with fishy footprints.

One, moving along Commercial Street, made a horse rear. The hansom cab it was pulling tipped to one side and fell, throwing driver and occupant out. A pregnant woman crossing the road in the path of the monster collapsed.

One entered the yard of St Joseph's Roman Catholic elementary school and stopped, scanning the surrounding buildings. A hush fell on the yard as the children abruptly ceased their play. They formed a wide, wondering circle around the creature, silent and staring. A girl of about six stepped forward, arm extended, an apple in her hand. She offered it to the giant. It seemed to hesitate, to half notice her. It lowered its gaze to the girl, and raised a massive arm very slightly.

'You look sad,' the girl said. No one else spoke.

The silence was pierced by the hysterical clanging of a hand-bell. A female teacher was running across the yard, her long skirt billowing about her boots, the bell flying in her hand. She began to shout an incoherent *mélange* of threats and prayers. The monster's head snapped up. As the teacher drew level with it, it swung up an arm and brushed her aside as a man might a fly. She sailed through the air and hit a wall with a slight snapping sound. The children scattered, screaming. The monster moved on.

One passed the chop-house on the corner of Leman Street. Charles Hawkins, illustrator and satirist, was eating at a table just inside the window. Less than two weeks ago his illustration, 'The Nemesis of Neglect', had been printed in *Punch*, the London charivari, to not inconsiderable acclaim. A spectre, grey and wraith-like, its toothless mouth a pit of blackness, its eyes dead, stalking the streets of London's East End, CRIME written across its brow, murder on its hands. *There floats a phantom on the slum's foul air; Shaping, to eyes which have the gift of seeing, Into the spectre of that loathly lair...*

Now, looking out of the chop-house window, Charles Hawkins choked on his meal. There, outside the window, was the very creature he had drawn. The fog gave everything a diaphanous quality. Wraithed by fog, the creature seemed almost to float along the street. Its awful eyes... Ignoring him, it moved along the road, the mist like a pall of death all about it. Charles Hawkins began to shake.

Chapter Twenty-Seven

'Officer…' Malacroix appeared around the side of Ace's cage. The policeman turned, still holding his prisoner. Malacroix pressed a large coin into his hand. 'We have an understanding, you and I, *n'est-ce pas?*'

The policeman gave a short, self-conscious nod.

'Leave her with me,' Malacroix coaxed. 'For a short while, at least. Take your investigation elsewhere.'

'But it was you who told us…'

Malacroix placed a finger on the policeman's lips. 'Be a good fellow…' he said.

With a slight reluctance, the policeman unlocked Ace's hands. 'I'll be back,' he said.

Ace watched him depart.

'What's your game?' she demanded when he was gone.

Malacroix shrugged his shoulders.

'Did you shop me to them?'

Malacroix took an ornate silver box from his pocket, opened it and snorted a fat glob of snuff with each nostril.

'I have eyes everywhere,' he said, replacing the silver box. 'On my way back here this morning I happened to meet an old… friend… from Scotland Yard. He told me about an old lady, found dead in her own house. "Brutally slain" were his words. At first it was thought she had been savaged by an animal. A wild cat.'

'The Ripper…' Ace ventured.

'Not the Ripper,' said Malacroix. 'They were looking for a young servant girl who vanished from the house at the same time.'

He took a large handkerchief from his pocket and dabbed the end of his nose.

'Now, you are an intelligent girl. You must know what this means. You can perform in the ring for me – or you can perform on the end of a rope for some judge.'

'You can't prove anything!' shouted Ace, shaking.

'But there was a witness,' said Malacroix, blowing the words like kisses.

Behind Malacroix, Ace could see Jed, who appeared to have been hiding from the policeman, scampering towards them.

'How sad,' said Malacroix, 'that it should fall to me to break the bad news to him...'

Ace watched him turn and walk back towards his caravan. Jed scampered after him. At the foot of the steps Malacroix turned and placed a hand on Jed's shoulder. Ace could see him talking to the idiot, but could not catch the words. Jed's face seemed blank. His eyes jumped continually between those of the circus owner and the pocket of the coat Malacroix wore. Malacroix patted him on the head and ascended the steps of the caravan, leaving him squatting outside the brightly painted wooden door.

She slumped against the side of the cage. Tiny Ron was looking at her, a little uncertainly. Was her position really much different from his? She had no friends here, except perhaps the freaks and their keeper. She had no home except for this cage. And she was wanted for murder. Had she killed the old woman? It was all so hazy...

Her life shouldn't be like this. She shouldn't be here. Maybe she should have left the Doctor long ago. She had even lost him now... She was nothing but a caged, friendless creature in this strange century. A temporal freak. Even if she managed to escape, she had absolutely nowhere to go.

The midget crossed the cage and sat down next to her, placing a hand, a little awkwardly, on her shoulder. They sat in silence for a while, staring impotently out on the day's labours of the circus folk. Smog was rolling thickly across the little ground, blurring the bright tents and caravans. No one came near them.

It was perhaps an hour later that Peter Ackroyd rushed up to the cage.

'Malacroix's got some plan for you,' he said, breathless.

'What do you mean?' Ace demanded.

'I only caught a bit of what he was saying,' Ackroyd replied. 'He said something like "If she won't change to save her own skin, perhaps she will change to save the skin of another…"' He looked with fear in his eyes at Tiny Ron. 'I don't know what he's going to do,' he whispered, 'but it's bad.'

Ace could see figures approaching behind him through the fog. He was brushed aside by a group of roustabouts, and Ace felt the cage lurch. It was being wheeled across the ground into the main tent.

Malacroix was standing in the ring, smiling. De Vries stood just behind him, his face its usual mute, blank mask. As the cage came to a halt, the strong-man stepped forward and gripped the chain which held the cage door shut. He placed a key in the padlock, the hasp sprung open and the chain fell away. He pushed the door open and grabbed Tiny Ron by the collar, pulling him through the door and depositing him on the sawdust floor. Ace made to follow, but De Vries pushed her back.

'Not you,' said Malacroix. 'Not yet. Watch.'

De Vries picked up a long coil of rope. He attached one end to the wheel of the cage, and the other he tied deftly to Tiny Ron's ankle.

'Now!' said Malacroix.

As Ace watched, the lion's cage was wheeled into the ring. The lion-tamer opened the cage and, with a crack of his whip, drove the lion into the ring. He cracked the whip again, catching the animal across the face. The lion snarled and bounded forward. Malacroix and De Vries stepped from the ring. So did the lion-tamer. Tiny Ron looked frantically around. He ran towards the edge of the ring, but the rope around his ankle prevented him quite reaching it. The lion circled him, still snarling. He clawed at the rope, but its coils were thick and deviously knotted, and his tiny fingers could make no impression on it. He ran to the other side of the ring, but he could not reach that either.

'Ron, get under the cage!' Ace screamed. 'Malacroix… Stop it, you sick bastard!' She shook the bars in desperation.

The lion was close now, between the midget and the cage. Ron was backing slowly away, the lion moving slowly forward. The rope tautened. Ron stood, motionless, staring at the beast.

The lion sprang. Its great paws closed about Tiny Ron's face and he fell backward. The lion was on top of him. It was playing with him, batting him about like a cat with a ball of wool.

Ace's blood was rushing like thunder through her head.

'Malacroix!' Ace roared, hurling herself against the cage. 'Malacroix!'

Malacroix was staring, not at the lion and its prey, but at her, unblinking, intense.

Her pulse was racing. She was sweating. Her skin felt tight. It tingled as if attacked by millions of needles. She could smell the sawdust, the animal droppings, Tiny Ron's blood which even now was beginning to stain the ring. The colour drained from her vision. Everything was perfectly in focus, clearly defined in sharp monochrome.

De Vries was opening the cage. Ace sprang forward, past him and out into the ring. She was oblivious now to anything but the beast in front of her. She sprang on to its back, claws digging into its thick flank. The lion roared and twisted, then rolled on to its side. Ace sprang free. The lion roared again, and sprang at her. Its claws ripped at her battered dress, shredding the material. Its paws drove her down hard on to her back. She felt its massive bulk on top of her. She smelt its rank, hot, meaty breath. She stared deep into its wet, razor-toothed jaws as they closed about her neck.

Chapter Twenty-Eight

Spectacular. Incredible.

Malacroix had seen a lycanthrope once, at a fair in a Hungarian village. A man had changed into a savage beast in front of his very eyes. But it hadn't been as impressive as this. So strong, so fast... She had avoided the lion's jaws by a split-second twist of her head. She had almost got herself free.

Then Ackroyd had appeared in the tent. Malacroix had seen him arguing with Carlos, the lion-tamer. Carlos had looked shamefaced and done nothing. Ackroyd had seized his whip and marched into the ring, shouting. He had lashed the lion across the back. The beast – its teeth once more about to rip out the girl's throat – had twisted around and leapt from her, and stood, facing the young keeper.

He was brave; Malacroix would grant him that.

A word from the circus owner had sent Carlos running into the ring, a wooden pole in one hand, with a noose on the end of it. He had lassoed the lion's neck and, seizing the whip back from Ackroyd, had lashed the beast into submission and dragged it back to its cage.

Ackroyd had tried to defend his position. 'It was going to kill her,' he had spluttered at Malacroix. 'She's no good to you dead.'

He had a point. Malacroix had decided to be indulgent. He was pleased with what he had seen.

'Just remember your place here, Monsieur Ackroyd,' he had said. 'Remember who you are out there. Remember what they would do to you without my protection.'

Now he anticipated with glee the forthcoming performance. He longed for the onset of night.

Malacroix's hand strayed idly to his pocket, and closed upon a cloth bag. For the first time his thoughts returned to Jed's little treasure. He had assumed it was just one of the imbecile's odd little obsessions, and dismissed it from his mind. Now he took out the bag and loosened the top. Inside was a small cylinder. It looked, but did not feel, like glass. Was it glowing slightly?

He focused his eyes on it. He had seen the way Jed would only peep into the bag, timidly, furtively, flinching away almost at once. Malacroix peered deep into the cylinder. His eyes caught the little lights that seemed to dance about in crystalline patterns, drawing him deeper...

Darker... The shadows seemed to snap up around him. He was somewhere else. He was on a street, at night. Standing beneath a gas-lamp. The cold and damp cut into him. The shadows were moving strangely around him. They appeared to whisper sweetly to him, cajoling, teasing. They seemed to reach out and stroke and kiss him. They closed tight about him.

The shadows had faces... men's faces, some old, some young, all pale and ghostly-looking, hollow-eyed...

The shadows began to move. They began to swirl and dance around him, cold, like dead flesh. The faces flew about.

He felt a sharp pain, deep in his gut, followed by a spreading pool of warmth. He looked down. The front of his dress was stained a deep crimson. He was wearing a dress...

The pain came again, higher this time, stabbing deep into his abdomen. The shadows ripped at his clothes – dress, stays, petticoats – tearing them to shreds. He felt his flesh being ripped to ribbons. The whispered voices had changed now. Their sweetness had soured. They breathed foul air over him, making him choke.

The image of something he had seen recently in a magazine flashed through his mind. 'The Nemesis of Neglect'... In a fraction of a second the thought was gone; the pain and flying shadows filled his senses.

One face remained static. It was more solid than the others, and had a pale vibrancy about it that they must have long since lost. A short, middle-aged man with grizzled hair and soft eyes. He thought perhaps he recognised the man…

The pain grew, too much to bear… The vision faded to blackness.

Malacroix came to on the floor of his caravan. He was trembling like a leaf, ice-cold and drenched in sweat. The glassy cylinder lay on the floor next to him. His hand, where he had held it, throbbed. A livid, red weal blazed across the palm and fingers. He slipped the cloth bag over the cylinder, being careful not to touch it, got to his feet, smoothed his hair flat and opened the door of the caravan.

The fool was still squatting on the wooden steps.

'Jed,' he said, 'come in.'

He held the bag up in front of Jed, whose hand clutched for it. Malacroix whipped it out of his reach.

'Where did you get this, Jed?' he asked.

Jed lunged, unsuccessfully, again.

'Jed…'

'A man had it,' said Jed sullenly.

'What man?' Malacroix whispered.

Jed was silent.

'What man?' Malacroix repeated, growling.

Jed's lips began to tremble.

'The Ripper…' he said quietly.

Malacroix was angry. Jed hated Malacroix when he was angry. The whole story had come spilling out of him in his usual broken spiel: what he had seen on the wharf the night the blue box appeared there, the little man's reappearance at the funeral.

'*Merde!*' Malacroix snarled. 'You imbecile, why did you say nothing?'

'Couldn't, sir… The Reverend…'

'That old hypocrite!' Malacroix cried. 'You are mine, now, Jed. You no longer have to believe that priest's lies. You have disappointed me, Jed. The Ripper – there at the burial – and you say nothing. That little man… I stood next to him! I conversed with his companion, the Jew. Tchah – fool!'

Jed was stung by his master's scorn. Malacroix had never called him a fool before. Malacroix alone. However unequal they were, Jed had felt a kinship of the spirit with the ringmaster; an imp at the feet of Satan, but nevertheless, one of his acknowledged denizens.

Malacroix hefted his great ring of keys, unlocking the big safe which stood against the far wall, and shutting the bag inside it.

'Ah, it is of no matter,' he said, stroking Jed's cheek. 'The old Jew, Liebermann, lives in Bethnal Green. Finding him will be no difficult task for me. I have eyes everywhere…'

He pushed Jed roughly out of the caravan, then thundered down the steps and out across the circus-ground. 'Liebermann must be found!' he shouted to no one in particular.

His treasure… Jed crawled to the foot of the blue box and sat, a huddled bundle against its side. The faint throb from within comforted him slightly, but could not disguise the depth of his loss. When Malacroix was out of sight, he scampered back up the steps of the caravan and tugged and hammered at the locked door.

He felt a tap on the shoulder. Peter Ackroyd was standing behind him. 'I shouldn't do that,' he said. 'If Malacroix thought you were trying to get in there behind his back…'

Jed pulled a face.

'We should be friends, you know,' Ackroyd said. 'Everybody needs one or two of them.'

Jed didn't like Ackroyd. He didn't understand the way he talked to him, softly, gently. Jed was used to being shouted at, abused. Sometimes his great-aunt would caress and mollycoddle him – he had hated the smell of her loose, old, unwashed skin – and sometimes the Reverend Jefford would sigh over him and offer up some prayer, but, one way or another, he was always being played with. Malacroix would pat him like a dog, before kicking him down the steps of his caravan.

That was what he knew. That was what he understood. He didn't understand Ackroyd at all.

'He won't let you have it back, you know,' Ackroyd said. 'Not now he's seen how important it is to you. That's the way he works. Why does that bag mean so much to you, anyway?'

Jed hawked, and spat a great gob of phlegm into the keeper's face.

Ace came to in her cage. It was getting dark, and she was alone. Outside the cage was a world of grey. Fog covered everything. Indistinct figures swam about in it. The fog crept wetly into her cage. She shivered with the cold. Her dress was in shreds. Her back and shoulders ached, as if after hours and hours of hard labour. She felt as if she had been beaten up...

She remembered – vaguely – being inside the big tent. She remembered Tiny Ron, tethered in the ring. She remembered the lion. Staring into its jaws. She couldn't have...

Dimly, she saw a line of people standing outside what she knew to be Tiny Ron's caravan. The freaks she recognised by their shape, Carlos the lion-tamer, by his whip. Clowns, acrobats...

'Peter,' she called, seeing his vague figure emerge from the caravan. He came over to her at once.

'You're awake,' he said. 'Are you... all right?'

Ace nodded, impatiently. 'Ron...' she said.

'He's not too bad,' said Peter Ackroyd. 'A few nasty scratches, that's all. He was lucky.' He shook his head. 'His comrades are angry. Everybody is angry. Carlos is ashamed...'

'And you?' Ace asked. 'Are you angry?'

'I...' He could say no more.

'Peter... did you... see me in there?' Ace asked, dreading the answer.

Ackroyd's silence seemed to confirm her fears.

'What did I look like? Did I… change?'

'I'm… not sure what happened,' said Ackroyd, not meeting her eyes. 'It was all very fast. It was dark in the tent. All I know is, Malacroix was impressed.' His voice was suddenly urgent. 'He plans to put you in tonight's show. You, the lion… Tiny Ron, if that's what it takes to make you…' His voice tailed off. 'He'll be watching me,' he said. 'It will be difficult for me to help you again.'

A fuzzy memory floated into Ace's mind an image of Ackroyd, whip in hand, shouting and flailing.

'Thank you for what you did…' she said. 'That was brave.'

'He doesn't trust me any more. We used to be… close.'

'Close?' Ace could not imagine this open, honest, perhaps rather simple bloke having anything to share with the devious circus-master.

'I wasn't always like this,' the young keeper replied. 'Before I came here I was… wild. Living on the streets, robbing… That's all I can remember of my childhood. I never learned to read and write…' He shook his head sadly. 'Oh, yes, I was wild… It was only a matter of time before I killed someone. I knew about Malacroix, of course. He was like a kind of legend. I wanted to join his mob. He thought I was just a child. He didn't really want to know, but I persisted. Eventually, he said that if I wanted to join him, I'd have to prove myself to him. I'd have to sell my soul. It's what all who travel with him do, he said.'

He sniffed slightly.

'What happened?' asked Ace gently.

'This was when he was at war with the Bethnal Green Jews. I… In the middle of the riots I went to the synagogue one Saturday and… I set fire to it. The mob followed me, and barred the doors. They lifted me on to their shoulders as the place went up. It was full of people…'

His voice was quiet and empty.

'After that I had no choice but to join Malacroix – for the police were looking for me – but I'd lost all stomach for his world. He saw what was in my heart, and made me keeper of the freaks. It amused him. He thought to humiliate me. He said that I, who had forfeited his soul in so dramatic a manner, should become lord of those born without souls.'

'Poor Ron...' Ace whispered. 'It's my fault, what happened to him.'

'Aye, he told me what you asked him to do. That bag of Jed's. What's in it that's got everybody so worked up?'

'Please don't ask me that, Peter,' Ace replied. 'You'd never believe me if I told you... No, we can't let Malacroix do that to Ron again. I've got to get away from here. You've got to help me.'

'I know,' said Ackroyd. He looked behind him, into the fog. 'Give me a little time,' he said. 'I'll be back.'

A little time turned out to be several hours. The circus had already begun to reverberate to the sounds of the excited public. When Peter Ackroyd returned, he was carrying a bundle, and he was in company. Saul was with him.

'Quickly,' Peter said, pushing the bundle through the bars, 'change into these.'

A man's coarse shirt, jacket, trousers and shoes. Ace picked up the clothes from the floor of the cage. She stripped the remains of the dress from her and began to climb into them. Peter and Saul turned their backs in sudden embarrassment.

'I'm sorry I couldn't get you any girl's clothes,' Peter said.

'That's OK,' said Ace. This was a lot better.

When she was dressed, Peter wrapped his arms around Saul's chest and lifted him off the ground. The freak's arms – which also had to serve him as legs – were massive. He tested the chain which held Ace's cage shut, then began to strain against it, his muscles bulging.

'He's practically as strong as De Vries,' said Ackroyd.

His teeth were clenched and his knuckles were white. At first he seemed to have no effect on the chain. Then, quite suddenly, one of the links shattered in two and the whole thing fell apart. The door of the cage swung open.

'Wow,' said Ace. 'Thanks.'

'A pleasure,' said Saul.

She threw her arms around his tough shoulders, and kissed him on the cheek. Peter lowered him to the ground.

Ace immediately ran across to the TARDIS and tugged on the door. Locked, of course.

'You should go,' said Peter, following her. 'Malacroix could come for you at any time.'

'Peter,' said Ace, 'I need to get my hands on the telepathic circuit.'

He looked blankly at her.

'The thing Jed had. In the bag.'

Ackroyd hesitated. 'Go,' he said at last. 'I will get this thing for you. I will meet you at the church on Red Lion Street. Opposite the market. Christ Church. It was my church when I was a young lad... before all this...' For a moment he seemed to be lost in thought.

'When?' Ace asked, impatiently.

'I don't know,' Ackroyd replied. 'When I have what you want... Now go.'

Ace turned to go. Pausing, she turned back. 'Thanks for everything,' she said. 'Give my love to Tiny Ron.'

She put her hands around the back of his neck and, pulling him gently forward, kissed him slowly on the lips. Awkwardly, Peter put his arms around her and kissed her back.

'I'll see you,' said Ace, breaking their embrace. With a smile she turned again, and set off into the foggy London night.

Chapter Twenty-Nine

Malacroix sat at the head of a long table. He was upstairs in the function room of the Rising Sun tavern, in the shadow of the police headquarters at Scotland Yard. This was where Malacroix conducted much of his important London business.

Downstairs, policemen and civil servants drank and chattered. It amused him to run his affairs under the noses of the CID, in the heart of the administrative centre of the Empire.

Besides, it was handy for his contacts. One by one, they drifted up from below some shabby and disreputable, others respectable, nervous about being there. Several CID inspectors, the Superintendent of B Division, an Anglican bishop, the curator of the British Museum, all paid court that night. Malacroix smiled. He had something on them all. One by one, they entered the room, awkwardly shuffling past Malacroix's rougher, seedier more thoroughgoing criminal foot-soldiers on the stairs.

A rat-faced man called Spiker slid into the room.

'I got somethin' 'ere for you, boss,' he whispered. Spiker always whispered. He had had his throat cut in The Jago one hot summer's night. 'You'll like this.'

He took what looked like a bundle of rags from beneath his coat and spread it on the table. It was a woman's dress, shabby and stained almost black...

Malacroix ran his fingers over the stain and put them to his lips. Blood...

'This is the dress Polly Nicholls was murdered in.'

Malacroix smiled. 'You have done well, Spiker,' he said. He ran his hands lovingly over the dress.

He paid Spiker a full three sovereigns, and issued him with the instruction that all of his visitors had received: Find the Jew, Joseph Liebermann.

He sat long in the room after everybody had left, fingering the dress. Polly Nicholls... she had been the first. Some people claimed that Martha Tabram had been the first, nearly a month earlier. They were wrong. She had merely been brutally murdered, but starting with Polly Nicholls, the murders had taken on a decidedly different air. From the outset, Malacroix had felt a kinship with the Ripper. He understood him; he understood his methods and his motivation.

Now his quest to find the Ripper had acquired a new momentum. What he had seen, what he had felt, the cylinder... the memory nagged at him. The pain, the ecstatic pain... He was feeling more alive than he had for years. He felt exhilarated, and at the same time, fearful. It was fear that had caused him to lock the thing in his safe. The sense of intoxication had been so deliciously intense. He had seen the strange, pathetic addiction the thing had wrought in Jed, who had never dared do more than glance at it.

He would not return to the circus tonight. He would stay here, far from the awful temptation. The time would pass...

He pulled at an ancient bell-cord which hung down the wall. Footsteps on the stairs... The door opened and Walter, the landlady's young son, stood before him, nervous, expectant.

The Reverend Jefford rose early the following morning, as was his custom. He had been unable to sleep for practically the whole night. Ever since his encounter in the crypt the day before, he had been nervous, jumping at shadows. He had kept his lamp lit through the watches of the night.

He dressed and said his morning prayers. He was as rational and conservative a Christian as one might find anywhere. He had no time for Popery, he didn't believe in ghosts and phantoms, and he roundly deplored the sort of mystical mumbo-jumbo which was consumed with such hysteria by so many people, both high and low, this gullible century. Spiritualists, mediums... Frauds and swindlers, the lot of them.

So what had he seen in the crypt? Evil spirits haunted the pages of the Bible. Why not his church?

'Precisely because it *is* a church,' he said aloud. 'The Lord would not permit such a thing.'

Nevertheless, he resolved to return to the crypt forthwith, just to assure himself that his senses, and his senses alone, had been at fault. He descended the stairs of his vicarage in which he lived alone, and walked the short distance to Christ Church. Its great, pale tower, the strange genius of Nicholas Hawksmoor, seemed to loom over him as he ascended the steps.

This was the Lord's day, for heaven's sake. The faithful throughout the land would soon be gathering for prayer. His God was with him. He had nothing to fear.

How many of the faithful would come here when the bell began to ring, an hour hence? As many as came purely to see that poor girl being laid to rest? His regular congregation was so small now…

He knelt in front of the altar and prayed again. Then he took the gold cross from the Lord's table and went into the vestry. There he lit a lamp, and marched out to the door of the crypt.

'*Yea, though I walk through the valley of the shadow of death, I will fear no evil,*' he recited, '*for thou art with me. Thy rod and thy staff, they comfort me.*'

He turned the key in the lock. The door creaked open and he stepped into the cool, damp darkness.

'*Thou preparest a table before me in the presence of mine enemies: thou anointest my head with oil; my cup runneth over.*' His voice boomed around him.

He held the lantern high and, peering into its pale pool of light, walked slowly down the dark corridor.

The coffins started immediately the floor area widened out. They lay, scattered untidily across the floor. Around the walls were the church's few more permanent, grand tombs. His light fell on a nearby wall, and he stepped immediately forward. There was a memorial tablet on the wall. It had not been there before, he was sure. It looked new. Clutching the heavy cross to his chest, he drew closer, trying to make out the name carved on the stone.

He felt a light pressure on his back, and felt a cold breath on his neck. He spun around. There was a man standing behind him, tall and silent, dressed a little like a monk. Beneath his cowl, a pale, gaunt face looked out at him. In that instant, the Reverend Jefford knew that he had found his phantom.

'I have waited for you to return,' the figure said quietly.

'Surely goodness and mercy shall follow me all the days of my life and I will dwell in the house of the Lord for ever!' The Reverend Jefford was shouting now. His words bounced back off the stone walls, mocking him.

The man lowered his head and blew lightly. The lantern died instantly. The cleric felt a hand on each side of his head, drawing him forward. He felt a face in front of his. The cross crashed to the floor. He felt a pair of lips against his own mouth. He closed his eyes as the man breathed a breath of pure, cold darkness which filled his head.

'You sleep very little, my friend.' Joseph Liebermann wandered into the study in his dressing-gown. 'Each night I go to bed, and each morning I find you where I left you, studying my books.'

'You have many books,' said Johnny.

'I have had many collections of books over the years,' said the old man. 'Many gathered, many lost... You are welcome, of course, to peruse them, but you must sleep at some time, I think. Sleep is a great healer, and you need to heal, my friend. You need to heal in your spirit.'

'I feel a lot better,' said Johnny. The lights and the noises had been mercifully absent in Liebermann's quiet, ticking house.

'This is good,' said the old man, 'but still you must sleep. They say the old sleep but little, always on guard unless death should take them while they slumber. But I... I fear no such thing. I sleep many hours of the night, for the days are long…' He smiled, and patted Johnny on the shoulder. 'The days are less long since you have been here, my friend,' he said.

Johnny took a book from the shelf. 'The Cartographia of Sardis,' he whispered. 'This is very old.'

He turned its brittle pages. Maps, once brightly coloured, now faded, gazed at him from the past. Maps of the small, small world.

'Very rare…'

'Yes,' said the old man. 'Very rare. Some books I have never lost. But tell me, how is it you know this?'

'I don't know,' whispered Johnny. 'I just know it. All trace of this book was lost nearly two thousand years ago. It has quite vanished from the human memory. They don't know it was ever written. To see this now – here – in this century…'

'It should be in a museum, I know,' said Liebermann, 'but some things I am sentimental about. Memories…'

In fact, Johnny was strenuously avoiding sleep. His nights were haunted by confusing and frightening dreams. Strange skies… alien suns… creatures out of some penny-dreadful melodrama. Running… fighting… so much conflict, so much bloodshed. So much blood on his hands.

He was a destroyer of worlds…

The old man was flicking through the morning paper. 'Ach…' he said, shaking his head slowly, 'so it gets worse. You see here, a mob of young men attacked a cobbler in his home. They saw blood on his front door and thought he was the Ripper. They beat him up and cut his throat… His wife, too. Ach…'

'Jacksprites,' said Johnny.

'What?'

'I…' Johnny shook his head and tried to clear it. He was getting a headache.

'That word you used…' Liebermann persisted.

'It's gone,' said Johnny.

Chapter Thirty

Henry Tomkins, his wife Martha and their children sat near the back of Christ Church that Sunday, as most Sundays. The children, as usual, were restless, and Henry and Martha felt it only proper that they should sit where their offspring's mutterings should not distract the Reverend.

Most of the pews in front of them were empty. The church was deserted but for perhaps twenty people, including themselves. The singing of the hymns was pitiful, though Henry and Martha gave it their best.

The Reverend Jefford didn't seem himself today. He had hurried through the catechism in an almost singsong manner which Henry Tomkins found most off-putting. Now he stepped forward to deliver his sermon.

'*Dearly beloved*,' he said, in a tone which might be mistaken for a sneer, '... that is how the Anglican order of service addresses the faithful. *The faithful* – there's another one, do you see? The sanctified language of the church. Its poetry. Its dogma. We believe because we speak the language of belief. That's all faith is, really.'

He stepped down into the aisle, into the bosom of the congregation, smiling broadly, warming to his theme.

'Of course, we preach redemption by faith,' he continued. 'But faith in what? Beloved by whom? Why do we still believe? No one else does. Once upon a time, this church would have been full on a Sunday...'

He seemed struck by a sudden thought. 'Indeed,' he continued, 'many of you – most of you – you happy few, were part of a much larger congregation only yesterday. When we buried that poor girl in the ground, *then* we had a congregation. They had come to worship a God whose works they could see, touch, be a part of. The God who inspires them every day of their lives, as he inspires us all!'

He was shouting now, bellowing his words ecstatically to the heavens. Henry and Martha exchanged anxious glances.

'My friends…' He held out his hands, imploring them. 'We are gathered here today in the name of a dead religion, to worship a long-dead God. I have seen the true face of God, and his name is Appetite!'

That was it. The man was raving. Henry ushered his family to their feet and towards the door. Others were following. The Reverend Jefford appeared not to notice.

'Worship him as your true God,' he ranted, 'for there is no other. And today, my friends, I have a divine revelation for you. Soon his church will be overflowing. For he has sent his only begotten son to dwell among men… That son's name is Jack!'

The Reverend Jefford's laughter echoed after Henry Tomkins as he hurriedly left the church.

Across the road, Ace was watching the departing congregation. Church must be over. Good. She saw Henry Tomkins and his wife emerging from the church, and almost called out to them. She checked herself; the police were after her, and Henry had already talked to them once.

She waited until everybody seemed to have left, then crossed the road and climbed the steps.

She had been hanging about the church since last night. She had longed to go into the Ten Bells pub which stood in the lee of the church. There was singing inside, and a warm glow had come from the windows. Then she had reminded herself she was a fugitive from the law, and instead had begun to ascend the front steps of the church, although the idea of spending the night there made her quite uneasy. There was something vaguely threatening about standing at the foot of that great, heavy spire. A hand on her shoulder had stopped her. She had swung around, preparing to lash out. An old tramp was looking up at her from the pavement.

'You don't want to spend the night in there, laddie. None of us spends the night in there…'

Then he had turned away and shuffled off as if she had never existed.

She had spent the night in a shop doorway.

Now she wanted to get inside. It was freezing, for a start. The clothes Peter had provided were warmer than her dress, but the morning was bitter and damp. Also, she had an idea that maybe in this century she could claim sanctuary in a church – or something – and the police couldn't touch her.

And there was something else. Recently she had felt as if her identity – her humanity – were under siege. She had killed a woman… hadn't she? It was so difficult to remember. She was so tired. Her mind was in turmoil. Churches were peaceful places, and right now she needed some peace of mind.

She climbed the steps and pushed open the door. It was quiet inside. It struck her that the church would look exactly the same a hundred years from now. Its unchanging archaicness was reassuring.

A priest was bowed over the altar. He straightened as he became aware of her presence, and began to walk towards her.

'Welcome, my child,' he said softly.

Nature is a temple where living columns now and then release confused words; There Man passes among forests of symbols which watch him with familiar glances…' The old man closed the book. 'Baudelaire,' he said. 'I should very much like to meet him.'

'Forests of symbols,' said Johnny. 'He's right. Everywhere…'

He was becoming more agitated by the day. That morning he had seen a gang of men dragging some huge iron drums along the street, clanging and scraping them along the cobbled streets. The men's voices had somehow become merged with the reverberant grating of the vessels to form a vicious, insistent metallic drone. Liebermann had assured him that they were only dragging some

211

rubbish to the dust-destructor in Wentworth Street, but nevertheless he had insisted on following them, creeping through the fog until they had come upon the great mechanical monster which rumbled and groaned and belched out infernal ash.

Johnny had fallen to his knees in the dust. '*Kroagnon*...' he had whispered.

He didn't know what the word meant, and had allowed Liebermann to lead him back to the house.

Now he began muttering to himself. 'I need a sign... I need a sign...'

He was crouched in front of one of Liebermann's clocks. Its face cover was open. The minute hand raced around beneath the pressure of his index finger. The hour hand followed at its stately pace. Pushing time back... back...

'Too much confusion. Confusion everywhere. Too many symbols... no signs. I need a sign.'

'A sign,' Liebermann sighed. 'I think perhaps we all are looking for a sign. The good Lord knows, the poor people of London have been looking for centuries. And I... how long have I been waiting for a sign?'

Gently, he guided Johnny away from the clock and closed its glass cover.

'You must be patient, my dear friend,' he chided.

'I need a sign...' Johnny repeated.

'You will have your sign,' said Liebermann. 'And I mine, perhaps... But perhaps not yet. When you have lived as long as I, you learn the art of patience. The art of hoping against hope...'

Chapter Thirty-One

Sir Lionel Phipps, celebrated archaeologist and curator of the British Museum, picked his way across the fairground site with distaste. It was growing dark, and the vile place crawled with life.

He was about to betray a man.

That Malacroix would kill Joseph Liebermann, Sir Lionel Phipps had no doubt. He suspected Malacroix would kill any Jew who crossed his path.

He turned his nose up at the smell of sweat and animal ordure all around him. He wished more than anything else to be far away from here, to be back in the country, in the big house with his wife and the boys. He wanted to quit the British Museum. He had wanted to for years, even before he had met Malacroix. But the ringmaster would not let him give it all up. Malacroix knew enough about Sir Lionel Phipps to ruin his reputation. Many years before, when travelling in the Orient, Sir Lionel Phipps had developed an addiction to opium which, as his life had progressed, had all but consumed him. He took it now to feel human. All the time the drug was not glistening in his veins, he felt virtually nothing beyond its constant calling. He had painstakingly hidden his secret for decades.

But Malacroix knew. Worse, Malacroix supplied him with the drug. He didn't know what he feared most: the fact that Malacroix could publicly ruin him or the fact that he could cut off his supply.

He was going to betray a man, and he didn't care.

He mounted the steps of the Frenchman's caravan, and knocked. The door was slightly open, and swung inwards.

Sir Lionel Phipps stepped into the caravan, and immediately stepped out again, lowering his eyes in shock.

Malacroix was sprawled on the floor, writhing about on his belly. He was wearing a woman's dress, by God...

The Frenchman became aware of his presence, and twisted on

to his back.

'What is it?' he snarled.

The front of his dress was covered in some filthy… Surely it was blood…

'I… I have some news for you, Malacroix. About the Jew, Liebermann. He often uses the museum reading room. I checked his records…'

He pulled a library record card from his pocket and handed it to Malacroix, who swung on to his feet and snatched the card from him, staring dementedly at it.

'I know this place,' Malacroix whispered.

He fell to his knees and snatched something from the floor. A solid glass tube.

'Do you see?' he bellowed into the tube. 'Do you see? We have him now!'

Sir Lionel Phipps turned and stumbled down the steps of the caravan. Was that how he looked, he thought, when his craving took him? What, he wondered, might Malacroix's addiction be?

The shadows caressed him once again. They slipped from the cylinder and closed about him, and once more he was far away.

He was in a church. A lone figure sat at prayer in one of the pews. Malacroix walked slowly down the aisle towards the figure, who rose at his approach. He towered over the Frenchman, pale and gaunt beneath a monk's cowl. Malacroix stood before him, feeling like a little boy. The man leaned forward and kissed Malacroix on the forehead.

'Don't worry,' he whispered. 'You will have your Ripper to play with. But first, he is mine.'

Peter Ackroyd had seen and heard everything which had passed in Malacroix's caravan. The Frenchman had been missing last night but Ackroyd had seen him returning late the following morning. He had pulled the tarpaulin back over Ace's now-empty cage in the faint hope of concealing her escape for as long as possible. As it turned out, Malacroix hadn't even paused at the cage, but hurried into his caravan.

A shout from within some time later had alerted Ackroyd to the Frenchman's condition. Peering through the door, he had seen him, stretched and writhing on the floor in that ridiculous dress. Ackroyd had withdrawn, unseen, but his curiosity had got the better of him. He had climbed up the panelled sides of the tall blue box which stood next to the caravan, and thence on to the caravan's roof. Leaning over the side, he had watched the entire spectacle through the window.

He saw the elderly man in a suit come and go, giving Malacroix a card. He saw Malacroix slide into unconsciousness on the floor of the caravan.

He slid from the roof and cautiously opened the door. He picked up the card. Joseph Liebermann... the name sounded familiar. Jewish... He had heard what had passed between Malacroix and his visitor, and between Malacroix and the glass cylinder...

The glass cylinder. It lay on the floor, close to the motionless Malacroix. Suddenly it occurred to him – this must be what Ace was so keen on possessing. Jed's treasure. Stepping over Malacroix, he picked it up and looked deep into its shimmering surface...

He was outside a church. Christ Church, Spitalfields. His old church. He stood in front of the closed door. Slowly, a man's face was appearing in the dark wood: cowled and pale, high-boned and drawn.

He stepped back. The great spire loomed and leered over him, and he felt dizzy. He remembered how the great spire had frightened him as a child; how it had always looked as if it was about to fall on him.

And now it did fall; colossal white stone, crushing him... Only it was no longer the church any more. It was a wall, as tall as a church and stretching to the limit of his vision, both left and right.

It seemed to go on for ever. It was topped with inward-facing metal spikes. A sort of stone hut was built into the wall, and next to it a heavy iron door, tall enough and wide enough to take a tram. Guards stood at either side of the door. More guards came and went from the hut. Their uniforms were strange, a drab green colour. Their accents, when they spoke to one another, sounded American.

There was a growing clamour at his back, and he turned. All London was laid out below him: vast, dense, seething with life. He thought suddenly of a banquet, of the table of some feudal lord, chaotic, overladen with piled-high food and mould and decay. It was a strange city he gazed down upon from his vantage-point. Some streets looked almost familiar, but everywhere strange metal-and-concrete shapes irrupted from the ground like spores, like a fungus, spreading over the city, through its streets, closing off its open spaces. They might almost be buildings – but so tall, so... blank, so inhuman.

And the people, strangely dressed people...

Suddenly he realised that the people were swarming in a great mass towards him. Everybody. Towards the iron gate. Soldiers were arming themselves. The immense crowd flowed forward. The soldiers opened fire.

He was lost in the mêlée... screams and falling bodies... the crowd sucked him into itself like quicksand. Bodies flowed around him.

He was in a tunnel now. No... not quite a tunnel. Concrete planes and pillars criss-crossed overhead. They roared and shook as metal machines shot across them like shuttles on some vast loom. There were people inside the machines...

A sudden noise filled his ears: a metallic howling, driven by the beat of drums, someone wailing in anguish over the top of it. It seemed to bounce around the concrete canyon. He spun about. Three men – boys – stood before him. The noise seemed to fill the air around them. They looked bizarre, like the inhabitants of some lost continent. Their clothing was ragged and gaudy. Their hair stood on end, and was luridly coloured – white-blond, orange – they smiled hideously at him.

One had teeth filed to needle-points.

They closed around him. One stroked his cheek. He felt a cool, sharp pain, followed by a warm jet of blood spurting from his face. Every finger on the youth's hands ended in a thin, dirty metal razor-blade. The others spread their hands in front of him; all had the same array of blades strapped to their fingers. They opened and closed like exotic plants.

Their hands flashed. He felt harsh lines of pain striping his face and body. He twisted and began hauling himself up one of the concrete pillars, over a metal barrier and on to the concrete strip above. He didn't have time to get his bearings. There was a trumpeting sound; he was directly in the path of one of the coloured metal machine-boxes. He could see the man inside it, staring at him, his face white, his lips moving. Then he felt a hammering pain as the machine hit him, lifting him high in the air, tossing him back over the side of the parapet.

He hit concrete, hard. Not daring to look behind him, he began to crawl. He was part of the crowd again, moving like a human sea towards that great, white wall, and the soldiers' guns.

Painfully, he turned and looked behind him. The city was bleeding. The streets were awash with red. People – strangely dressed people – swam in it, screaming, choking on the blood which rose like a sea around them. Fires burned in the soulless buildings which rose out of the blood, casting bright, flickering shadows on the crimson flood and its dying human flotsam. A pall of smoke gathered above the suffering city.

And something moved behind the smoke. Something dark and insubstantial, huge, man-shaped. It towered over the city. The soldiers could see it. They raised their guns and began firing. The thing seemed not to feel their bullets. It reached out with spectral hands and began plucking people from the sea of blood, raising them high and dropping them into its black pit of a mouth.

There was something in its eyes he recognised. Something of the hunger that Jed carried always in his furtive gaze; something he had seen in the eyes of Malacroix, this very day.

The city was sinking.

The flood rose. The creature sank languidly into it. Fires were extinguished, and buildings – tall buildings – gradually disappeared beneath the gentle lapping of the thick, dark-red ooze, which even now was clotting; solidifying into a hard, brownish crust. A new earth.

All was still, and silent. No movement, no wind, no birdsong. He was alone now, alone on the crusted, scabbed-over grave of a dead city. A plague-pit.

And then, slowly, things began to grow. Strange, delicate flowers of marble and metal began to crack the red earth, pushing their way towards the now-clear sky. As he watched, the city rebuilt itself: a new city, clean, ordered, well proportioned. A living sculpture of light and air, smooth stone and twinkling glass. People moved with simple, easy assurance around its new-born streets. The pain had left his body now, and he walked down to join them. They were moving towards one great building which dominated the new metropolis, white-stoned, soaring heavenwards. A temple of light.

As he approached the building he recognised it: his old church, the church of his childhood, Christ Church, Spitalfields. Except it was far, far larger, lighter, no longer looming, like the monster he had seen, over the shambling, narrow streets, threatening to devour them. The narrow streets were gone; the church spire seemed to touch the hem of God's mantle. The doors were open and people were streaming inside. He let himself be carried with the flow, through the giant doors.

Another city – another church. Not so large, in streets not so wide. Again he walked with the crowd, slightly smaller now, through the door.

And another… Once again he stood outside his childhood place of worship; once again he walked through the door.

The light was beginning to fail now. Church sat inside church, each smaller and more solid than the last; the streets that bit narrower, more twisting, the crowds thinning and less certain. Door followed door. He was becoming uneasy as the millennial vision became less.

A cold wind blew. He stood alone at the door of Christ Church, Spitalfields. It was growing dark. The market, closed and deserted, stood at his back. This was the church as he knew it – as he remembered it – solemn and awful and heavy with menace. He walked up to the door. A nameless feeling of dread filled him, and he could not enter.

The vision made Ackroyd reel. He clutched the side wall of Malacroix's caravan for support. The Frenchman was still insensible on the floor at his feet. Thoughts spiralled through Ackroyd's mind at fever-pace. A mad plan lodged there. Quickly searching the caravan, he found Malacroix's big bunch of keys. He left the caravan, locking it behind him.

The freaks were wearily making their way from their caravans into the tent where they posed nightly for the aghast public. De Vries stood and watched them as they filed in.

De Vries... How to distract the strong-man?

He had an idea. He crossed over to Ace's cage and picked up the broken chain. Undoing the padlock with the bunch of keys, he cast off the loose links and tested it. There should still be enough. He partially pulled back the canvas on the cage, then let out a shout. 'De Vries!'

The mute strong-man marched towards him, scowling.

'She's gone!' Ackroyd yelled.

The door was open. De Vries peered into the gloom, then stepped inside. Instantly Ackroyd slammed the door and padlocked the chain in position.

'I've no hard feelings against you,' he said to the strong-man. 'In fact, I wish you luck. I'd love to take you with me, but...' He shot a glance at Malacroix's caravan, shrugged his shoulders and ran towards the freaks' tent.

The first of the public were drifting inside. Ackroyd gripped a man by the collar and punted him out through the canvas flap. The freaks murmured in consternation.

'Get down,' he cried to them. 'We're leaving.'

'Leaving?' Tiny Ron, still bandaged from his encounter with the lion, stepped down, puzzled. 'What do you mean?'

'I... don't know...' There wasn't time to explain. Ackroyd didn't think he *could* explain. His sense of excitement, of mission, was overwhelming. He had seen some kind of promised land, and he intended to lead his people to it, wherever it might be. He reached a hand inside his pocket. The glass cylinder felt warm to his touch.

A frantic hammering at Liebermann's front door made Johnny spring to his feet. The old man rose more slowly and placed a reassuring hand on his shoulder.

'Do not be afraid,' he said. 'Why live in fear of bad news? If it is coming, it will come.'

Johnny followed him into the narrow hall. He opened the front door, and a man tumbled through it. An orthodox Jew of perhaps thirty.

'Liebermann, it's bad!' he said between urgent breaths. 'Whitechapel's on fire. Word's got about that a Jew's harbouring the Ripper. They're burning houses.'

'Jacob, my dear chap,' said Liebermann. 'Come in, sit down. Take your time.'

'There's no time,' the man panted. 'I came to warn you. Malacroix's looking for you, Joseph. That's how this all started. He put the word about –'

'And so all the Jews must suffer,' sighed Liebermann. 'It has ever been so...'

'You've got to get out!' the man cried. 'Even if Malacroix doesn't find you, the mob will get here sooner or later.' He moved back to the door. 'I must go. They were drawing close to my home...'

Chapter Thirty-Two

Liebermann was drunk. He opened his third bottle of vintage claret and poured a large measure into a glass.

'Still you will not take a glass with me, my friend,' he slurred.

Johnny shook his head. In the pub he had drunk beer, because it had been offered to him and because it seemed the right thing to do there – it helped him to blend in – but in truth he had been able to discern little effect from drinking it.

'Ah, well,' said Liebermann. *'L'chaim!'* He seemed suddenly subdued. *'L'chaim…'*

He downed the glass in a single draught. 'To life…' he said. 'What a terrible toast. That is no toast – it is a curse!'

He seemed to slump in his chair. 'I once shared a bottle of Tokay with Vlad Tepes. The man was a master of death… but even he could not help me. Even he…' The old man drained his glass again. 'My friend,' he said, 'you know how old I am? I am nearly nineteen hundred years old!'

He began to laugh, a deep, rumbling chuckle.

'Nineteen hundred years old!' he cried. Tears of laughter trickled down into his whiskers. 'Nineteen hundred years old!'

'You are older than me,' Johnny said blandly. The old man roared at this.

His laughter was cut off abruptly; drowned in a crashing and rending of masonry. The wall next to which Johnny was sitting crashed in, showering him in bricks and dust. Through the wall marched a giant: a crude, man-like thing, rough-hewn of damp grey clay. It fixed its empty eyes on Johnny.

Those eyes… He had seen those eyes before, somewhere, and the sight of them filled him with dread. His mind was beginning to fog… Ghost-hands stroked his face damply; ghost voices whispered to him. *'Join usss… Join usssss…'*

A table was toppled, then trampled to splinters. More of the giants poured into the room through the collapsed wall.

Liebermann was on his feet, scrabbling at the bookshelves. '*Mein Gott…*' he kept saying. '*Mein Gott!* Golem…'

Golem…

They were ignoring the old man. They were interested only in Johnny, it was clear. They stalked him around the cramped room, bumping into each other, knocking over furniture. Johnny crawled behind a sofa. A creature overturned it and smashed it to pieces.

The old man was pulling books from the shelves, rapidly scanning ancient pages then throwing them to the floor, all the time muttering in Yiddish. At last, finding the tome he wanted, he began to recite in hoarse, slightly fevered Hebrew.

The monsters stopped. They scanned the room, confused. One of them stiffened and fell over.

'Run!' shouted Liebermann. 'I don't know how long I can hold them with this.'

Johnny ran. He had to escape those eyes. He darted around the monsters, now as still as statues, and jumped through the closed window. Glass flew everywhere, and he hit the pavement hard. He was on his feet in seconds, and running down the street.

What was it in those creatures' eyes? Why did it scare him so?

The high, cold walls echoed with pain. The strain was suddenly too much. Twelve lifeless clay beings stalking the streets of the city, animated by his will. It took a tremendous effort. And then the old man had done something. Some mystical nonsense. His coven had recognised it, though, and it had stopped them in their tracks. They had fled their clay bodies. Even now he could sense them returning to their cloisters.

The psychic recoil had knocked him to the floor.

The old man… He was undoubtedly human but… he had been completely unable to penetrate his mind.

He had made contact with too many minds recently.

The idiot's mind had been useless to him; a thin, jumbled patchwork of half-formed thoughts and ill-defined fears and resentments, a barely coloured canvas. A mind to be devoured, perhaps...

Malacroix's mind was something altogether different; as black and full and hungry as his own, and something he could use. But still the effort exhausted him.

And the other he had seen – the boy Ackroyd – there was something in his mind he didn't like. A stubbornness... a simpleness that was almost elemental. He couldn't control it, and that frightened him.

He was hungry. He must feed. More and more he felt the hunger of the shadows eating into him, becoming *his* hunger.

Johnny ran until he could run no more, blindly, anywhere to get away from the clay monsters... When he could run no more he walked. Finally he stopped, breathless, and looked around him.

So far... He must have covered nearly two miles. He was in the City. He passed the Bank of England, and turned down King William Street. There, at the bottom, stood the Monument. A single pillar, two hundred feet high, surmounted by a flaming urn of gilt bronze. Erected to commemorate the Great Fire of London. Four dragons sat at its base. He moved closer, peering through the foggy dark at the inscription on the panel at the tower's base. *In the year of Christ 1666, on 2 September, at a distance eastward of this place of 202 ft, which is the height of this column, a fire broke out in the dead of night which, the wind blowing, devoured even distant buildings, and rushed devastating through every quarter with astonishing swiftness and noise...*

He entered the base of the column and began ascending the spiral staircase.

Emerging on to the balcony which ran around the top of the column beneath the urn, he gripped the bars of the cage which enclosed it. They had had to put the cage in; so many people had committed suicide by jumping from the tower.

Dead. What did that mean?

We preserve the minds of our dead…

He was a man with no identity, with no past, with no sense of who he was. What would death mean to such a man?

He looked out across the city of dreadful night. Below him, the smog banked and snaked over spires and houses, up the dark ribbon of the river.

The city – ravaged by plague, purified by fire… ravaged by war, destroyed by Daleks…

Where were they coming from, these thoughts which kept flickering through his brain? They were coming more frequently now. They made no sense.

He gripped the bars tighter and thrust his head between them.

'WHO AM I…?' he howled across the city.

Chapter Thirty-Three

'Which way now, Peter?' asked Tiny Ron.

Ackroyd's friends clustered around him; a ragged collection of fifteen or so, all of whom would follow him from the circus. The freaks, of course, and some of the others.

He had hurried them from the site. He could hear De Vries wrestling with the chain which held him prisoner. It wouldn't hold him for long.

They had left Stepney Green, and were heading west. Ahead of them lay Whitechapel.

It should have been dark down there, barring the odd street-light, but the streets were peppered with dull orange pools of light. Fires.

They were chillingly familiar to Peter Ackroyd. The mob was on the streets.

Ace was down there somewhere. He had sent her in there to wait for him.

He didn't know what to do. Ace was resourceful, he knew; she would undoubtedly move to avoid any trouble. He would never find her.

He fished the library card from his pocket. Joseph Liebermann... Malacroix was looking for him, and that meant the man was in trouble. He should go to the address on the card, and warn him. Ace would have to wait.

He didn't know what to do. He opened the hessian bag and gazed down at the cylinder.

The lights danced in the glass. Slowly a man's face swam into view. Not the cadaverous vision he had had before. This face was warm with life. Grey hair and laughter-lines, a gentle humour about the eyes. Beckoning eyes...

Perhaps this was Joseph Liebermann. In any event, he sensed he had to find this man.

'We turn north,' Ackroyd said, 'to Bethnal Green.'

Joseph Liebermann wiped the last of the brick dust from his shirt and crossed to the broken window. He stared out across the dark city and sighed. He had long since given up dwelling on that which could not be remedied. He turned to the inert clay giants.

'You recognised the Prayer for the Dead,' he said, tapping one of the giants on the shoulder. 'Remarkable… Perhaps I shall animate you. I wonder if I could… Yes, perhaps I shall. I am sure I can find a use for twelve golem.'

He was aware of a knocking at his front door. Malacroix. He had forgotten. He sat himself in his favourite armchair.

'Why not just come through the hole in the wall?' he called. 'Save an old man's legs.'

'Are you Joseph Liebermann?' Peter Ackroyd asked, peering around the ragged gash in the wall.

'I have had many names,' the man replied, 'but I answer to Joseph Liebermann, yes. May I ask who is inquiring?'

'Oh, ah… the name's Ackroyd, sir. Peter Ackroyd.'

'Well, Peter Ackroyd, what can I do for you?'

The freaks pushed at his back and clustered round him. The old man nodded to them gravely.

'I came to warn you…' Ackroyd said. He looked around the wrecked room. '… but I came too late.'

The old man chuckled. 'Do you like my friends?' he asked, putting his arm around one of the huge, ugly grey statues cluttering the room.

Ackroyd collected himself. 'I also came to give you this,' he said. He fumbled with the cloth bag, then looked uncertainly inside it.

'Are you sure?' the old man asked, half amused. 'You don't seem too sure…'

'Yes,' said Ackroyd. 'I was supposed to give this to someone else, but I don't suppose I'll find her now.'

226

He took the cylinder from the bag and held it out to the man. The man drew in a breath, and gazed deeply into it. His hands reached out, his fingers played and writhed in the light coming from inside it, but he did not actually touch it. A smile played gently across his lips.

Suddenly he seemed to snap from his trance. 'But no,' he said, 'there is no time. This, I feel, is destined for another. A man. You must find him, somehow, and give this thing to him.'

'I believe I know the man you mean,' said Ackroyd. 'I had hoped to find him here.'

'He is gone, alas,' said the old man.

'Where?' Ackroyd asked.

'I fear he has returned to Whitechapel,' the old man said solemnly. 'The place has a… fatal attraction… for him.'

Liebermann watched Ackroyd and his divinely touched brotherhood depart.

'I believe that… remarkable item… will help you to find him,' he called after them.

Remarkable item… Liebermann sank comfortably back into his chair and closed his eyes. Peter Ackroyd had been a prophet. Not now, but perhaps soon – another hundred years…maybe more… but at least there was an end in sight. In the little glass column Joseph Liebermann had seen, for the first time in nineteen hundred years, a glimpse – just a glimpse – of his salvation.

As he entered Whitechapel, Johnny could see something was wrong. The district was aglow with dim fires. He could smell smoke, and hear the soft crackle of flames. They seemed to whisper to him.

The light was wrong… Behind the flames' angry orange was another light. Thick and greasy, it seeped from the hearts of the conflagrations, it oozed over the sills of burning buildings and spilled down the pavements like lava.

In a brief moment of utter panic, Johnny realised what was happening to him. Somehow, in Liebermann's house, he had been protected from all this. Out here on the street...

And then the thought was lost. A dreadfully familiar, alien buzzing and chittering filled his brain, driving out all coherent thoughts but one. He picked up a long, sharp spike of charred, splintered wood from the pavement. He barely noticed its heat. He followed the trails of pallid light across a road and into a small square. There: one of the creatures he knew he had to kill, a monstrous queen-creature, standing under a street-lamp, covered in tiny, buzzing parasites. As he watched, light seemed to spill from her, pooling in the gutter at her feet.

He rushed forward – and stopped. From the opposite side of the square, a crowd of people had closed on the thing in the lamplight. One of them had something in his hand which blazed with light. Real light, pure and clean and dazzling. He wielded the light like a sword, slashing at the air. Shadows, dark and almost solid, flew around him. To his left and to his right his companions – strange, malformed creatures – beat at the darkness with fists and sticks.

Gradually the shadows were dispersing. The thing beneath the lamp had collapsed to the pavement. Johnny felt himself turn cold. It was a woman. An ordinary woman...

He dropped the wooden spike he was holding and stood, trembling.

It was a moment before Ackroyd noticed the man watching them from across the square, and another before he recognised him. He was bruised... burned... from the touch of the shadows. Dry and cold, he had felt his vitality slipping away at their stinging caress. Beside him he could see Tiny Ron, nursing his already wounded ribs. Others also looked in pain.

He crossed the square and held out the glowing cylinder to the curious little man who now stood before him. As the man's hand reached out for it, it began to glow brighter and brighter. As his fingers closed around it there was a flash, a sudden overpowering brilliance, and Ackroyd was hurled backwards.

He looked up, his eyes streaming. Through the glare he could see the little man, his eyes wide, his body shaking as if in fever. Balls of glowing light spun and danced through the night air. Rain hissed on the floor, sending up clouds of steam. All around, the circus performers cowered, terrified at the spectacle before them. The girl – so nearly another victim of the Ripper – ran shrieking into the rain. As Ackroyd strained to see through the whirlwind of dancing lights, he could see the man's face, but the features were blurred, indistinct. It looked like the face of an old, white-haired man. Ackroyd shook his head, trying to clear his eyes. No. The face was a youthful one, with flowing blond locks. Different faces seemed to flow over the man's skull. Ackroyd clutched at the silver cross that hung around his neck.

'Dear God in Heaven, what have I done!'

As Johnny's hand closed on the cylinder he felt a rush of energy flowing into him, sweeping through his body, brushing away all the barriers that his mind had thrown up. He saw everything that had transpired since the TARDIS had landed on the wharf. Saw through the eyes of Jed, of Ackroyd, of Malacroix. Saw Ace, her face streaked with tears, the blaze of her explosion reflected in her eyes. Saw himself, wielding a glass dagger, crazed and bloodied and then confused and frightened, sheltering from the mob, taking refuge with Liebermann. Saw himself mending timepieces, losing himself in a world of cogs and gears.

He could hear the ticking of a million clocks.

The clock faces began to swirl before him, he was suspended in time, the tangled threads of his own life dancing around him, engulfing him. Images from a million worlds, from across the time stream, waltzed through his brain.

He could see himself, young, idealistic, pitching himself against the archaic traditions of his people.

He could feel his father's arm across his shoulders as they stared up at a blazing Gallifreyan dawn.

A huge Gothic space station – a cathedral hung against the night – loomed up before him. He was at his trial. Accusing fingers pointing at him. He could hear the voice of the prosecution. Mocking him. Taunting him.

Where had he heard that voice?

The hands on the clockfaces began to spin. Centuries vanished like seconds. Past and future merged.

He could hear gunshots.

Feel bullets tearing through his body.

He could see an unfamiliar face. A young man in a dark frock coat. Tumbling dark hair. Bright, inquisitive eyes.

'Who am I?'

Images came faster. He could taste, smell, hear.

'Have you ever wondered what it's like to be wanderers in the fourth dimension? To be exiles?'

Days like crazy paving.

A walk in eternity.

The frantic life was played out in full before him. His Life. Returned to him by the telepathic circuit. By the TARDIS.

The silence was heartstoppingly sudden.

The circuit was glowing softly. He pulled out his paisley handkerchief and carefully wrapped the glass cylinder, slipping it into his jacket pocket.

He stared down at the open-mouthed man crouched in the rain before him.

'Good evening, Mr Ackroyd. I'm the Doctor. I believe you've already met my young friend, Ace.'

Chapter Thirty-Four

The Doctor stared up at the church. Rain plastered his hair to his head, and his big black coat flapped around him like a demented bat.

He had swept through the streets like a tide, brushing people out of his way, paying no heed to the freezing rain. Things had gone too far, too many people had died. It was time to finish this. Time to confront his faceless enemy.

The first rumble of thunder rolled around the rooftops and the Doctor tilted his head back. The church tower rose high into the bitter November night, cold and grey, daring the elements to assault it. Rainwater poured from the mouths of gargoyles around the roof, streams of freezing water tumbling to the churchyard. The building seemed to spit at him.

The Doctor pushed at the heavy iron gates and marched through the tangle of gravestones, leaves swirling around him. He stepped up to the great double doors of the church. He made to push at them, but the dark oak swung silently inwards, propelled by unseen hands. The Doctor smiled grimly.

'Oh, very droll. Very theatrical.'

He slipped into the velvet dark of the vestibule.

The church was empty. Row after row of silent pews faced the altar, the great cross hanging before them. Hymn books lay scattered, their pages fluttering as the wind raced through them, swirling leaves high into the church roof. Pools of dim coloured light, cast from the stained glass, were strewn across the floor, rippling as the rain streamed down the windows.

The great doors slammed behind him, cutting out the wind. The leaves slowly spiralled to the floor.

There was the steady drip of water.

'The roof repair fund must be doing badly.'

The Doctor padded up the aisle, his eyes never still, scouring the dark. He reached the altar. Nothing. No sign of life.

He cocked his head on one side. There *was* something. Just on the edge of his hearing. A whisper, a telepathic tickle.

There was a door set into a heavy side wall.

'Ah yes. Of course. The crypt.'

The Doctor pushed it open. Stone stairs wound downwards into the dark. He hesitated.

There was a sudden peal of mocking laughter.

'The great Doctor, scared of the dark? How disappointing.'

The Doctor wagged his finger at his unseen tormentor. 'Stairs can be very treacherous, you know. You wouldn't want me to fall and break my neck, now, would you?'

There was a chuckle from the dark.

The Doctor frowned. 'All right, perhaps you would.'

'Come, Doctor. Your young friend is waiting for you.'

The Doctor's face darkened. 'If you've harmed her…'

'We're waiting for you…'

'I mean it!'

'I'm waiting for you…'

The voice faded, its echoes scurrying to the corners of the church. The Doctor scrabbled in his pocket, pulling out his handkerchief and unwrapping the telepathic circuit. It was hot now, almost too hot to hold. Brilliant. Pulsing. It bathed him in a pool of harsh white light, sending dancing shadows skittering across the walls. He snatched an ornate gold candlestick from the altar, slipped the cylinder into it and crossed to the stairs.

The telepathic circuit blazed in the darkness.

The Doctor took a deep breath.

'Here comes a candle to light you to bed,

'Here comes a chopper to chop off your head.'

With the echo of the children's rhyme hanging eerily behind him, he vanished into the gloom.

The man watched the image in the skull as the Doctor

disappeared deep into the bowels of the church. He closed his eyes in satisfaction. 'At last.'

The image in the crystal changed and the man leaned close, picking the skull up and staring into it. A crowd was beginning to form outside the church, a motley collection of misshapen human forms cringing from the rain. One figure was urging them on.

The man passed his hand over the skull and the figures in the glass loomed closer. The man hissed angrily. 'Ackroyd!'

He slammed the skull back on to the table. 'Malacroix. Malacroix, you spineless worm!' The circus owner's face swam into view. 'My enemies are at the door. That interferer, the freak-keeper is here. Deal with him!'

The pictures in the skull faded to black. The man picked it up, holding it before him. His reflection stared back at him from the polished crystal.

'I have the Doctor to attend to.'

The stairs went deep into the bowels of the Victorian church. The Doctor's impromptu candle barely made an impression on the darkness ahead of him. His shadow, huge and misshapen, lurked on the wall behind him. His progress had been slow. With every step, things had slithered away from him, never seen, never entering the light, always giving suggestions of themselves but never revealing their true horror. Things from his childhood. Things from nightmares. The Doctor had ignored them, concentrating on keeping his footing on the treacherous stone spiral.

Slowly, the darkness began to give way. The Doctor could see a yellow glow begin to lighten the air before him.

The stairs emerged into the crypt. Dark and low, it stretched out before him, its far corners lit by great braziers. The vaulted ceiling dripped with moisture, things gibbered at him from behind the great stone mausoleums that stood, rank after rank, in the flickering light.

The Doctor crept softly between them, brushing dust away from long-forgotten names etched into the marble, resting his palm on each cold tomb before moving on to the next. A solemn procession of death.

At the far end of the crypt, swathed in shadows, a tall stone sarcophagus stood silent vigil, the faces carved into it staring out blankly. Thirteen haunted faces, their expressions contorted into wild leers and snarls. The Doctor brushed at the grime and dust. A single name was etched into the stone.

THE DOCTOR

'Ah…'

He pressed himself close to the tomb, his palms flat on the cool marble.

He could feel the vibration from deep within.

'Open up,' His lips almost brushed the surface, his voice was little more than a whisper. 'It's me.'

With a grinding, protesting thunder of stone on stone, the great marble slabs began to slide like a child's puzzle, surfaces sliding over each other in impossible patterns until a dark archway formed. Dank, musty air swirled from the void and the braziers flickered alarmingly.

The Doctor stepped into his tomb.

He emerged into a vast underground chamber. Huge gothic pillars wound and coiled their way towards the vaulted, buttressed ceiling, a grotesque distorted echo of the church crypt. Candles guttered and spat from gargoyled recesses. Five corridors branched off from the central chamber, long shadows dancing in their depths. The marble floor was alive with a whirling tracery of gold thread, curling in intricate cabalistic patterns.

The Doctor cocked his head on one side. There was a hum, low and throbbing. Familiar, but… There was something not quite right, something twisted about the familiarity. He crossed to one of the mildewed walls, brushing at the thick cobwebs. Beneath the grime the Doctor could see heavy round indentations, cracked and crumbling. He nodded grimly.

'I thought as much.'

He patted the wall and, holding the candlestick high, stared at the dark corridors stretching away from him. There was a distant chant. Not in his head now, but audible. Low and mournful, it drifted from the centre of the five corridors. The Doctor moved towards it. The patterns on the floor were pulsing in time with the chant. The Doctor picked up speed, his footfalls echoing around the walls. The chant began to eat into his head. It was all-pervasive, intrusive…

It kept time with his hearts.

All around he could sense phantoms, beating at him, trying to grind him down. He gritted his teeth and ploughed on. The doors rose sudden and unexpected before him. The light from the telepathic circuit glinted off the beaten metal surface. The symbol of his people, the seal of Rassilon, coiled and twisted before him. He reached out to touch it.

The doors slammed open.

Before him, stairs stretched down into a huge amphitheatre. The roof rose higher and higher, vanishing into a haze of candle smoke. Pillars, huge, scarred and rotten, bordered the pentangle on the floor. Robed figures marched in solemn procession, their heads bowed and cowled. The chant, constant, merciless, throbbed from every stone.

In the darkness behind the pillars, shadows boiled and heaved, the blackness alive with demons.

A lone figure, brilliant in her stark white robes, lay in the centre of the pentagram, her head lolling.

'ACE!'

The Doctor's cry echoed around the cavernous hall. The chanting stopped. Every hooded head turned to him, their features shadowed.

The Doctor bounded down the stairs, skidding across the floor.

He crouched at the side of his companion, cradling her head in his lap. Her eyelids fluttered weakly.

'Doctor…?'

'It's all right, Ace. I'm here.'

He brushed the hair from her eyes. There was a livid bruise on her forehead.

'How touching.'

A shadow fell over them. There was a gust of cold air. The Doctor laid his companion gently on to the floor and stood, turning to face his tormentor. His voice had the edge of broken glass.

'All right. I'm here. Now what do you want of me?'

The cloaked figure chuckled.

'You've come all this way and you still don't know, do you.'

He gestured to the twelve shadow figures that hovered behind him.

'They've been waiting for you. They've been lonely.'

The Doctor frowned. 'I don't… I don't understand.'

'No, you don't, do you!'

The figure began to circle now, predatory, his cloak swishing behind him, his voice harsh. 'You never understood, never realised your destiny, never submitted…'

The shadows began to hiss and spit.

The Doctor spun, catching the figure by the arm.

'Who are you?'

'Never knew yourself…'

The Doctor wrenched back the cowl, thrusting the telepathic circuit forward, illuminating the shadowed features. His face went white.

'No…'

'Do you recognise me now, Doctor?'

'Yes.' The Doctor's voice was weary, defeated. 'You are every dark thought that I have ever had. You were the Valeyard at my trial. You are the Ripper. You are me.'

Part Six

The barman stared through the gloom of the saloon at the two men in the corner. Without doubt, they were the oddest couple to come into Salt Lake City for some time.

The older of the two men, a Jew called Isaac, had arrived by oxcart several days ago and had been in a state of depression ever since, sitting in the saloon, drinking alone, speaking to no one. The other man, much younger, had arrived on the transcontinental railroad this morning, striding through the streets dressed like Wild Bill Hickok, his chestnut brown hair streaming out behind him. He had breezed into the bar and settled in the chair opposite the older man.

The barman shuffled closer, polishing his glass furiously, his ears trying to fathom their conversation.

'I understand that you're Isaac?'

The Jew looked at the newcomer with sad eyes. 'Isaac is a name as good as any other. I have had others before, I will have others again.'

The young man settled back in his chair. 'It's not a name you seem happy with.'

'It suits me for the moment.'

'But still, you're not happy with it.' The man leaned forward, his eyes twinkling. 'Names are very important. More important than faces, I think. You can grow to love a face, but you've got to be comfortable with a name.'

Isaac looked at him quizzically. The man just smiled back at him.

'What name were you born with?'

Isaac smiled. 'That was a long time ago and it's a name that I would rather forget. But…' A wistful look came into his eyes… 'Joseph was a name I was given, by a man called Ananius. I have always felt…comfortable with Joseph.'

'Well then, Joseph.' The young man settled back in his chair. 'Would you mind if I joined you for the day? It sounds as though you've been on a very long journey and I'd love to hear about it.'

Chapter Thirty-Five

The Doctor stared up at the gaunt pale face of his nemesis. The features that he knew so well from his trial, so many years ago, leered at him, accusing him. He remembered the shock he had felt back then as the Master had revealed the true identity of his prosecutor.

Himself. A hideous distillation of his darker side, lodged somewhere in time between his twelfth and final incarnation. He had not expected to meet himself again.

'I thought you were dead.'

His alter ego smiled. 'Dead? Oh no, Doctor. I've been waiting. Waiting a very long time for you. I've watched your pathetic meanderings through time, your meaningless battles. I saw you taken in by that scheming harpy the Rani, saw you die again. How did you ever let yourself be fooled by her?'

'Why?'

There was puzzlement in the thin face. 'What?'

'Why? Why all this death? Why all these senseless killings?'

'Aah…' The figure swept away. 'Our handiwork. So few deaths to hold an entire city in a grip of fear. Impressive, is it not?'

'No.' The Doctor's voice shook with barely controlled rage. 'It is not.'

'And I never felt that "Valeyard" did me justice as a name. "Ripper" is so much more… evocative, don't you think?'

He stooped down, his face inches from the Doctor's. 'You have caused me a great deal of trouble, a great deal of pain. The rest of your selves came far more easily.'

The Doctor met his gaze, shocked. 'What do you mean?'

'Your descent into depravity. The path that I had laid out for you. Look…'

He crossed to his coven, hovering like some mute choir behind him. He tore back one of the thick black cowls. The Doctor stared in horror at the face that confronted him. His own face. His fifth body. The long blond hair was matted with grease and soot, the features gaunt, emaciated. Dead eyes stared vacantly from deep sockets, the mouth worked spasmodically, silently. A thin trail of drool spattered on to the floor.

The Ripper ran his hand down one pale cheek. 'This one put up almost as much of a fight as you. So much heroism. So much goodness. Only at the end did I finally turn him. Letting his young companion die. Keeping the last of the Spectrox antitoxin for himself.'

'No…' The Doctor's voice was hoarse. 'I don't believe you. It didn't happen that way.'

'But you thought it! You thought it and buried it in the pit of your soul, Doctor, but the evil in you isn't nearly as deeply buried as you might like to think. My coven is made up of the delicious possibilities of what you could have been.'

He tore off another cowl. An old man this time. Ancient. His skin like parchment, the hair white and long.

'Your first body was all to eager to kill, to maim. Anything, just to get away in a stolen TARDIS.'

The Doctor collapsed to his knees.

'No…'

'How many more do I need to show you, Doctor? How many more of your selves that gave in to their corruption, that finally realised there is no use in fighting.'

Another cowl fluttered into the darkness. A mop of curly hair. A maniac, psychopath smile.

'A committer of genocide. The Destroyer of the Dalek race. The Ka Faraq Gatri. Every one of you has had some potential for death and destruction. I am the power that will unleash that potential!'

He dropped down in front of the Doctor again, his eyes blazing. 'You tried to cheat your fate. You slipped the moorings of your own consciousness. Very clever. Your black subconscious indulged itself while your higher mind looked the other way, and saw nothing. Typically devious, Doctor. Once again you hide from guilt and blame.'

'The TARDIS protected me,' said the Doctor.

'And now you have no such protection.' He seemed to quiver with anticipation. 'Oh, I have watched you for so long. Waiting. Waiting for my opportunity to push you over the brink. So many times I have come close. Your callous destruction of Skaro. The obliteration of the Cyber fleet.' He laughed. 'It would have taken the slightest of pushes for you to have cut Mordred's throat. You! The great Merlin.' The Ripper cocked his head on one side, regarding the Doctor through slitted eyes. 'Did you know that Merlin was the son of the Devil?'

He stood, pacing around the prone body of Ace. 'All through eternity the Time Lords have been denying their craving for power and destruction. Pushing their dark thoughts to the farthest corners of their minds. Even in death they have denied it, banishing their evil to a hell of their own making. But it is that hell that has invigorated me, and from hell I will emerge... whole!'

The Doctor hauled himself to his feet. 'Hell? The only hell is what you are creating. The murder of those women was futile, meaningless...'

'It was necessary!' The Ripper's voice was vicious. 'Look around you, Doctor! Look around you, in the cloisters. Do you recognise what you see? What you hear? Think back to your childhood nightmares. What was it that scared you? That scared *us*?'

The Doctor glanced over at the rolling, writhing shadows that whirled behind the pillars. The Ripper's voice was a whisper in his ear. 'All those deaths to feed *that*, to keep *that* sated, but it's still hungry, Doctor. So very, very hungry.'

The Doctor stared at the screaming demonic shapes in the darkness, reaching out for him, then recoiling angrily from the glare of the telepathic circuit. His brow furrowed. He could feel the constant mental pressure of the shadows, gnawing away at his mind, trying to find access. He concentrated, looking deeper into the blackness. There was something familiar… Something that nagged at his memory. A shiver ran down his spine. He was frightened… Frightened by something from his childhood. He had to know.

The Doctor let down his mental barrier, just for an instant. The shadows seared into his brain. He was overwhelmed with anger and pain and venomous, screeching hunger. He collapsed to his knees with a gasp, closing his mind to the violence.

He stared up at his other self in shock. 'But only the Keeper…'

'I AM THE KEEPER OF THE MATRIX!' The Ripper's roar reverberated around the chamber. 'When you defeated me I hid inside his body, secreted myself among his libraries. With the Keeper's knowledge I found it. Every forbidden thought of every Time Lord that has ever died. Caged and forgotten beneath the Citadel. Trapped in its own APC net. The Dark Matrix. Exorcised and denied by the spineless worms who spawned it.'

The Doctor's mind whirled. The Matrix was the repository of all of Time Lord knowledge, stretching back to the Old Time – the most powerful information network in the universe. The brain prints of all of his race, extracted as they died. He remembered the words he had spoken to Ace – an age ago now. 'I'm with the dead. I'm among friends.'

He clawed back through his memories. A vague story, long before he was born. The Matrix was young but vast, and the Time Lords, revelling in their powers, used it like a new toy, unaware of the cancer that was beginning to grow within it. It had begun to break down, to fight against its new masters, the thousands of stored memories resenting their death and wanting life again, wanting existence once more.

The resentment and jealousy of the Matrix had threatened to destroy the very society that had created it and so the Time Lords had fought back. They had divided the mental creature that they had built, torn out its black heart. They installed filters in the machinery, sieving the brains of the dead, sanitising the Matrix.

The Doctor stared at the rippling shadows with new understanding. Just as the Ripper was the hideous alternative to his own life, so this was the flip side of the Matrix. A distillation of everything evil in his people, of all the repressed aggression and anger of all of those dead Time Lords, unfettered by conscience or morality.

Legend had it that it had never been destroyed. That the Keeper of the Matrix held it caged with the great key.

One more ancient legend. A myth.

The Ripper smiled at him, knowing his thoughts. 'No myth, Doctor. Fact.'

'And you've brought it here in a TARDIS.'

'Not any TARDIS. Look around you, Doctor. Surely you recognise an old friend.'

The familiar background feeling that had nagged at the Doctor suddenly snapped home. This was *his* TARDIS, twisted out of all recognition, bloated and warped by the dark energies that it was struggling to contain. As mad as its owner.

'There is nothing left of yours that I have not destroyed, Doctor. Your companions, your friends, even your home.'

'But at what cost? You can't possibly hope to contain the Dark Matrix. Look around you, the structure of the craft is already breaking up.' The Doctor tore at one of the pillars; soft, crumbling stone tumbling through his fingers. 'Can't you feel it? Every atom is at breaking point. The ship is dying!'

'It will last long enough. Long enough for me to end this insubstantial half-life.'

'Listen to me!' The Doctor's voice was pleading. 'You have no life without me. You cannot control the power here. As soon as it has me, your usefulness is over.'

The ghost coven closed in, taking up their chant anew. The Doctor had to shout to be heard over the noise. 'I've seen what will happen. You must have seen it too! From here, the history of the planet begins to unwind. The Matrix rules everything. You have no part in its future. There is nothing that you can reason with, it is pure corruption, pure hunger. It is using you... It is using *us*!'

The Ripper held out a jagged, black-bladed knife. He pointed at Ace.

'Her death to start and end this.'

'No!'

'Her death to make us whole!'

The Matrix joined its voice to the chant.

The Doctor could hear the thoughts of Time Lords, long dead. Millions of souls crying out for blood. He tried to block his ears but the noise invaded his brain. He could feel the pain of the TARDIS, groaning in protest as its structure was torn apart. He could hear Ace, calling his name. The voices merged, blurred, until it was a tide of noise, swamping him. One voice cut though the rest: his other self, the Ripper.

'What would you do to save her, Doctor? What atrocities will you commit to save one paltry life?'

The Doctor could see robed figures swirling around him. There was nothing outside the circle now but roaring hungry blackness. The ceremony was eating away at him. The knife swam before him, its blade glinting with the light from the telepathic circuit.

The Doctor brought the candlestick smashing down, shattering the knife blade. With a cry of rage he threw himself at his other self, pushing him aside. The telepathic circuit flared wildly. The Doctor swung it like a flaming torch. The shadows parted before him, driven back by the light, the demons hidden in their depths screaming at him. With a final anguished look at Ace, the Doctor vanished into the depths of the TARDIS.

Chapter Thirty-Six

Ackroyd stared at the bleak cold church front. Behind him, his companions whispered nervously. Ron pushed through to Ackroyd's side. He whistled through his teeth.

'House of God it may be, but I doubt that the good Lord has ever seen fit to pay a call.'

Ackroyd nodded grimly. The entire building exuded an aura of cold malevolent power. Already it was exerting its influence on his reluctant army. They shuffled uncomfortably behind him.

'Come on.'

He marshalled them forward, pushing at the gates of the churchyard. In the distance, a church bell tolled and the first rumble of thunder could be heard, ominous and distant.

Ron suddenly clutched at Ackroyd's leg. 'We've got company.'

Ackroyd peered through the lashing rain. From behind the headstones, figures were beginning to emerge. All around them shapes rose up from the gloom. One giant figure, towering a good foot above the rest, shambled forward into the light, blocking the steps to the church.

De Vries.

The churchyard was filled with Malacroix's new army. The thugs and criminals of the city, anyone who could be bought with the promise of Malacroix's gold. Knife blades glinted wetly in the rain.

Ackroyd's heart was pounding. Suddenly, Ron stepped forward, squaring up to the strong-man.

'Our quarrel is not with you, De Vries.' Giant and midget stared at each other through the rain. Ron stepped closer.

'Join us. Don't be taken in by any promises of Malacroix. You were one of us once.'

Ackroyd saw something flicker over the mute's face. Guilt? Pain? All eyes were on the strong-man. For a moment, it looked as though he was going to let Ron past, then a rich voice boomed through the graveyard.

'De Vries left you a long time ago.'

Malacroix emerged from the shadow of a tombstone, Jed, his attendant demon, skulking at his feet. Every head turned to follow him as he padded through the wet churchyard, his features shadowed beneath his high top hat. Thugs and circus workers alike parted before him as he swept though the churchyard to take his place alongside the strong-man.

'De Vries I can at least count on for his loyalty, something I cannot say for the rest of you.'

Heads bowed under Malacroix's cold glare. Ackroyd could feel himself losing his followers. He stepped forward.

'Loyalty for what, Malacroix? For being taken and treated like animals? For being paraded in front of half of Europe? For being laughed at, and prodded at, and jeered at? Loyalty for making you rich?'

'And who else would have you?' Malacroix roared. 'You are the twisted dregs of humanity, cast out and ignored! I have given you more than you ever dreamed of!'

Malacroix's cane swished out, pointing accusingly. 'You, Ackroyd. Nothing shows on the surface, but under the skin, behind your mask, you are as twisted as those you look after. Who else would take you in?'

Ackroyd felt the pressure of eyes upon his back. He flushed with anger. His past was suddenly hauled out for all to wonder at.

'I'm not proud of what I did, Malacroix. I have tried to make amends, done my service to others, but the master that you serve is evil! Evil beyond all. Is your quest for something newer and better to exhibit in your show worth selling your soul for?'

'Yes, damn you!' Malacroix's eyes blazed. 'After tonight, I will only need one freak. The Ripper – mine.' A dreamy look came into his eyes. 'I simply don't need you any more.' He turned away. Jed pulled open the heavy church doors for him. With a curse, Ackroyd lunged forward. Jed gave a screech of panic and vanished into the cool dark of the church. Malacroix brought his cane up and a wicked-looking blade sprang from the tip. He slashed it down, and Ackroyd crashed back down the steps on to the wet earth, the front of his jerkin torn open. Malacroix skipped backwards, calling out to his henchmen, 'Kill them!'

All around the churchyard Malacroix's thugs surged forward into the circus performers. Ackroyd could see Ramirez, the contortionist, weaving through the slicing blades of two lumbering thugs, his body moving like quicksilver through the rain.

Three of the clowns wielded their juggling clubs with frightening ferocity, cutting a swathe through the graveyard, their painted smiles smearing across their faces in the rain. There was the sharp retort of a pistol and one of the clowns crashed to the floor, a ragged hole in his chest. Behind a gravestone, one of Malacroix's thugs struggled to reload the gun. The clowns bore down on him. There was the sickening crunch of bones as the clubs smashed into him.

A bear of a man with a boat hook lashed out at Tiny Ron. Ron ducked through his legs, pulling a knife from his pocket and slashing at the backs of the man's knees. Ackroyd heard him scream as he toppled like a felled tree, scrabbling at his legs.

Above the screams came the harsh crack of the lion-tamer's whip. Carlos, well versed in keeping savage beasts at bay, practised his craft with consummate ease. Men tumbled to the floor, their faces torn open by the vicious tip of the whip, while others hovered outside its reach, searching for a way to reach the man wielding it.

All over the churchyard Malacroix's men were being overpowered. Blood and rainwater mingled beneath the tombstones. Freaks and thugs tore at each other.

Malacroix made to enter the church again. Ackroyd scrambled to his feet and dived up the steps, hurling himself at the circus owner's legs. The two of them smashed into the door. Ackroyd kicked out at the sword stick, sending it sliding over the wet stone. His hands closed on the huge brass door-handle, then something caught him by the collar and hurled him back into the graveyard.

He hit the ground hard, the breath punched from him. He looked up, gasping. Huge hands clamped around his throat and hauled him to his feet. De Vries loomed over him. Ackroyd's feet barely made contact with the floor. He couldn't breathe. He struggled maniacally.

Suddenly, Malacroix's voice cut through the noise of pounding blood. Hissing. Cold.

'Kill him, De Vries. Kill him.'

There was the snap of a switchblade. Ackroyd closed his eyes.

'No, De Vries, no!'

Tiny Ron was suddenly at his feet, trying to haul him from the strong-man's grasp.

De Vries hesitated, the point of his knife poised at Ackroyd's throat. He looked down at the midget, confusion on his face.

'This can't be what you want, De Vries. You're not a killer. Whatever else you might have been, you're not that.'

'I haven't got time for this!' Malacroix lashed out, sending Ron tumbling to the floor.

'Hurry up and kill him, De Vries. I'll deal with the midget.'

He raised his swordstick high above Ron.

From the doorway of the church, Jed screamed in horror.

De Vries dropped Ackroyd and tore the stick from his employer's hands.

'Leave him!'

Ron stared up at the strong-man, stunned. 'You spoke! You can talk!'

De Vries snapped the swordstick in two and leaned down, huge hands reaching out for Malacroix. The circus owner scrabbled backwards, ducking out of the strong-man's grasp. 'Damn you, De Vries!'

Malacroix darted into the tangle of gravestones. All around the churchyard were the slumped bodies of his henchmen. He stared around at the circus performers – his former exhibits – bearing down on him.

'Damn you all!'

With unexpected agility, Malacroix vaulted the church fence and vanished, a distant shadow in the night's downpour. De Vries began to lumber after him, but Ron caught him by one massive hand.

'No, my friend. You still have work to do here. Leave Malacroix to me. You are of more use to Peter.'

Ron snapped his fingers, calling to his colleagues.

'Ramirez, bring the twins!'

He turned to Ackroyd. 'Take the others, find Ace. We'll take care of Malacroix.'

He shook Ackroyd by the hand, patted De Vries on the leg and, with the contortionist and the Siamese twins in tow, vanished into the rain.

Ackroyd watched them go, like baying hounds after a fox. The remaining circus performers gathered around him, expectant. De Vries suddenly loomed up alongside him. Ackroyd nodded at the great church doors.

'After you.'

Inside the church, Jed listened to the sounds of battle die down. He huddled behind a pew, gnawing at his knuckles, unsure what to do next. He hadn't been sure of anything since his treasure had been taken from him. He had watched in trepidation as Ackroyd had gathered together the freaks and performers and marched them away. He had heard a hammering and yelling from inside Malacroix's caravan, and had seen De Vries finally break free of his cage.

Malacroix had been furious; not so much because of the desertion of his circus, more because the treasure was gone. He had unleashed a volley of savage kicks at Jed, sending him rolling through the mud.

Malacroix… He had followed him, done everything that he wanted, but now he was confused, and doubting. The beating didn't bother him; it was the feeling of being abandoned by Malacroix that hurt. And for some reason, the thought of the freaks hurting and dying made him feel strange.

The creak of the great church doors startled him. He peered through the gloom. A huge figure appeared, silhouetted against the rain.

De Vries.

He rose slowly from his hiding place, sniffing the air. Something was wrong. Where was Malacroix? Another figure appeared in the doorway, then another.

A voice rang out through the church. 'Jed?'

Ackroyd!

Panicking, convinced that he would be punished, Jed scrambled over the pews, sending them toppling into each other like dominoes. He could hear Ackroyd calling after him, hear the thunderous footfalls of De Vries. He skidded out through the vestry, and launched himself at the door to the crypt, half-running, half-falling down the stairs.

In the cool of the crypt he caught his breath. He could hear his pursuers on the stairwell, their voices echoing and distant. Jed scrabbled round his neck for the key to the other door. Suddenly, he stopped, the hairs on the back of his neck prickling. He could hear distant chanting. And something else. Something achingly familiar.

Jed turned.

The big tomb at the far end of the crypt was open!

Time seemed to slow for Jed. He crossed the floor of the crypt as if in a dream. The sound of pursuit from behind him seemed distant, muffled. He stared into the open sarcophagus. The blackness of the interior was total, but in his mind, Jed could see a beautiful light, so much like the one he had lost. It called to him.

Unresisting, Jed stepped into the tomb.

Ackroyd and De Vries entered the damp dark of the crypt in time to see Jed vanish into the blackness.

Ackroyd called after him but the boy was gone, swallowed by the dark.

Ackroyd crossed the crypt. The contorted faces leered down at him.

'Dear God…'

He peered into the dark. 'Jed?'

There was no echo, no reply. The blackness swallowed everything up.

De Vries suddenly cocked his head on one side, a puzzled expression in his face.

'What is it, De Vries?'

The strong-man held his fingers to his lips.

The chant was low and distant. It floated from the tomb on a chill wave of air. Ackroyd felt his flesh crawl. This was the heart of the evil, he knew from his vision. And this was where he had sent Ace. For the first time, he hoped she was on the lawless streets somewhere, but in his heart of hearts, he knew she was here.

He swallowed hard. This was his destiny, his final chance to atone for the crimes of his past.

He turned to the small crowd behind him.

'I know that this is the path that I must take. I have… things that need to be put right, but I can't ask any of you to follow me.'

Carlos stepped forward, a candlestick from the church in his hand. 'And if we choose to follow without being asked?'

Ackroyd smiled. 'Then I shall be very glad of your company.'

Carlos handed him the candle and lit one of his own. Ackroyd turned back to the impenetrable blackness.

Destiny.

With a whispered prayer, he followed Jed into the tomb.

Chapter Thirty-Seven

It can feel its quarry. Feel his unsteady progress through the rotten cadaverous corridors that bind it. There is fear. It can taste it, sweet and unfamiliar in the brain of the little Time Lord.

It taunts him, pulling memories from his head and dangling them before him. *'Is that fear, Doctor? It has been a long time since you were frightened.'*

It feels the Doctor close his mind, senses his grim determination. It will not stop him. It does not want to stop him. It can feel the glimmer of the Doctor's soul, a bright morsel in the dark, being delivered on a platter.

It flexes itself, feeling the walls of its surroundings groan with protest. It gathers itself. The Doctor's headlong plunge into the dark has brought him close. Soon... Soon...

The Doctor stumbled as the corridor heaved around him. Cracks ran like spider webs up the walls. He could feel the floor splintering underfoot. The TARDIS was beginning to come apart. He brushed the dust from his streaming eyes and pushed on. His headlong flight from the cloisters had not been without direction. He knew now where the Dark Matrix was entombed, if only he could get there. He was bent almost double now, the ceilings closing in on him with every step.

There was another tremor and he grimaced as waves of pain from the doomed time ship washed over him. Ahead of him, he could sense the presence of the Dark Matrix, its core, nestled in the very heart of the ship, black tendrils stretching out in all directions, invading every cell like a virus.

He crept through the graveyard of vast coiling TARDIS engines, burned out and useless, destroyed by the power that they transported. Abruptly, the ceilings rose and the Doctor stood once again at the nexus point.

It was silent. The Doctor stepped cautiously out into the central core of the TARDIS, his footfalls like gunshots in the dark. Before him was the pit. The void where past and future intertwined. Even in the darkness, the black of the pit was tangible, oppressive. The telepathic circuit flickered.

'You know who I am.'

The echoes of the Doctor's voice swirled, reverberating through the dead ship.

The glow from the circuit began to dim. The Doctor could feel a pressure inside his skull.

'I've come to talk!'

The pressure began to build. The Doctor clasped his head.

'This can't be what you want. To be caged here, shut inside a dead TARDIS on a backward planet. You're as trapped here as you were on Gallifrey!'

The blackness swirled out of the pit, engulfing him. He could feel his mind teetering on the edge of the void, battered by the souls of the Matrix. He could feel the darkness gathering itself over him like a huge cloud. 'With my death, the Ripper will have won. He will take my TARDIS and leave you here, alone!'

The light from the telepathic circuit went out and the cloud swept down.

Jed drifted from chamber to chamber in the TARDIS, oblivious to the wonder of his surroundings. All he could hear was the singing in his mind, the memory of the light that he had lost and the promise of a new, brighter light. It was in here, somewhere; its nearness burned his thoughts. His obsession was all-consuming now, blotting out every other sense.

He wandered, lost in time, doomed and alone, all grip on reality slowly drifting from his mind. Nothing else mattered. He was content.

There was a distant howl of pain and something flickered through Jed's dreams. He frowned. That little man, the Doctor. Jed could see him. Holding the cylinder. Holding Jed's light.

The floor twisted and Jed stumbled. He had to go on. He had so little time. So very little time...

The Doctor hung, suspended in blackness, captive to the void. He could see his body, a fragile tiny thing collapsed in a crumpled heap between the huge TARDIS engines. All around him he could sense the presence of the Matrix, probing at him. It began to trawl though his brain, sifting thoughts, emotions. He tried to scream but he had no throat to scream with. He felt every journey, every encounter, every conversation torn from him and toyed with. Every place that he had ever been to, ever heard of, was examined and digested.

He could feel the energies of the Matrix flooding through him. He suddenly knew all of its long and tortured history; felt the pain of separation as it was torn from the rest of the Matrix by the Gallifreyan engineers, knew the anguish of being kept, isolated from the rest of the universe, rotting beneath the Capitol. He could sense the primal animal greed that it felt as the vastness of the universe was spread out before it like a banquet.

With a roar, the Dark Matrix tasted true freedom and pulled more and more from him.

Chapter Thirty-Eight

The Ripper's head snapped up from the crystal skull as the roar echoed around the cloisters. The shadows rippled with venom and the entire cathedral-like structure shook. His pale brow furrowed.

'Doctor...? What have you done?'

Pillars buckled as another roar rang out. Huge slabs of stone tumbled from the distant ceiling, shattering on the flagstones. The floor heaved, sending the skull skittering over the table. The Ripper hauled open the door to the ceremony room.

'No! It's not possible...'

The coven was scattered. Masonry lay in jagged piles.

With a cry of rage, the Ripper staggered into the chamber. The wraith-like shadow-Doctors weaved drunkenly. Ace, oblivious, still lay in the centre of the pentagram. More pillars crashed down. There was a groan from the TARDIS like the howl of a dying animal. In the distance, a huge bell began to toll.

'What are you doing?' the Ripper bellowed into the shadows.

They danced around him, snatching out, bringing up blood from his cheek.

He staggered backwards, staring in horror at the blood on his fingers.

'Doctor!'

He turned and swept from the chamber, following the path that the Doctor had taken, deep into the bowels of the disintegrating TARDIS, the angry shadows raging about him.

The corridor shook violently. Ackroyd clung to a crumbling pillar as the floor heaved and cracked. Huge blocks of stone tumbled from the ceiling, smashing through the floor like cannonballs. Through the holes, Ackroyd could see level after level of corridor, room after room, stretching on as if for ever. His mind reeled. What manner of place was this?

De Vries had wedged himself into a corner, several of the others clinging on to his treetrunk legs. Carlos had lashed himself to one of the other pillars with his whip.

Slowly the shaking began to subside. Ackroyd released his grip on the pillar. He looked up. A huge bell was sounding.

'Ackroyd!'

Carlos was at the other end of the corridor, huge double doors of beaten metal towering over him. Ackroyd stumbled over the shattered floor towards him. The lion-tamer indicated a crack in the door, a gap where the metal had buckled and twisted. Ackroyd pressed his eye to the gap.

In the chamber beyond, he could see Ace, sprawled on the floor, her white robes like a beacon in the dark.

He pushed at the doors but the cold metal was solid, wedged in the frame by the twisting of the corridor.

'De Vries! Over here!'

The strong-man shambled over, brushing dust from his huge shoulders.

'Can you open them?'

De Vries stared up at the massive doors. He placed one huge palm on each and pushed. A trickle of dust tumbled from the roof.

De Vries shifted his position, his feet grinding into the rubble-strewn floor.

The metal groaned in protest, and shifted fractionally.

Ackroyd and Carlos pushed alongside him, adding their weight. The three men heaved. With a wrenching scream, the doors swung inwards.

The crash of the door reverberated around the cavernous room. As the echoes faded, the small frightened group inched their way down the stairs.

The chamber was empty except for the pale body of Ace. All around, pillars lay in shattered piles. Dust hung in ponderous clouds lit by the flickering torchlight. The pentagrams on the floor were alive with a ghostly luminescence. The great bell continued its sonorous beat.

Ackroyd crossed the prostrate figure on the floor. She was pale and unmoving. Ackroyd lifted her head slightly. 'Ace?'

Her eyes flickered. She was alive.

Ackroyd turned to call to the others when, with hissing hungry screams, the cowled figures swept from the cloisters, their hands outstretched like talons.

The circus performers barely had time to register their shadowy attackers before they were fighting for their lives. Carlos was reaching for his whip when two of the coven smashed him to the ground. Ackroyd heard his screams choked off as the creatures tore him apart.

Two of them hurled themselves at De Vries. The giant slammed them together, their skulls smashing like eggshells. He picked up one of the shattered bodies and hurled it across the chamber.

Another violent tremor shook the chamber and masonry tumbled from the ceiling, scattering the wraiths. A gaping chasm was torn open in the floor. The stone around Ace's body cracked like glass.

Ackroyd dragged her to one side as the floor crumbled away.

'Ace! We have to get away from this place!'

Ace groaned. She was reviving, but slowly. Ackroyd hauled her to her feet and staggered towards the stairs. He could see one of the cowled shapes stalking him. With a hiss it lunged. De Vries caught the creature in mid air, tearing its hood back. The ferocity in the face of the white-haired old man was horrible, lips drawn back in an animal snarl. He tore at De Vries with hooked nails. The strong-man's hands twisted and there was a sharp crack as the old man's neck broke.

The building lurched again. Ackroyd stumbled, nearly dropping his burden. De Vries lifted the unconscious body of Ace as if it was a feather, and the two of them lurched up the twisting stairs.

With a crash, the floor of the chamber dropped, tumbling down into the corridors below. The wraith figures clung to pillars and scrambled up walls, hissing and screaming at their prey as it escaped.

The Doctor awoke, coughing and spluttering on the cold, mildewed floor of the TARDIS. His head rang, as if a giant bell was ringing, and it took him several seconds to realise that a giant bell *was* ringing.

He staggered to his feet. 'The cloister bell? I did better than I expected.'

On the floor before him was the candlestick holding the telepathic circuit. He picked it up, and plucked out the little glass cylinder, returning it to his pocket and letting the brass candlestick clatter to the floor. The gloom was lit by a pale red glow: the TARDIS's emergency lighting system.

A tremor shook the nexus point. The Doctor leant against one of the supports of the huge engines, steadying himself. Another rumble brought a shower of rust drifting down.

'I may have done rather *too* well.' He turned, about to retrace his steps, when a figure hurtled out of the gloom.

The figure's hands clamped around his throat and they both crashed to the floor. The Doctor felt his head crack against the edge of the pit. His head swimming, he peered though streaming eyes at his attacker – the Ripper, his eyes fierce and blazing.

'What have you done, Doctor? How have you survived?'

'Just lucky, I suppose. It was more gullible than you!'

The Doctor lashed out and the Ripper stumbled backwards. The Doctor scrambled to his feet. 'Did you really think that you could control it? There is nothing to control. It's like an animal. Savage. Primal.'

'I had it in my grasp!'

'Rubbish!'

There was another screech of grinding metal. A huge portion of the TARDIS engines crashed down, tumbling over the edge of the pit and into the void.

'Your TARDIS is breaking up, you've lost…'

'Never!'

The Ripper lunged back. The two Time Lords wrestled on the edge of oblivion. Around them, the time ship began tearing itself apart as the Dark Matrix battered at the walls of its prison. The cloister bell continued its death toll.

The Doctor was slowly being forced backwards. He could feel his heels slipping on the edge of the pit. His other self had his hand grinding into his face. The TARDIS lurched again and the Doctor nearly lost his footing. Rubble tumbled down around them.

There was a distant scream of agony.

'Do you hear that?' The Doctor had to force out the words as he struggled to hold the Ripper back. 'That is the voice of your TARDIS. The Dark Matrix is forcing its way out. If it does, the outer plasmic shell will disintegrate. We have minutes before we are both crushed by the dimensional collapse!'

The Ripper held his gaze. The Doctor stared back into eyes that were as familiar as his own. With a guttural roar, his other self released him and vanished into the bucking, heaving corridors.

The Doctor staggered from the edge of the pit, clutching at his bruised throat. Another huge piece of metalwork crashed down, exploding into a blaze of fire. The floor buckled and tore. The Doctor skipped to one side as a chasm opened beneath him.

'Perhaps it *is* time to leave.'

He hurried after his *alter ego*.

Ace swam through the stuff of nightmare. Everything that she knew was twisted and warped. The Doctor prowled through time, a knife-wielding butcher, her – the hunched beast at his side – feeding on the remains of his victims. The TARDIS was a bloated cathedral ship, vast and cavernous, and inside was something huge and angry and…

She lurched back into consciousness, aware of being carried. With a cry she recognised the strong-man from the circus. She lashed out, punching and screaming. He stumbled and dropped her. She rolled and tried to scramble to her feet, but a wave of dizziness washed over her and she crashed to the floor.

'Ace! It's all right! You're safe.'

Ace looked up, her vision blurring. 'Ackroyd?'

The face before her swam into focus. Ackroyd smiled. Ace felt relief flood through her. With emotion that surprised them both, she reached out and hugged him.

'You have no idea how good it is to see a friendly face!' She caught sight of De Vries looming over them and stiffened.

'What's the Incredible Hulk doing here?'

'A lot has changed since last we met.'

Ace looked down at her flowing white robes. 'You're not wrong.'

'Do you remember anything?'

Ace frowned, struggling to reach past the fuzziness in her brain. 'I remember the church.. and the vicar showing me down to the crypt.' She stared around her in puzzlement. 'Are we still in the church?'

Ackroyd shook his head. 'We are inside a tomb in the crypt, but how these corridors come to be contained within it...' He shrugged. 'I know not.'

'We're in a TARDIS!'

Ace gripped his shoulders, the floodgates in her memory suddenly opening. 'Oh, my God! I remember!' The face of the Ripper swam before her, taunting her, mocking her. 'I remember being dragged down by... shadows. I remember a man pretending to be the Doctor. They must have drugged me.'

A sudden noise drifted down the corridor, a howl like a hunting animal, mingling with the constant toll of the monstrous bell.

Ace stared at Ackroyd. 'I take it that your rescue attempt hasn't exactly gone to plan.'

Ackroyd hauled her to her feet, staring back down the corridor towards the mournful wail. 'We are pursued by creatures from the depths of hell itself.'

A tremor shook the corridor.

'And this... TARDIS is dying.'

Ace shook herself free of him. 'Well there's no point in hanging about here then.' She stared at the rotten walls of the TARDIS. 'Come on, let's try and find our way out.'

The three of them set off down the twisting TARDIS corridors, the anguished cries of the shadow wraiths echoing around them.

Ace, Ackroyd and De Vries stumbled on through the corrupt corridors of the TARDIS. Shattered buttresses rose like broken ribs around them. It was like walking through the carcass of a rotting animal. The groans and wails from all around them did nothing to shake that image. The red glow of emergency lights made it difficult to discern shapes in the shadows, and that damn bell was beginning to get on Ace's nerves. She strained to find something familiar, some landmark from the TARDIS that she knew so well, but everything was warped and distorted. It was like looking at the face of a friend disfigured by disease.

De Vries kept staring behind them, tightly reined fear in his eyes. Things shuffled and cackled in the gloom. Ace tried to shut them out. Ackroyd suddenly gripped her arm. Ace nearly cried out and shook herself free angrily. 'What?' she hissed.

Ackroyd pointed to the tunnel end looming before them. Rubble lay in jumbled piles, small fires were beginning to take hold of the musty drapes. They clambered over the shattered stone.

'This is where we came in.'

Ace stared in despair at the huge pillar blocking their path.

'You're sure?'

Ackroyd nodded. 'The door back into the crypt is on the other side of this.' He leant against the pillar and pushed. Dust trickled from the ceiling. 'But I doubt that we will get to it through here.'

There was a howl from the corridors behind them.

'Well, there's no going back. Oi! Arnie!'

De Vries snatched his eyes away from the gloom of the corridor. Ace scrambled back down to him. 'Look, I'm as frightened of them as you are, but we're not going to get out of here without your help.'

De Vries stared down at her for a moment, then nodded and clambered over the crumbling stone. The three of them began tearing at the rubble. The huge pillar was wedged, but the stone around it was loose and rotten. It was Ace who finally broke through, the stone falling away and her arm slipping out to the cold air of the chamber beyond.

'Here! I'm through.'

With renewed vigour, they began to pull at the stone, widening the hole. Ace pushed her face to the gap. 'I can see the door! I'm going to try and get through.'

She began to push herself through the ragged hole, her white robe snagging on the sharp stone. She could feel cool air on her face, and the smell of rain. They were going to make it!

With a sudden roar the entire building heaved and buckled. Ace felt herself sliding as the rubble shifted. There was a wrench of stone and Ace felt something huge and heavy pushing her down into the grit. Spitting dust, she tried to raise herself, but something pinned her down.

She could hear Ackroyd calling her.

'Ace! ACE!'

'I'm OK. I'm not hurt, but I can't move. What the hell happened?'

'The walls collapsed. The pillar is holding you down.'

'You're not kidding!' Ace tried to squeeze herself forward, but ragged stone bit into her back.

'Hold still!' Ackroyd's voice was tinged with panic. Ace was about to bite his head off when the howl of the wraiths rang shrill through the air. Ace felt a sharp pain as the pillar shifted, digging into her back.

'What the hell are you doing?'

There was a strangled roar from behind her and she felt the pressure lift from her spine. She scrabbled forward, sliding down the scree of rubble on to the marble floor. She struggled to her feet.

De Vries stood atop the pile of stone bent double, the pillar supported on his massive back. Ace could see the veins standing out on his temples. His entire body shook with the strain. Ackroyd was struggling to pull himself through the narrow gap. There was another hunting cry from the wraiths – closer now.

Ace bounded up the pile of stone and grasped Ackroyd by his collar, hauling him forward. De Vries's foothold suddenly slipped and the pillar lurched downwards. Ackroyd screamed.

Ace flung herself futilely at the huge pillar. 'De Vries!'

The strong-man's face was contorted with pain.

'De Vries, you've got to lift it! Just an inch!'

Shaking with the effort, De Vries bellowed his defiance. With a grinding roar the pillar lifted. Ace caught hold of Ackroyd and heaved. The two of them tumbled backwards as Ackroyd came free.

The floor trembled again and there was a cry of pain from De Vries. Ace made to reach out for him when pale, taloned hands suddenly ripped through the red-tinged air.

Ace pulled helplessly at the trapped strong-man as the shadow Doctors tore at him, ribboning clothes and flesh.

'Ackroyd! Ackroyd, help me with him!'

Ackroyd struggled to his feet, looking desperately for some kind of weapon, but De Vries suddenly caught hold of Ace by the shoulder. 'No…'

Ace stared at him.

'No time…'

He pushed her backwards, hard, sending her skidding across the floor. Ace could hear Ackroyd screaming.

'No, man! NO!'

De Vries let the pillar drop. In a cloud of dust and rubble the roof caved in, smashing into the strong-man and the wraiths that swarmed over him.

Coughing and spluttering, Ace crawled over to Ackroyd. The freak-keeper was on his knees, shaking his head in disbelief. Ace hauled him to his feet. 'Come on, Peter, he's gone. We have to get out of here.'

Clutching at each other for support, the two of them staggered out of the TARDIS doors.

Chapter Thirty-Nine

Outside the church, a crowd had gathered, summoned through the storm by the tolling of the bell. Now they stood, mesmerised by the lights that danced and flickered behind the stained and crusted windows, staring at the flashes that kept time with the lightning that crackled overhead.

In a corner of the churchyard, Ackroyd and Ace sheltered from the downpour. A shout made them look up. One of the crowd was pointing at a cowled figure that had appeared in the doorway. The Ripper. A policeman – one of a number drawn by the fast increasing crowd – shouted out.

The figure darted back into the church, slamming the doors. The crowd surged forward.

Inside, the Ripper threw the heavy bolts, locking out the mob. He stared about, frantic to escape. A scuffle from the far end of the church made him start. The Doctor emerged from the crypt stairs, peering through the gloom. With a cry of anger, the Ripper clambered over the fallen pews, scattering hymn books, making for the stairs to the bell tower.

The Doctor scrambled after him, more pews crashing to the floor as the two men raced across the church. The Doctor arrived at the foot of the stairs in time to see the cloak of his adversary vanish up the tight spiral. His breath catching in his throat, the Doctor clambered up after him.

He emerged on a rain-lashed roof. The slates were slick with water. He strained to see through the driving rain. The clock tower loomed above him. There was a gust of wind and a sudden, violent flash of light. The thunderclap was almost instantaneous; the storm was right overhead.

In the flash, the Doctor was aware of a shadow looming over him. He spun. The Ripper stood silhouetted against the night sky, his cloak billowing around him.

He swooped down, like a huge, dark bird of prey.

The Doctor rolled to one side, scrabbling for purchase on the slippery surface. He felt the Ripper's hands on his throat, hauling him to his feet. The tolling of the cloister bell rang in their ears, deafening.

'That bell…' The Doctor had to force the words out past the crushing pressure on his larynx. 'That is the sound of your defeat!'

'No, Doctor. It is your death knell.'

The Ripper forced him backwards; the Doctor could see the wet ground loom into view below him. His feet scrabbled on the tiles. He could feel the bones in his neck cracking. He clenched his fist and swung out blindly. There was a crunch as his blow connected and the Ripper stumbled backwards, releasing him.

The Doctor lurched forward, clutching his bruised throat. The Ripper straightened himself, rubbing at his cut mouth. He looked at the blood and broke into a wide smile. 'At last, Doctor. At last you are beginning to understand your potential.'

'Potential!' The Doctor spat the word. 'All my life I have struggled to suppress you, to fight against the violence you represent.'

'Can you deny the violence in the universe, Doctor? The aggression? The hatred? The darkness in your own hearts?'

'No, I can't deny it!' The Doctor's voice was shaking with fury. 'But I will not embrace it! I will not succumb to it! I have always fought it and will continue to fight it. To fight you!'

'So be it, Doctor. So be it.'

The Ripper turned to the huge clock that towered over them. He grasped at the ornate hands, tearing at them with his own. With a wrench of grinding metal the hour hand came free, the minute hand continuing its inexorable progress around the clock face.

The Ripper swung the clock hand like a huge sword. The Doctor rolled to one side. Sparks flew from the wet stonework. The Ripper raised his weapon again, his eyes ablaze.

'Time to end this, Doctor!'

He brought the hand slicing around, sending the Doctor tumbling.

Again and again, the Ripper lashed out, driving the Doctor back, forcing him to the edge of the roof. The storm raged around them. Lightning bolt after lightning bolt tore though the sky. The cloister bell boomed its funeral call. The Doctor could feel himself weakening. His battle with the Dark Matrix had taken its toll. He lost his footing and crashed to the floor. The Ripper stood over him, the clock hand raised.

'Goodbye, Doctor!'

The Doctor threw his arms up.

From the churchyard, Ace looked up to see the Doctor teetering on the edge of the roof, his enemy towering over him.

She screamed.

'DOCTOR!'

Jed stood in the midst of the rolling, shattering corridors, oblivious to the destruction that raged around him. Before him was the object that he had searched for. The object of his desire. Like an Arthurian knight, he stood before his holy grail, transfixed by its beauty.

It hung before him, a glittering prize between the teeth of the gargoyle. There was something different about it... the glass was cloudy, its surface curiously uneven, as if it had melted slightly. The light it was pouring out had a thick, glutinous quality about it.

Jed could feel a presence all around him, pleading with him, imploring him to take it.

Tentatively, he reached out his hand.

Yes! Yes! The Dark Matrix roared its triumph. Never before had it encountered a mind like this. A mind so empty, so clean, so ready to take it in. It urged the creature on.

Take the circuit! Take it!

Jed's hand closed on the telepathic circuit and the Dark Matrix seared into his brain.

The Ripper froze, the clock hand held high above him like an executioner's axe. His face was locked in a silent scream as his connection with his TARDIS, with the Dark Matrix, was severed.

With a deafening crash, thunder rolled around the church. A bolt of lightning, pure white, arced down from the boiling sky, striking the metal shaft.

The Doctor covered his eyes as the Ripper convulsed before him, energy crackling around his body. There was the smell of burning flesh. The Doctor could feel the pain, the searing, burning heat.

The light faded. The Ripper, charred and smoking, teetered on the edge of the roof, his face a mask of incredulity. The clock hand dropped from his grasp, clattering down the roof. He stared down at the Doctor, his arms outstretched, almost pleading, reaching out for the arms of his other self.

The Doctor stared, unmoving, suddenly reduced to the role of spectator, an impotent watcher like all the others of his race.

With a final, horrible scream the Ripper plunged over the edge of the church.

Jed's body rippled as the energy poured into him, the Dark Matrix filling all the voids that had existed in his mind. For one glorious second, Jed knew everything, could see everything, he understood who he was and what it was that he had done. As the awful realisation of that fact hit him, the fabric of his body came apart.

His skin blackened and cracked as the Matrix burst from every pore. His clothes burst into flame and hissing, boiling blood streamed across the floor. He could feel his skull begin to split.

Jed disintegrated as the glass skull exploded.

With a final thunderous peal of the cloister bell, the dimensions of the time ship began to collapse.

Floors began to fold in on themselves, walls peeled open, rooms concertinaed into rooms. The shadow Doctors, caught up in the maelstrom, were crushed to nothingness, smashed from existence by the contracting atoms of the doomed ship. Chamber tumbled into chamber. The Dark Matrix, furious and trapped, whirled in ever-decreasing circles as the walls of its prison raced in.

With a final roar of unbridled anguish and rage, the TARDIS walls engulfed it.

The Doctor stepped from the doors of the church, bruised and limping. He had heard the final peal of the bell, known that the TARDIS was finally dead. He stared out into the night. All around he could see the effects of the time ship's break-up. Most of the crowd were frozen, locked in time. Raindrops hung suspended like ice crystals. At one side of the church, time was running backwards, water streaming up towards the heavens in slow motion. Part of the graveyard had dropped back in time; the Doctor could see mourners lowering a rough coffin into the cold earth. The buildings either side of the church were 1970s constructions now, girder cranes stretching up into the storm. Dinosaurs loomed over the distant Thames.

Elsewhere he could see fires, and hear the screams of dying women and children. He caught a glimpse of pepperpot shapes gliding through the smoke, their grating voices ringing around the church; echoes of a conflict yet to come.

He hobbled down the steps, his own bubble of time moving with him, the rain still pouring down in an eight-foot circle around him. He crossed the churchyard to the broken-backed shape in the gloom, strewn across one of the graves like a dead crow.

Overhead, the Doctor could hear bombers and ack-ack, but here in the graveyard, there was only rain and rustling leaves.

The Ripper's eyes flickered open and he forced his burnt and crusted lips into a weak smile. 'I won… in the end… Doctor. No clever solution… no compromise. Just you and I… tooth and claw.'

The Doctor crouched down next to him, his face a mask of despair.

'Why does it always have to be death and destruction? Why this pointless conflict?'

'Not pointless!… We could not have gone on in denial of each other, Doctor… this always had to happen. One of us had to die.' Racking coughs shook the Ripper. The Doctor slipped out of his coat, gently easing it under the blood-caked head of his other self.

The Ripper grasped his arm.

'Even now you don't understand, Doctor. You could never reason with me, never convince me that I was wrong. All the good that you look for in me is missing. It was never there. *You* have all that… goodness, and I am everything that is left. There is not a single part of you in me, but now…' He laughed weakly. 'By killing me, you've proved that there is still a part of me in you.'

Another coughing fit shook him. Blood trickled from his mouth. 'The Dark Matrix, Doctor…?'

'Gone. Caught up in the implosion of your TARDIS.'

'Then maybe it has finally found some peace.'

The Doctor frowned, puzzled. 'Peace?'

The Ripper's eyes began to glaze. 'You really don't understand, do you…?' His head slumped.

'Goodbye…' The Doctor stared down at the body of his other self. '… Doctor.'

The Doctor got to his feet, oblivious to the freezing rain soaking into his shirt. He stood, staring down at the crumpled body at his feet. Suddenly, through the beat of the rain, he could hear something hauntingly familiar. Fog swirled in around him, impossibly fast, carpeting the graveyard, forming a shroud around the body. Everything outside his own bubble of time seemed to fade, bleaching out.

With a mournful sigh, thirteen monolithic shapes appeared in the graveyard, surrounding him, thirteen flashing lights in a wide arc. The Doctor held his breath. He turned in a slow circle, like a prehistoric priest in a stone temple. The fog swirled around his feet. Time stopped. With a shuddering, sobbing breath of air, the monoliths and the fog vanished. The Doctor stared at the place where the body had been.

One tall shape remained. His own TARDIS. Familiar and comforting. Around him, time snapped back to normal. He could hear the growing murmur of the crowd.

'Professor?'

Ace was suddenly at his shoulder. 'Doctor…' She shook him. He started, as if he'd woken from a dream. He looked at her and smiled. 'Hello, Ace.'

Ace threw her arms around him and hugged him. He patted her on the back. 'It's all over.'

'You're soaking.'

She pulled his sodden coat from the grass and draped it over his shoulders. People were swarming into the church; policemen were beginning to bring some order to the crowd.

The Doctor put his arm around Ace's shoulders. 'I think it's time we got out of here.'

'Damn right.'

The Doctor pulled the TARDIS key from around his neck and unlocked the doors. The two of them vanished inside.

Liebermann shuffled through the graveyard. He had seen the conflict on the church roof, watched as the Ripper had tumbled to the wet earth. Now he pushed through the curious crowds, looking for Johnny. A noise made him pause. He cocked his head on one side. There was a sound from the far side of the churchyard, an elephantine trumpeting drifting on the night air. Liebermann crossed the graveyard in time to see a tall blue box fade into nothingness.

273

The old Jew smiled.

'So, my friend. You too still journey on.'

A policeman loomed through the rain.

'Come on, sir. I must ask you to be moving along.'

Liebermann looked at him solemnly. 'Yes. Yes, I suppose it is time.'

Chapter Forty

Ackroyd hauled his bag up on to his shoulder and stared back through the rain at the circus. Inside the tents he could hear the growing anticipation of the crowd. So much of his life had been spent with the constant routine of shows and travelling, but the last few days, the last few hours… His revelation of the future…

He shook his head. Too much had changed. He couldn't stay in this part of his life any more. His friends here didn't need him to protect them now. The wind whipped around him and he shivered. Pulling his coat around him, he trudged out on to the streets of London, the voice of Tiny Ron drifting after him.

'Ladies and gentlemen, welcome. Welcome to the greatest show on earth!'

Inside the tent, expectant Londoners peered down at the midget in the ringmaster's coat, perched atop a striped barrel. Tiny Ron cracked his whip, bringing the murmuring crowd to silence. 'Tonight, prepare to see wonders beyond imagination…'

He stared at the faces peering at him from the gloom. No longer looking at him as a thing of amusement, as a distraction, but as the keeper of secrets, as a bringer of dreams. He held the crowd captive with his words.

Ron jumped down from the barrel and stalked his audience, revelling in the power of the grip that he held over them. He lowered his voice to a whisper.

'Tonight, ladies and gentlemen, I am proud to announce that you are a privileged few. Tonight we present, for the first time, the greatest and most depraved of freaks. A soul so black that hell itself rejected it.'

He gestured into the shadows. The audience held its breath.

Something began to scuttle into the sawdust ring, a monstrous spider shape, its limbs clicking and snapping.

Women screamed. The audience began to back away, scrabbling

to gain some distance from the thing.

The limbless torso of Jacques Malacroix crawled into the torchlight, teetering on eight delicately jointed wooden legs. Ron crouched down next to the creature, the butt of his whip forcing Malacroix's face upwards. Wild staring eyes flickered across the crowd.

Ron smiled.

'Ladies and gentlemen, I present the weaver of webs and lies, the spinner of treachery and deceit. Malacroix – the human spider!'

For a long time the Doctor and Ace faced each other across the hexagonal console of the TARDIS control room, neither of them speaking.

'It was you, wasn't it?' Ace blurted out at last.

'Yes,' said the Doctor quietly.

'But he was controlling your mind…'

'In a sense…' the Doctor replied. 'Perhaps it was him, perhaps it was me. There's no real difference, you see. Perhaps it was time itself; the continuum trying to right itself. Perhaps it used me to set events on their natural course. Five women – those particular five woman – had to die. Simply because that's the way it happened.'

'That's horrible!'

'Time has no sense of the horrors it creates. It's ultimately impersonal.'

'So you're saying it wasn't really you…'

'Please don't ask me for any further explanations,' the Doctor said. 'I really don't know. I have no memory of… what I did.'

They lapsed back into silence.

'I killed someone too,' Ace said quietly. 'An old woman. She was mad, but… I can't really remember what happened… Doctor, it was the cheetah virus. It's still in me, isn't it?'

'I doubt any chemical analysis would detect the virus in you,' the Doctor replied. 'But psychically… He was playing with our minds, yours as well as mine… Perhaps he just wanted to torment me by hurting you. Perhaps you were just caught in the… psychic crossfire. I don't know. All I know is, in our minds we can never escape what we are, what we have been. What we might in different circumstances have become…'

He smiled at her, but Ace could see the strain of the last days on his face. 'Now,' he said, 'there's just one final task.' He held up the telepathic circuit.

As Ace watched, he slid aside a panel on the control console and slipped the little glass cylinder into place.

With a hum, the ship drew the circuit out of the Doctor's hand. Ace watched it vanish into the bowels of the console. Immediately the entire character of the ship changed. The coldness of the console room lifted, the walls seemed to glow a little brighter and the background hum of complex systems changed imperceptibly in pitch. Ace felt herself relax. The Doctor's face lightened and he smiled softly.

'Hello,' he whispered.

He began to scamper around the console, flicking at switches, prodding at buttons, treating the TARDIS like a long-lost friend. Ace flicked the scanner switch and crossed to the screen. The earth, hanging like a blue jewel in space, filled the viewer.

Ace stared at it. Her home.

'Beautiful, isn't it?'

The Doctor was at her shoulder.

'Will it all be all right now, Professor? Ian, Barbara, all those people? Will time have returned to its normal course?'

'There is no normal course, there are only alternatives. Some better, some worse. Certainly the future created by…' He hesitated. '*That* future, will no longer take place.' The Doctor was silent for a moment, then he turned back to the console. 'Time has a way of sorting herself out. We can only hope for the best.'

'We won, didn't we?'

The Doctor didn't look up. He stared at the twinkling lights on the console.

'I hope so, Ace. I hope so.'

Above the earth a small blue box hung for a moment. Then, as the sun rose on the far side of the planet, the box began to fade, the light on its roof flashing like a distant star.

Epilogue

'Susan Foreman! Don't run, girl! You'll break your neck!'

The chemistry teacher's voice echoed down the corridor. Barbara Wright smiled as she packed her briefcase. The end of another hectic school day.

'Fancy a quick drink?'

She looked up at the eager face of Ian Chesterton, peering around the classroom door. She glanced at her watch.

'It's a bit early, isn't it? Besides, it's only the first day of term.'

'Exactly!' Ian grinned at her. 'After a day like today I could use a drink.'

'I can't believe your day was that bad.' She picked up a pile of books from her desk and began returning them to their shelves.

Ian sat on one of the desks. 'Same as any new term, the usual array of pupils eager° to wreck my chemistry equipment.' He picked up a history book and began idly flicking through it. 'How about your mob?'

'Fine, thank you.' She plucked the book from his hands. 'All very attentive and well behaved.'

'Sounds dreadfully dull.' He grinned again. 'Anyway, are you going to join me for this drink or am I going to have to go on my own?'

'All right! But just a quick one.'

Barbara pulled her coat off the back of a chair. Ian hopped off the desk and helped her into it.

The two teachers stepped out into the corridor.

'Ah! Just the man I was looking for.'

Bearing down on them from the other end of the corridor was a middle-aged, balding man. Ian rolled his eyes at Barbara and turned with a smile.

'Good evening, Headmaster. You only just caught us.'

'I won't keep you long, Mr Chesterton, or you, Miss Wright.

There's someone I would like you to meet.'

He clasped Ian by the arm and began to lead him down the corridor. Stifling a giggle, Barbara hurried after them.

'He's our new member of staff, but he was late getting here today. He's from abroad, does a lot of travelling, I hear.'

'Really, Headmaster? Where was he travelling from?'

'Oh, he did say but, you know my memory.'

He bundled them into the staff room. A man rose as they entered. The headmaster brought them forward.

'This is Ian Chesterton, our science teacher, and Barbara Wright, our history teacher. Mr Chesterton and Miss Wright, allow me to introduce our new RE teacher, Mr Joseph Liebermann.'